# A MATTER OF PROFIT

## *Hilari Bell*

*An Imprint of* HarperCollins*Publishers*

Eos is an imprint of HarperCollins Publishers.

A Matter of Profit
Copyright © 2001 by Hilari Bell
All rights reserved. No part of this book may be used
or reproduced in any manner whatsoever without written
permission except in the case of brief quotations embodied in
critical articles and reviews. Printed in the United States of
America. For information address HarperCollins Children's
Books, a division of HarperCollins Publishers,
1350 Avenue of the Americas,
New York, NY 10019.

Library of Congress Cataloging-in-Publication Data
Bell, Hilari.
A matter of profit / by Hilari Bell.
p.   cm.
Summary: Sick of the horrors of conquering beings on
other planets, Ahvren will end his service as a soldier and
save his sister from an unhappy marriage if he can discover
who is behind a rumored plot to assassinate the emperor.
ISBN 0-06-029513-9 — ISBN 0-06-029514-7 (lib. bdg.)
ISBN 0-06-447300-7 (pbk.)
[1. Science fiction. 2. Mystery and detective stories.] I. Title.
PZ7.B38894 Mat  2001                      00-050555
[Fic]—dc21                                         CIP
                                                   AC

Typography by Larissa Lawrynenko
❖
First Eos edition, 2003

Visit us on the World Wide Web!
www.harperteen.com

*For my first reader*
*and best friend—*
*who also happens to be*
*my mom—who*
*loves this story as*
*much as I do*

# Chapter 1

**H**E WOULD HAVE TO tell his father. He couldn't tell his father.

Ahvren hoisted his three overstuffed gear bags and tried not to let his reluctance slow his feet as he boarded the shuttle that would take the spaceliner's passengers down to T'Chin. The voyage from Mirmanidan had lasted five interminable months. Ahvren was probably the only one aboard who wished it had been longer.

He might not even have a choice about telling his father. If the bizarre compulsion that had seized his tongue so often during the last few months overcame him, he'd blurt out the truth to Viv Saiden the moment he opened his mouth—whether he wanted to or not.

*Hello, Father, I realize that this will disgrace our family, perhaps even end our line if I'm declared unfit, but I just can't help them conquer anyone else . . .*

When had his own people become *them*?

Ahvren dropped his bags onto the seat beside him. The shuttle wasn't so crowded that he had to leave room, and he was in no mood to make idle conversation. After all these months in space, he should be accustomed to recycled air, but it still smelled stale and dead. It would be good to be on a planet again. A planet where there was no war.

Maybe all he needed was rest. Rest on a world that wasn't engulfed in violence—where it was safe to wear a sword instead of the disrupter whose weight had become so familiar on his belt over these last blood-stained years.

Ahvren opened his eyes and looked out the viewport. The brown-and-green sprawl of T'Chin's largest continent loomed below. T'Chin had a wide range of ecosystems, but its principal city, K'Moth, lay in a desert at the edge of one of the planet's three seas. Not the best climate, but K'Moth had the only space-port large enough for the shield fleet's auxiliaries, so Emperor Lessar—and Ahvren's father who served him—had settled there. Most of the shield fleet, like the ship Ahvren had traveled in, wasn't built for atmosphere.

By now Ahvren could make out the river that bisected K'Moth like a curved blade lying on a rough brown sack. The sea must be on the shuttle's other side.

Ahvren had paid little heed to his family's messages, except to be grateful that the people he cared most about were trailing after the shield fleet instead of being where he was. Everyone knew that the fleet had found and conquered something called the T'Chin Empire, though it wasn't an empire but something the linguists translated as "confederation." There were forty planets in the T'Chin Confederation, each inhabited by a different sentient species. All the planets traded with one another. All the species traveled freely from world to world and lived on whatever planet they chose, atmosphere and climate permitting. And all but one of them had surrendered to the Vivitare without a fight. Ahvren's lip curled in contempt. At least the Mirmani had courage—for all the good it had done them.

K'Moth was the largest city on the planet T'Chin, for which this whole chaotic-sounding mess had been named. His family had lived there for almost a year now, and they all said it was fine—except for his mother, who complained about the heat. His father and Sabri never mentioned weather.

His parents were still fine, but just six months ago, Sabri's face had appeared on Ahvren's message screen.

"Hello, heart-sib." She was smiling, but a note of stress in her voice had arrested Ahvren's attention. Her long-boned face, framed in wings of flaming hair, looked the same. Or was there something . . . controlled in her expression? Ahvren wasn't sure.

"We heard about your victory—congratulations! You always did get all the fun."

She grinned, but Ahvren grimaced. Sabri really would have enjoyed it. Such a pity, such a *waste*, she'd been born a girl.

"Actually, heart-sib, I'm missing you."

Ahvren straightened, staring at his foster sister's face—if Sabri had ever said she missed him, he couldn't remember it.

*"I really wish you were here."* She'd tried to sound casual, but the intensity in her eyes crept into her voice—it quivered. Then she glanced over her shoulder, looking for all the world as if someone Ahvren couldn't see was listening to her, and burst into aimless chat-

ter—very unlike her usual crisp directness.

Ahvren was halfway out the door before the echo of her farewell died. It was a parent's right to monitor a daughter's messages, but if someone was controlling what Sabri said to *him*, there was something very strange going on.

The shuttle's engine began to whine, and drab brown buildings, a city, took shape below. Sabri had saved him. With the Mirmani rebellion crushed, his service oath for that campaign had ended. His commander was becoming more and more impatient for him to swear himself to the next one, but urgent family business was a perfect excuse to leave. And of course he couldn't renew his service oath until that business was resolved. He hadn't even had to lie. Yes, Sabri had saved him; now it was up to him to help her. And then himself. If he could. If he could keep the truth from his father.

The engine's whine swelled to a shriek, and Ahvren's stomach lifted. They touched down with a bump. Wrestling his gear bags down the aisle, Ahvren wasn't even thinking about the strange planet until he stepped through the door and a wave of heat slapped him like a giant palm.

"Shackles! Is it always this hot?"

"Yes." The shuttle attendant grinned. "Enjoy your stay."

Ahvren grimaced and staggered down the ramp. He was sweating before he reached the pavement; the heat soaked into his skin, his feet, his fingers, driving out the clammy chill that had become part of his bones on Mirmanidan. He decided he liked the heat and the vivid, cloudless sky—or he would, as soon as his eyes adapted and he could stop squinting. Under the ship's exhaust fumes, he smelled the brininess of an alien sea.

A small crowd emerged from a cluster of ground cars parked at the edge of the landing pad and rushed toward the disembarking passengers. Ahvren scanned them, one hand going reflexively to the butt of his disrupter, but he didn't see his father. The flash of relief faded quickly. He'd rather get it over with. And he might not blurt out the truth. He usually had enough control over himself to keep his mouth shut unless someone asked him a direct question.

The passengers mingled with the crowd, clasping wrists, embracing, smiling. No one greeted Ahvren. He'd sent word ahead, the shuttle was on time, his father had promised to meet him—if he couldn't make it, surely he'd have sent someone else. No one seemed to be looking for him. Perhaps his father was waiting in the terminal.

Ahvren looked across the plain of sun-baked concrete. Heat waves cast ripples over the scene; there were ships of every variety from the sleek private cruisers of the very rich to squat, scarred freight-lifters. The busiest part of the field held the hordes of repair and maintenance flyers that were preparing the shield fleet for the conquest of Zodan. The Zo was the only species of the T'Chin confederacy that hadn't surrendered at the Vivitare's first request. Some of the others had surrendered before they were even asked to do so.

In the distance Ahvren saw a long, low roof, its supports reaching out to caress the ground. A swarm of flitters rising and descending behind it, well out of the port's traffic patterns, marked it as the terminal. Some of Ahvren's fellow passengers were boarding a spaceport van. Not knowing what else to do, Ahvren heaved his bags in and sat on one of the padded benches. The people around him chatted with the easy excitement of arrival, but Ahvren didn't join in.

It was unlike his father, not to have met him.

The van released its passengers between two of the sweeping roof supports. The terminal's double doors were nine feet high, but they whisked open politely as Ahvren approached. It was cool inside, and Ahvren sighed with relief as he shuffled through.

The ceiling arced over a huge room filled with counters, behind which baggage popped into and out of the floor. The rest of the space was filled with . . . not people, Ahvren decided. Beings. Creatures. Ahvren had seen pictures and read reports on most of the aliens who were part of the T'Chin Confederation, but seeing them in the flesh . . . or fur . . . or feather was something else again. And nothing had prepared him for the grunts, squeaks, and whistles echoing off the vaulted ceiling.

Ahvren's hand clenched on the hilt of his nerve disrupter. All the reports claimed the T'Chin natives were harmless. Suspiciously harmless, some said. Ahvren was safer here than in his own room on Mirmanidan. Was that a *beak* on that thing?

8

A few hundred feet away, Ahvren noticed, was a knot of dark heads—Vivitare, wearing the gold-trimmed scarlet sashes of the emperor's personal guard. Gripping his bags and his disrupter, Ahvren hurried toward them. In the center, reeling off a string of orders, was his father's fit, stocky form. Viv Saiden saw Ahvren at the same time, and his scowl lightened, but he didn't stop speaking. The guardsmen scattered as Ahvren approached.

"Father, what—"

"Thank the old gods you're here, Son." His father swept his outstretched hands aside and hugged him, bags and all. "I'm delighted to see you well, and I'm sorry I didn't meet your shuttle, but we've got a problem— Sabri's run off."

"She's *what*?"

"Run away. When we got here, she said she had to relieve herself. She went into the humanoid facility, but she didn't come out. When I went in to look for her, her clothes were in the disposal bin and she was gone."

"Her clothes were . . . What makes you think she ran away? She could have been kidnapped! She could—"

"No, she's run. This is the second time. I should have suspected, but—"

Ahvren caught his father's arm. "What is Sabri running from? What's going on?"

Viv Saiden sighed. He looked older than Ahvren remembered.

"I'll explain later, all right? The important thing now is to find her. I've drafted a dozen of the emperor's guard—I showed them a picture, but they don't know her. You and I have the best chance of recognizing her, whatever disguise she's—"

"Disguise?"

"I found her clothes, Ahvren. What do you think she's wearing? Will you please stop repeating what I say and look for your sister?"

Ahvren took a deep breath. "Suppose she's already on a ship? How long—"

"She's not. The first thing I did when I realized I'd lost her was order all passenger ships groundlocked. Nothing is leaving this terminal for space until we find Sabri."

Ahvren stared. "You have the authority for that?"

"No, but Emperor Lessar does. I got his edict when I called for the guard. But he doesn't want to tie up shipping indefinitely, so we'd better start searching."

"Right." Ahvren took another deep breath. "We should stay together. Which way first?"

His father's brows lifted. "We'll cover more ground if we . . . ah. Ahvren, this isn't Mirmanidan; we'll be safe on our own. You go that way, I'll go this."

"But—"

His father turned and walked off through the crowd as if every odd being in the place could be trusted. Perhaps they all could. Everyone said they could. Ahvren threw his bags into a corner—nothing in them mattered much. Nothing mattered at all, compared to Sabri. He took the direction his father had indicated, trying to still his whirling thoughts so he could concentrate on looking for Sabri. Sabri, who'd never run from anything in her life! Why in the world would she be running now? And what—

A being, creature, thing . . . a nightmare was coming through the crowd toward him. Ahvren backed aside as a globe of murky water undulated past on a mass of writhing, rubber-coated tentacles. Any sound they made was obliterated by the thrum of a hover-lifter. A Daquee, a water worlder. Ahvren hadn't dreamed they could leave their unique, poisonous environment. He stared after it for several moments before he realized that no one else was acting as if anything unusual had happened. Then he realized that in the last few minutes Sabri could have come up and tapped him on the shoulder and he wouldn't have noticed.

He was a Vivitar, a warrior of the Vivitare. This aimless fear was beneath him. Sabri was the first priority. To help her, he had to find her. And ask her what was going on *without* the emperor's guards breathing down their necks. But to find her before the guards did, he couldn't start running in panicked circles. He had to think. Ahvren went over to a wall niche and sat on the floor. The crowd of bizarre creatures distracted him, so he shut his eyes, trusting his ears to warn him if anything came too close.

Think. Think like Sabri. She knew their father would close down the port. He'd said she had tried to escape before—from what? No, go on. She'd had other clothes, a disguise, waiting. But what disguise would get her off planet? No ships were allowed to leave the terminal . . . no *passenger* ships. What about freighters? Could she stow away in a crate? Yes, she could. Even the emperor couldn't tie up traffic forever. At least, Emperor Lessar wouldn't. It would have to be a load that was stored with atmosphere and in moderate temperature, so she'd have to choose it carefully. How could she find out what . . . ah, that fit. And a disguise that was part of the terminal scenery would be more likely to be overlooked. Ahvren started searching for a way to get down to the basement, where the baggage went.

The dimly lit basement was full of clattering machinery that sorted and routed baggage, but some freight had to be handled manually—freight that needed special conditions of atmosphere, temperature, or pressure. It took Ahvren twenty minutes, wandering down deserted aisles and ducking under rumbling ramps, to find the area he was looking for.

Its floor was a full story lower. Ahvren stood on the steel-railed landing, watching small carts scuttle through a maze of crates. Baggage handlers perched on the empty carts and walked behind the full ones. The light seemed bright after the shadows of the automated sorting area, but it still took Ahvren several minutes to locate Sabri. She wore grubby green coveralls, like most of the humanoid workers, and her fiery hair was tucked into a cap, but her long, easy stride was familiar enough to tighten Ahvren's throat. What had driven her to this? Now he could ask.

Dodging carts, Ahvren was fifty feet away when she saw him. Her eyes widened in recognition and he swore he saw welcome there. Then an expression of dismay so intense it was almost horror crossed her face, and she turned and ran.

Ahvren was so startled at the spectacle of *Sabri* running from *him* that he froze in his tracks until two of the emperor's guardsmen raced by. She must have seen them behind him!

Ahvren set off in pursuit, but he knew it was too late. She might have outrun the guards, but she'd never escape the range of the comm-unit one was yelling into.

They caught her on a staircase, two at the bottom, one at the top. At least she had the sense not to fight them, which would have

14

given everything away. Not that it mattered—she seemed to have lost her mind, anyway. No, thought Ahvren, as he jogged up to the group on the stairs, not lost her mind, been driven out of it. Her face was white in the gloom, her jaw clenched against useless protests. Against tears?

*I'll fix it, heart-sib*, Ahvren swore silently. *Whatever it is, I'll make it right. I promise.*

# Chapter 2

TWO MONTHS LATER, nothing had changed.

"... you'd command a seven-ship fighter wing on the *Survivor*, directly under the squadron commander." Ahvren's father had left his desk and was pacing before the high arched windows. The light silk of his tunic glowed as he crossed the bands of morning sunlight that pooled on the creamy stone of the floor. His hair was almost entirely gray, but his body was still muscular, and his face was alive with enthusiasm as he told Ahvren how wonderfully lucky he was.

Ahvren bit back a sigh and slumped in his chair. *Say nothing*, he told himself.

"It's a lot of responsibility for a young man of eighteen," Viv Saiden continued. "Ordinarily, you wouldn't see ship duty for two more years, much less command. But you did well during the Mirmani revolt, so they were willing to take you."

Words flashed into Ahvren's mind like a sword from its sheath. *Don't say it! And if you must say it, say it* tactfully!

"It takes three months to get to Zodan—I understand it's one of the newer planets in the T'Chin Confederation, on the outer reaches. The voyage will give you time to familiarize yourself with the ship, your wingmen, and your duties, so you can—"

"I don't want to go." Ahvren heard his own voice say the words and winced. He'd said it before over the past two months, compulsively, but he'd been wrong about the problems that saying it would bring. Or rather, wrong about the nature of the problems. His father wasn't angry with him. Instead, his father refused to listen to him.

He'd hoped that, given a couple of months of peace, a chance to let his guard relax, his strange compulsion to tell the truth would diminish. It hadn't, leaving him torn between annoyance and a growing fear. It wasn't that his nerve had broken. He'd seen that happen— mostly to boys in training, but sometimes even to seasoned Vivitars. Some of them developed strange reactions. Ahvren knew one man who broke out in a rash whenever

17

he touched a weapon, no matter what substance it was made of. But he'd never heard of anyone whose war-weakness took the form of an inability to lie.

And Ahvren's nerve hadn't broken. He could still fight. He didn't fear the call to come to his commander's office. He would never see contempt or pity in other men's eyes.

But eight months ago at the victory celebration, when the Mirmani revolt was finally crushed and the last of those stomach-churning executions over with, Barad had been talking about finally getting off this cold, wet world and going on to conquer something with a better climate. A wave of nausea had swept over Ahvren, so intense he'd had to run from the room to keep from disgracing himself in front of his friends. No one commented. Executions were worse than clean battle, even if you didn't participate in them personally. It took a lot of people that way—you got sick, you got over it, you got on with it.

Later, shivering in the warm privacy of his own bed, listening to the distant sounds of celebration and the rain dripping from the eaves, Ahvren wondered if any other Vivitars were struggling with a shamed, soul-wrenching wish that the Mirmani had won.

Not three days after that, the regional commander had asked him about the status of a report Pahdrec was working on. Ahvren had opened his mouth to speak the smooth excuse he and Pahd had worked out and blurted out the truth. It was as if something else had seized his tongue, used it without his consent while he looked on in horrified astonishment.

When Pahdrec, flushed with shame and fury, had emerged from their commander's office, Ahvren had had to explain why he hadn't covered for his friend as they'd agreed. As Pahd had covered for him in the past. But he'd had no explanation.

He still didn't. In the three months that followed, he'd walked a knife edge, never knowing whether he'd be able to control his tongue or not. And there were some truths he couldn't speak, not if he wanted to retain his honor. The day he was to renew his oath to the emperor and the shield fleet had drawn nearer and nearer, and the compulsion had worsened. Only Sabri's message had saved him.

He still wasn't afraid that his nerve would break, at least not much. But who knew what other weird reaction might crop up? Or what wrong thing he might say, to what wrong person, at what wrong time? He didn't want to fight on Zodan. And he knew he wouldn't be able to get through the service oath without blurting out that truth.

His father scowled. "This is an honor, Ahvren. The finest chance to serve the emperor and win renown that you're likely to see for years. A chance most young men would *kill* for. You've said that you don't want to go, but you still haven't told me why."

"Because it's all a lie," Ahvren blurted out. "It wasn't glorious, like the bards are saying. It was ugly and ghastly and I can't do it anymore. At least, not now."

His father's expression became grave and still. Ahvren's heart flinched, waiting to see scorn or, worse yet, pity in his eyes.

Viv Saiden sighed. "You're right, but war is what it is. And as the Karg taught us, those who aren't conquerors are the conquered."

"I know that. It's just . . ." Ahvren's voice trailed off. He wasn't quite sure what it was. He just knew that he couldn't go to Zodan.

"Ahvren." His father's voice was soft. "Did your nerve fail you on Mirmanidan?"

"No sir," said Ahvren truthfully. "Just my stomach."

"Ah, that happens to everyone at first," said his father. "You'll get over it. You're an excellent swordsman—"

"Only fair," Ahvren inserted.

"—and you'll find that those reflexes will let you fly a fighter, too. Space combat is cleaner than ground war. In a few years, you'll look back on this and wonder what you made such a fuss about. I'll tell the *Survivor*'s captain to expect you—"

"No," said Ahvren. "I'm sorry, sir, but you can't force me, even if I am your heir. You can have me thrown aboard a ship, but you can't make me fight."

His father took a deep breath, struggling for patience. "What do you want then? To fight in the emperor's service is the highest honor there is. If that doesn't matter to you—"

"It does. I want to serve the emperor. As a Vivitar, a warrior. I do." And he did. He wanted the honor, for himself, for his family. But . . . "But I want to serve with my wits and my sword, not a disrupter. I can't do that on Zodan."

His father frowned. "There are other

21

honorable professions. If you're being drawn to engineering, for instance, or to be a bard—"

Ahvren winced. "Not a bard. It's not that there's anything else I want to do. I just want . . . I want . . ." In truth he didn't know what he wanted, except to stay away from Zodan.

A brooding silence fell. Ahvren's father walked back to his desk and sank into his chair. "I think that both my children have gone mad. And picked a shackling inconvenient time for it."

Ahvren bit his lip, hesitating. This wasn't the best time, but he'd promised to try again. "Father, about Sabri—"

"No!" His father's hand slammed down on the desk, and Ahvren jumped. "I've heard more than enough from both of you, and I don't intend to hear it anymore! She's even crazier than you are—she's going to be the emperor's first wife when Lessar dies and Dravik inherits. She—"

"She doesn't like him."

"She hardly knows him. They've met, what, half a dozen times? Most girls are afraid of marriage—your mother was terrified, and we've been happy together for almost thirty years."

"She knows him pretty well. She's one of Jennah's friends, remember? And she's my age. She knows what she wants." Unlike Ahvren.

"Yes, and she wants to be a *warrior*. I hold you directly responsible for that, Ahvren. What were you thinking of, teaching her to fight? Wearing a tunic and trousers! I take it back, you haven't suddenly gone crazy— you've both been mad for years!"

"She couldn't move in long skirts, and those trailing scarves tangled us up. If you'd just watch her, you'd understa—"

"I understand that it's a miracle no one ever caught you. She'd have been disgraced! She may be only your foster sister, but she's a member of our household—her disgrace would affect us all. If Grem had seen you—"

"Grem taught her, too." The words were out before Ahvren could stop them, and his heart sank. It was one thing to let his impossible compulsions mess up his own life—to betray a friend was different.

His father's jaw sagged. "*Grem* taught her?"

Ahvren opened his mouth to try to deny it, to say he hadn't meant it, but the words wouldn't come. "It was because she was good," he said passionately. Memory flashed in his mind. Sabri's sword twisting against his, strong and supple as a cobra. Her laughter as his sword levitated out of his grip and flew across the practice floor. It had clattered to a stop at Grem's feet. "I'm only a fair swordsman, but Sabri *is* excellent. Master class, Father. That's why Grem taught her."

His father shook his head. "Maybe the madness is infectious," he muttered. "Some sort of mutating virus. Ahvren, I don't care if Grem taught her. I don't want to discuss it, and I don't intend, ever, to see my foster daughter dressed like a man—much less fighting like one! She's going to marry Dravik; then she'll be his problem and all I'll have to worry about is you, on top of this other mess."

Ahvren didn't want to argue about his affairs. The compulsion to say so rose murkily in his mind. Quick, say something else! "Ah, what other mess?"

The exasperation on his father's face turned to grimness. "There's a rumor that someone is plotting to kill the emperor."

Ahvren nodded. "Yes, I've heard it."

His father's hands clenched. "Heard it where?"

"I don't know. In the market, in the bath-house, at the spaceport . . . Everyone's talking about it. Do you mean the emperor is taking this seriously?"

The exasperation returned to his father's expression, so intense it bordered on anger. Ahvren sat up straighter.

"Ahvren," said his father with dangerous restraint, "you were on Mirmanidan during the revolt. Over four thousand Vivitare died. You don't expect us to take this *seriously*?"

"Well, no, I don't. But that's *because* I was on Mirmanidan. Serious assassins don't let rumors of their plans spread all over the planet before the attempt. Even if there is a plot, anyone but an idiot would give it up, once they knew we'd been warned."

"I know that. But you said it yourself—we've been warned. We'd have to be idiots to ignore it." His father rubbed his chin with his knuckles, and Ahvren eyed him watchfully. His father only rubbed his chin when he was plotting something. "So you genuinely believe there's no danger?"

"Oh, someone may have planned an assassination, but anyone stupid enough to go on with it now would be caught by the emperor's security. No matter what fool they put in charge of it."

"Hm. It might interest you to learn that *I* have been given charge of the emperor's security, until this plot is exposed."

Hot blood flooded Ahvren's cheeks. His father laughed.

"Sorry, sir. I thought Viv Redahd still had charge of it. Don't tell me the emperor finally dismissed the man?"

His father sobered. "No, unfortunately. *He* is assigned to find out who is involved in the conspiracy."

"Viv Redahd? But he— Father, that's a mistake! It was following his policies on Mirmanidan that caused half our problems. The T'Chin don't resent us; at least, most of them don't. If that shackling slaver-bait employs his usual methods for gaining information . . ."

His father grimaced in rueful agreement. "Redahd won't discover anything until the assassin walks up and points a disrupter at Lessar's head—and maybe not then. That's why I'm in charge of security. If it's any consolation, I understand Redahd's stuck. He hasn't even found anyone who knows enough to be tortured for it." He rubbed his chin again. "Ahvren, you say you still want to serve the emperor. Is that true?"

"Yes," said Ahvren warily. Where was this leading? "I'm still a Vivitar. I just . . ."

"You deal fairly well with the T'Chin, don't you? I know you've spent a lot of time in the town."

Ahvren shrugged. "They're . . . friendly people."

He'd spent as much time as he could roving the streets, to avoid confronting his father. Until this bizarre compulsion released him, he wanted to spend as little time as possible with his family, his friends, and especially his military superiors. But the T'Chin were friendly. After the hostility he'd encountered on Mirmanidan, it made him deeply nervous.

"Then you've learned something about them? Their culture? Their society?" Mischief danced in his father's eyes. "If I offered you a chance to serve, without fighting, would you be interested?"

Ahvren opened his mouth to ask "What do you mean?" but it came out, "What are you up to, Father?"

His father grinned. "I'm going to propose a wager. You say you want to serve with—what was it?—your wits and your sword? Prove it. Prove to me that your wits and sword are worth more to Emperor Lessar than a disrupter, and you win."

"Prove it how? Win what?"

"I want you to find out the truth of this conspiracy. Uncover these rebels—and if in doing so you showed Redahd up as the incompetent slaver-bait he is, that wouldn't hurt."

"But what if there is no conspiracy? How can I uncover something that isn't there?"

"By *proving* it doesn't exist. If you can do that, I'll accept it as a win for you. You won't have to go to Zodan. And we'll look into another career for you, as an intelligencer, perhaps."

Ahvren grimaced. "I'm too old to think being an intelligencer is romantic. In real life, all they do is sort through data files. They might as well be scholars, who never lay hand on a sword."

His father cocked a curious brow. "I thought that was what you wanted."

"I'm no coward, sir," said Ahvren. "I think

28

what I'm looking for is . . . a clean fight."

"In my experience," said Viv Saiden, "there's no such thing. Not real fights, anyway. But if you win your wager, I'll give you a year to try to find one. Or to come up with some other career we can agree on."

Ahvren eyed his father with deep misgivings. "What do you win if I fail?"

"Compliance." His father leaned forward. "I can't force you to serve. But if you give me your word, as one Vivitar to another, that if you lose you'll go to Zodan willingly and do your best, I know you'll keep it."

"And if I win," Ahvren asked slowly, "you'll give me a year to figure out what I want to do?"

His father gazed at him, the humor gone from his expression. "Yes. If you can either discover the T'Chin rebels or prove there aren't any, I'll give you your year."

Hope stirred in Ahvren's heart. His father didn't think he could do it. Maybe he couldn't, but even if he failed, how much worse off would he be? And if he succeeded . . .

"Done." He reached out and clasped his father's wrist. "As one Vivitar to another. Where should I start?"

His father leaned back in his chair, smiling slightly. "I have no idea."

"But surely there's something, some lead you want me to pursue."

"If I had any leads, I'd pursue them myself. And that part of it is Redahd's job, anyway."

"Then what am I supposed to do?"

"What, wits and sword already at a standstill?"

Ahvren scowled. "I haven't even started yet. I suppose this means you won't supply me with equipment or funding, either."

"You'll have your usual stipend, and room and board. But I don't see why I should help you win. Or don't you think that's fair?"

"Fair enough, sir." Ahvren rose and nodded farewell, then strode across the smooth stone floor and hit the bar that released the door latch. The mansions of the wealthy T'Chin, which the Vivitare had taken over, were so old that their doors opened manually. The whole family had spent their first days in the house bumping into the tall, carved panels that refused to open unless you pushed them. Even Ahvren, who had become accustomed to manual doors on Mirmanidan, had lost the habit on the long voyage to

T'Chin and had to relearn it.

He could have a year—a whole year—to lose that accursed compulsion. To let the tense wariness of the war zone fade. To find some way to serve his emperor, retain his honor, and never again have to see children kill and die. All he had to do was find out the truth, or lack of truth, behind that rumor. On a conquered planet, dealing with another culture. And if he lost . . . Ahvren's steps slowed. It would certainly prove a test of his wits.

He was almost out of the house when he remembered Sabri. He might be able to solve his problem, but hers . . . Wait a minute. Suppose there really was a plot—and given the rumors, there probably had been. If these people had intended to kill the emperor, they'd probably try again if they weren't discovered. Later, when the rumors died down, when the emperor's security wasn't so alert. If Ahvren could find them, he'd be saving the emperor's life! Ahvren grimaced. As logic went, it was pretty sloppy. But if he could convince the emperor that in uncovering the plot Ahvren was saving his life, then Lessar would surely offer him the traditional reward—any boon in his power to grant. And he could ask for Sabri's freedom! He could save himself *and* Sabri. Ahvren frowned. It was a long shot, but it was a lot more hope than he'd had this morning.

Ahvren turned and hurried toward the women's wing, his steps echoing against the arched ceiling. Some Vivitare found these rooms of subtly inlaid stone too bare, for they seldom held more than the minimum amount of furniture—exquisitely woven cloth slung over wooden supports. Their cool austerity seemed restful to Ahvren, and intensely sensible in a desert climate.

Sabri and his mother were in the garden, an oasis of narrow-leafed trees and sinewy shrubs—some still in flower. His mother sat quietly on the bench that bordered the central fountain, but Sabri paced in front of her, ignoring the sun's streaming heat. In the privacy of their own garden they'd removed their head scarves; Sabri's hair gleamed like copper, swaying with the rhythm of her long stride. The ancients said that the god of the volcano had taken human form, breeding this strain of red hair and tawny eyes into the black-haired, bronze-skinned Vivitare. Now they understood recessive genes, but Ahvren, contemplating the temperament that came with the hair, sometimes wondered if they hadn't dismissed the volcano-god theory too quickly.

He started toward them—he'd have sworn his footsteps couldn't be heard over the splash of the fountain, but Sabri stiffened and spun on the balls of her feet like a panther . . . like a swordsman.

"Well?" she demanded as Ahvren drew near.

He had to look up to meet her steady eyes; she was three inches taller than he. Too tall, too thin, far too unfeminine—why would an emperor's son choose her for his first wife?

"Mother, may I speak to Sabri alone?"

"Certainly, dear." She smiled at them placidly as Ahvren dragged his sister out of earshot.

"What's happened? Don't tell me Father changed his mind."

"I'm sorry, heart-sib. I don't think he'll ever do that. But listen. I've got another idea." Ahvren told her about the wager, and the conclusions he'd reached.

The brooding stillness that settled over Sabri's strong-boned face as he spoke made her look like a stranger, and Ahvren's enthusiasm chilled. "Sabri? Do you think I can do it?"

Her lips twisted ironically. "I don't know— I think you might. Though it sounds like a lot to accomplish, with just seven days until the wedding. Especially dealing with a conquered, alien culture. Where can you start? Besides, what if there is no plot? What if it's nothing but a rumor?"

"There has to have been something behind it," Ahvren argued. "Even rumors don't just start from nothing. I'll need to find an interface with their culture, someone who can explain things to me. I know it's a long shot, but if I can find some conspirators, then . . ."

The barest echo of her rueful grin flickered over Sabri's face. "Well, the old gods know how much luck I wish you." She turned back to their mother, and Ahvren followed her. "Mother, may I visit Dara? She asked if I could come today."

"Of course you may, love. If the storm catches you, just stay there; we won't expect you home till sunset. You can take Brrric with you. Grishik make such fine guardsmen."

His mother's face was unclouded. Sometimes Ahvren wondered if she really understood that the guards assigned to Sabri when she left the house were jailers as well as guardians. Sabri certainly knew it, but no trace of resentment showed on her face as she swooped down and kissed her foster mother's cheek.

"Thanks. I won't be late. And thank you, brother—I know you're trying." She gripped his shoulder, as if they'd just finished a practice bout, and he answered the gesture before he had time to think better of it. Then she strode off, forgetting, as always, to pull the scarf up to cover her hair.

Ahvren turned to his mother. "What in the world was that about? If I didn't know better I'd say she was . . . *resigned*."

"I don't know," his mother murmured. "It worries me."

Ahvren dropped to the bench beside her. The handful of lines that creased her plump, pretty face seemed deeper than usual. If he failed . . . "Mother, do women adjust to marriage? If they truly don't want it? Father said so, but . . ."

"Some do," his mother admitted. "Most do, I think."

"Yes, but Sabri isn't 'most.' Could you talk

to Father? He loves Sabri. If he believed she'd be unhappy, he wouldn't do this. He'd . . . he'd . . ."

His mother sighed. "That's the problem, isn't it? He and Emperor Lessar have agreed. If Dravik was the one who wanted out, and Lessar asked for it, he could comply, but as it is . . ."

Ahvren hated it when his mother made sense. "Maybe Dravik will back out. I can't imagine why he chose her in the first place. It's not as if she's— Why are you smiling like that?"

"You're her brother." She was still smiling.

Ahvren scowled. He also hated it when his mother didn't make sense. But maybe there was another way. "I'll talk to Dravik. He might back out, if he knew she was unwilling. I would. Most men would."

The hidden laughter left his mother's face. "Most men."

A chill swept through Ahvren. Dravik wasn't most men, any more than Sabri was most women. But for different reasons.

"I'll talk to him anyway."

# Chapter 3

**A**HVREN TOOK LEAVE OF his mother and headed for the front door. He would talk to Dravik. Uncovering a plot that no longer existed was a lot less certain—or maybe it wasn't.

Pomo was on duty at the door. He peered at Ahvren as he approached—then his wrinkled, turtlelike face broke into a beaming smile of recognition. "Are you to be going out, Viv Ahvren? What will you be needing?"

"Just my sword and pouch. Oh, and make sure there's money in it, will you, Pomo? I keep forgetting."

Pomo nodded and waddled off. Ahvren had had his doubts when his father hired the Olopoli. Their reptilian faces didn't disturb him, though he found it a little disconcerting to deal with an adult whose head was barely higher than his waist. And the fact that the Olopolis' photobiotic skin made it necessary for them to spend at least four hours a day sunning themselves hadn't proved nearly as inconvenient as he'd expected. Still, hiring a servant who literally thought all Vivitare looked alike, unless he knew them well, who couldn't even tell men from women, seemed madness. But Pomo had proved efficient and cheerful, and he solved the gender identification problem by addressing all strangers as mem/ser. No one had objected to it so far. He came waddling back with Ahvren's sword, which was almost as tall as he was, dangling awkwardly from his shoulder.

After two years of wearing a disrupter all the time, it felt odd to be wearing his sword again. Odder still to know that on T'Chin he probably didn't need any weapon. Even the street patrols were growing careless, since no one ever challenged them.

"A sand cape is here for you," Pomo announced cheerfully. "The day is warm, but the storm is already there, over the desert."

Ahvren buckled the sword belt and clipped on his money pouch. "Thanks, Pomo, but it's too hot for a cape."

"It's your choice, but foolishness is there." The mixture of kindness and disapproval on his lined face was irresistible.

Ahvren grinned. "All right, but just the head cloth."

It had seemed strange at first to wear a scarf like a woman, but the Zo-woven head cloth was so thin that Ahvren could see through it, breathe through it, and roll it into a ball half the size of his fist. Yet it was so tight-meshed that it screened out even the finest particles of dust. After their first few weeks in the city, even the most conservative Vivitare had abandoned the breathing masks and goggles that had been their initial solution to the merciless sandstorms that blew off the desert and inundated the city of K'Moth.

"And is it making sense to cover the head and not the body? The head is being most important, but without the body, it—"

"All right, all right." Ahvren accepted the cape and stepped into the courtyard, the late-morning sunlight enveloping him as if he'd opened the hatch of an engine core. Beads of sweat were pricking his skin when he opened the tall wrought-iron gate in the outer wall. Many Vivitare hated the fierce heat, swearing to leave on the first ship they could get, but Ahvren didn't mind it. The market was only half an hour's walk.

The streets of the wealthy quarter were quiet; Ahvren passed only a handful of people, most of them Vivitare, as he made his way past the high walls and intricately patterned gates. As he drew near the high-priced shops and offices of the old town, the amount and variety of traffic increased and the incessant drone of flitter engines overhead formed a familiar background to the snatches of incomprehensible gabble that reached Ahvren's ears.

On Mirmanidan, Ahvren had become so accustomed to the translator bracelet that he barely noticed that a person's voice came from his lips in multisyllabic gibberish and simultaneously from just above his left elbow in perfect Vivitare. Well, almost perfect, and only if you happened to have the right data clip in the translator at the time. But most T'Chin, like Pomo, were learning Vivitare with astounding speed. Ahvren's data clips were in his pouch, so the conversations of the strange beings he passed came to his ears in their original growls, squeaks, or clicks, depending on what was speaking. Forty species in the T'Chin Confederation. Forty planets. And all but one of them had surrendered to the shield fleet without firing a shot. Despicable. Cowards all.

But passing from the high stone walls of the wealthy quarter into the low clay and timber buildings of the old town, Ahvren was forced to admit that their cowardice had its advantages. No building on this planet was gutted and burned. No cities had been torn to rubble by shock waves. No rolling firestorms had swept through the arable lands. The transparent silicon coating they sprayed on the ancient clay walls protected them from nothing worse than the blasting sandstorms that blew out of the desert and into the sea. But for this peace, they had traded autonomy and honor. No, he couldn't accept it.

Looking down one twisting street, a little straighter than the rest, Ahvren caught a glimpse of the low brown storm cloud hovering on the western horizon. It looked like it might reach the city early today.

He started to pick up his pace, but an informagoth booth caught his eye. The ad on its side, whose writing shifted from language to language as he watched, claimed that a Darzix Corporation informagoth had access to all the information in the known universe. Information—lots of it—was what he needed.

Ahvren preferred getting information from people, but this might be a good place to start.

He slid into the booth and fed it the one-ounce copper cube that would activate it. The T'Chin insistence that some physical token change hands in any financial transaction was annoying. For people who cared so much about physical money, they had accepted the varied metal blocks of the Vivitare currency system with astonishingly little protest. The screen in front of him lit and began to babble, as face after alien face appeared.

"I'm Vivitare," he told it, having no desire to go through forty renditions of "What language do you speak?"

"Thank you." The face of a handsome Vivitare man appeared. "How may we help you?"

"I need some information about T'Chin society and culture."

"Will you be paying in currency or credit?"

"Credit," said Ahvren, setting the credit identification bracelet on his right wrist against the correct portal.

"Credit account accepted. Society and culture, T'Chin, lists 4,879 references. Do you wish to see an introductory article, or do you wish to narrow your topic?"

Ahvren sighed. "If I want to find some specific information, how should I go about it?"

"For information, ask a Darzix Corporation informagoth. We have access to all—"

"Stop. I need access to nonlisted information. I need to figure something out. How would a T'Chin do that?"

This was evidently a hard question. The face on the screen frowned slightly, and the machine hummed for several seconds. "Lessons in logic and deductive reasoning are offered by bibliogoths. Bibliogoths sell knowledge, while informagoths provide information. A Darzix Corporation informagoth can provide access to—"

"Stop. Please. A bibliogoth is a person, right? A scholar of some sort?"

"Bibliogoths are biological entities. Bibliogoths study information on a wide variety of topics, and—"

"All right, stop."

A scholar. A book-bound clerk. But also a teacher, who must know the society he lived in well enough to suggest a place Ahvren might start. "That sounds like what I need. Who's the best bibliogoth in K'Moth?"

"The city directory lists fourteen biblio-goths in the city K'Moth, planet T'Chin. None are named, listed, or referred to as 'best.' Please restate your request."

"I want to know which of them is most highly regarded," Ahvren told the face on the screen, without much hope. Informagoths always seemed to have either too much information or too little.

"No such data is available. Please restate your request."

"Can you rank them in order—most rec-ommended to least?"

"No such data is available. Please restate your request."

"Never mind. At least . . . Which one makes the most money?"

"No such data is available. Financial trans-actions are confidential. Please restate your request."

"Forget it. End . . . wait." It was stupid, but why not?

"Who are the leaders of the T'Chin rebel-lion?"

The face frowned. The machine hummed. "No such data is available. Please resta—"

"How can I contact the leaders of the

T'Chin underground?"

"The nearest access to the underground transit system, city K'Moth, planet T'Chin, is two blocks north of this location." A map replaced the face on the screen.

"End transaction," said Ahvren. It was a stupid idea.

"Three silver ounces have been charged on your account for this transaction. May freedom be yours and your children's, and thank you for choosing a Darzix Corporation informagoth."

Ahvren didn't know whether to laugh or swear.

The "new" market was the oldest part of the city that wasn't a slum. The carefully preserved stalls and shops could have come from medieval, or even earlier, technology— until the weather changed and glowing force fields snapped up to protect the wares from the driving sand or the rare rain that blew off the sea.

"Sand from the sunset, rain from the sunrise," the furry waiter who gave Ahvren his midmeal told him cheerfully. For a copper bar, he was delighted to give Ahvren the address of the best bibliogoth in the city. Thirty-three Shakka Street.

"What's his name?" Ahvren would have sworn he saw amusement in the round, squirrel-like eyes.

"I'm really not . . . equipped to say, Viv. But he's known as the bibliogoth of thirty-three Shakka Street, and unless he's out of town, you should find him there. It's a home office."

The moderate traffic of the old town streets had fascinated Ahvren, but the seething mixture of species crowded into the narrow lanes between the shops made him uneasy, though he knew most of them were tourists. The Wabani spicergoth gave him the same name, or rather address, as did the Olopoli electrogoth selling laser welding tools. A N'Ssser vegigoth gave a different address, but its eyes shifted. And the next two beings told Ahvren 33 Shakka Street. He had quite a reputation, whoever he was.

Ahvren went up to the nearest clerk, waited till its eyestalks turned toward him, and paid two copper ounces for directions to 33 Shakka Street. It was in the old town, on the other side of the market from his house;

he thought he had time to make it.

The wind was eddying through the twisting streets when Ahvren reached 33 Shakka Street, but there was no sand in it yet. He pushed open one of the high double doors and jumped as a brass chime rang—loudly.

The room he entered was obviously a waiting room; it held chairs and stools designed to fit a variety of beings, and reader screens lay on a desk by the door. Two closed doors concealed the rest of the building. The windows had already shuttered themselves against the coming storm, and the lights that flooded the ceiling were rather dim, so the computer terminal on the desk cast a visible light into the room when it lit. The familiar string of languages began to sound.

"Vivitare," Ahvren told it crisply.

"Thank you." At least there were no faces on this screen, just a series of curves replacing one another. "Do you have an appointment to see the bibliogoth?"

"No. Do I need one?"

"If you have no appointment, you may make one today. The first available appointment is on eighteen Vrisish, eleventh hour."

"But that's almost three weeks—I can't

47

wait that long."

"The next available appointment is on—"

"Stop." Ahvren looked around the empty room. "Hasn't anyone canceled this afternoon, because of the storm?"

"In the summer, all afternoon appointments are tentative." There was a pause while the computer processed. "Input from the bibliogoth will be required. Please wait."

Having little choice in the matter, Ahvren did so, pacing restlessly around the austere room. There was no dust, but it felt strangely unused, as if people seldom spent much time there. No paintings hung on the patterned plaster walls. The only ornament was a large vase, whose deep green-gold glaze and graceful curves proclaimed Cutachan manufacture. Ahvren was reaching to touch it when the terminal spoke again. "The bibliogoth will see you shortly." The screen blinked off.

A few minutes later one of the doors opened, and a stocky being swathed in a sand cape hurried across the room and opened the outer door. The wind whirled in, and the chime clanged. The outer door closed again.

The terminal on the desk remained silent, but the inner door was open, and Ahvren was tired of waiting. The hall beyond the door was short; two arched openings led into dark rooms on either side, and at the end of the hall, light glowed from a half-open door. Ahvren strode forward, shoved it wide, and froze in his tracks. He had no objection to the various forms of most of the T'Chin species, but he'd never really been fond of bugs.

"You're a T'chin, aren't you?" Ahvren asked the creature behind the desk. "Your people founded the Empire."

Ahvren had read about them on his voyage to the planet. These people had endoskeletons as well as exo- and eight legs instead of six, and their antennae were set behind their eyes instead of in front, but Ahvren always thought of them as ants. Eight-foot-tall ants. They were the reason the ceilings and doors were all so high.

Ahvren had seen them in the market-place, stalking slowly on their four lower legs, togalike scarves wrapped intricately around their upper limbs. This one was naked, except for the synthavode that hung like a breast-plate on its slender thorax. Ahvren had never studied a T'chin up close before . . . and he'd never had one study him.

The long antennae—five feet long? six? and covered with what looked like very short fur—swept forward, quivering in the air over Ahvren's head. It took all his self-control to keep from stepping back. Then the antennae lifted away, without touching him, much to his relief. They remained cocked forward, but relaxed, oscillating slowly.

"We are the intelligent species native to this planet, and the Confederation began here, so you might say we founded it. After a fashion." Three sets of chitinous fingers—claws? talons?—pressed together, pointed downward, and then rotated up. It had three talons per hand, and virtually no palms. Ahvren assumed this was a gesture of greeting and nodded in return before it occurred to him that he had no idea what the motion really meant—the creature could have just implied that his father was unfit! No way of knowing.

"But it's you the Emp—Confederation is named for."

"Indeed, though we spell the word that refers to our species and culture with a small c, to differentiate it from the planet—and from the Confederation, with

50

its multispecies culture."

"But they're pronounced the same. Isn't that confusing?"

"Not to us," said the T'chin. "Now, how may I enlighten you, young Vivitar?"

"I need your help. I mean, I want you to tell me something."

"I will probably tell you a great many things." One antennae curved in a soft spiral. Ahvren hadn't known they could bend like that. He knew he was staring, but he couldn't stop.

"But before I do," the creature continued, "will you answer a question for me?"

"Um, sure. What is it?" The voice coming from the synthavode, which translated its pheromones into speech, didn't sound mechanical. Ahvren had heard that T'chin chemical analyzers were so advanced that the Vivitare engineers hadn't even begun to figure them out.

"What is the difference between an informagoth and a bibliogoth?"

"An informagoth sells information, a bibliogoth sells knowledge. At least, that's what the informagoth said."

"Do you understand the distinction?" The

antennae spiraled again.

"Not entirely," Ahvren admitted.

"Then I will explain. In the beginning, informagoths were the keepers of great libraries, who sold bits of information from the books they gathered and hoarded." One set of talons gestured to the walls around them, and Ahvren saw they were lined with shelves holding antique paper books, as well as racks of data clips, chunks of bone and pottery, and scientific instruments, some ancient, some modern, and some he didn't recognize. "A bibliogoth, on the other hand, sold books. The source of the knowledge. Guess which cost more."

"The books, obviously."

"Yet informagoths have been replaced by computers, and I am still here. The fruit is often sweetest at the top of the tree."

"Huh?" Ahvren blinked.

Both antennae drooped forward, then lifted again. "Never mind. To summarize: An informagoth will *tell* you any fact you pay for, a bibliogoth will *teach* you how to figure out what facts you need, find them, and organize them in a manner in which you can use them and then put them to use. It's a long process.

So, young Vivitare, are you certain you need my services, or shall I direct you to the nearest informagoth?"

"No." Ahvren stepped forward, his excitement growing. "An informagoth can't give me what I want. What you just described . . . I think you can."

Both antennae cocked forward, quivering a little, but not hovering over him. "Then take a chair, young Vivitare, and we'll discuss my fee."

Ahvren looked around. The chairs that lined the wall were much the same mixture as he had found in the waiting room. He chose a low-backed chair and adjusted its height. The T'chin, he noticed, was seated as well, in a cup-shaped apparatus that cradled its abdomen and left three pairs of its limbs free, though it still rested the lowest pair on the floor. They were shorter than its upper limbs, and the talons were stubby.

"Before we talk about money, I'm Viv Ahvren—"

"Ah, a fit male. I've heard something of that. Should I congratulate you?"

"Don't bother. And I'm not that young."

"An infant is old compared to a sunrise,

but the sun will rise on the infant's grandchildren's graves."

"What?"

"I, Viv Ahvren, am almost six hundred of your years old, so I beg your forgiveness if I find you young."

"Six hundred *yea*—" The antennae were lifting. "Uh, yes, I guess I am young then." Someone had told him the T'chin were long-lived, but they'd never said *how* long-lived.

"Then perhaps we may return to the matter of my fee, youngling." Both antennae spiraled this time. Ahvren scowled. If that meant what he was beginning to think it did . . .

"I generally charge one gold brick per session. Sessions are two hours, and they may run over—I don't charge extra if they do. How many sessions do you wish to schedule?"

Ahvren struggled to find his voice. "A gold brick? That's a hundred and twenty-five ounces! *Gold* ounces? I can't . . ." His whole stipend, four silver bricks a month, was less than that. Ahvren had used most of his prize money from the fighting on Mirmanidan to pay for his passage to T'Chin. At a gold brick per session . . . "I can't pay that. I could only afford one session, maybe two. But I might not need many sessions. Don't you ever charge less?"

"Of course I do. Only death is nonnegotiable, and sometimes there are exceptions even to that. For an apprentice there is no charge at all, at least not in currency. But nothing of value comes cheap, Viv Ahvren, and currency is the cheapest form of tender. Even a humble bando nut will sprout and bloom more beautifully than one of your gold ounces."

"What . . . never mind. In most worlds, apprentices pay in labor. Can I be your apprentice? Just for a short time?"

"A pebble can turn an avalanche. An extra drop of rain in the Ama Sea can avert a sandstorm in K'Moth. A single crushed beetle can change the course of history."

Ahvren waited for the unspoken "but" that belonged on the end of the sentence. It didn't come. The creature had raised the smallest talon on one of its hands.

"But?" Ahvren asked.

The talon sank. The antennae drooped and lifted. "But apprenticeship is not a short-term proposition. I take as apprentice only those I think worthy to become bibliogoths themselves, those whom I am willing to teach the secrets of my craft. I have not taken an apprentice in over a hundred years. I don't plan to take one in the near future."

How distant was the "near future" to a creature six hundred years old? "I see. Couldn't we make some other arrangement?"

One antennae reached out to hover over him, very close, and Ahvren flinched. The antennae withdrew.

"By your scent, this is important to you." How could a mechanical voice sound so gentle? "May I ask why?"

"I made a wager with my father that I could find . . ." Your people's rebellion. ". . . ah, solve a certain problem. But I don't know how to start. And the stake was . . ." Sabri's happiness. And my soul. He hadn't realized that.

"High?" the creature inquired.

"Very high."

"Hm. Let me think."

Ahvren waited in silence. How could he find anyone to help him? The T'Chin had surrendered, but no honorable being would betray its own people. Why hadn't he thought of that before?

The creature's exoskeletal face was

unchanging. The great eyes never blinked. But the agile antennae were completely still for the first time since Ahvren had entered the room.

*Their antennae are their most important sensory organ.* The voice in his memory was from one of the taped presentations he'd seen on the voyage to T'Chin. *They smell, feel, and hear with their antennae, though they can't hear well enough to distinguish words. They are very nearsighted, relying on scent to give them distance information. Their antennae are their most vulnerable point, though their exoskeletons aren't as tough as they appear—a hard blow with a club will crush one. They are also slow moving, so don't be intimidated by their size. They are vulnerable.*

The creature's antennae whipped around. Ahvren jumped—surely *thoughts* had no scent. But the antennae weren't focused on him—they were cocked toward the west wall . . . West?

Wind slammed into the building, rattling the steel shutters, and Ahvren jumped again. The sandstorm had arrived.

The antennae relaxed and the creature turned back to him.

"I'll propose an exchange, Viv Ahvren,

which should bring us both profit. Your people are new to T'Chin, and there is much about your history, culture, and beliefs that I don't know."

"But we gave that information to the informagoth companies," Ahvren admitted before he thought. "Or rather, sold it to them."

"And far too cheaply, too."

"Well, we didn't . . . I thought financial transactions were confidential!"

All the creature's talons turned outward. "Word gets around. As even you have discovered, there are things you can't get from an informagoth."

Hope stirred. "So you'll help me, in exchange for information about the Vivitare? Just general information, not technology or . . . or . . ." The kind of information I want from you.

"Your military secrets don't matter," the T'chin told him. "And the technology will come in time, from more qualified sources. It is a T'chin custom to exchange some physical token in each transaction." It reached out and tapped the barter bowl on the desk before it— a clay bowl, not metal like the others Ahvren had seen. It looked old. "So I shall also charge you three silver ounces for each session. I don't have much time available during the day, so I'd like you to come in the evening, at the nineteenth or twentieth hour. I know this is late for some beings, but it has the advantage that our sessions need have no time limit, and you may come any night you are free. If I am unavailable, I will warn you. Is this acceptable?"

"Yes," said Ahvren. "That will be fine."

"Excellent. We have a bargain." The antennae reached for him, hesitated, and withdrew. "May it bring us both profit."

"It isn't a matter of profit," said Ahvren. "Not for me."

"Really? For the T'Chin, everything is a matter of profit. Since we have ten minutes before my next client arrives, perhaps you will tell me about this problem on which you've wagered so high. I can give it some thought before I see you this evening."

"You have a client coming during the storm?" Ahvren stalled. How was he going to phrase this?

"She lives nearby."

No more time. The compulsion to blurt out the truth gripped him. Say something, quick. "Ah, it's not a problem exactly. I have to solve a crime." It *is* true, he told himself, gritting his teeth.

"Hm. A detective might charge less than I do, but they would be less open to negotiation. On the other hand, they do have greater expertise in that particular area."

"No." Ahvren shook his head. "Our own intelligencer is working on it. And he's not getting anywhere." The compulsion was subsiding. Sometimes it let him get away with partial truths when it wasn't important. Trying to get this T'chin to betray its people wasn't important?

"Very well, tell me about this crime. A detective first considers motive, method, and opportunity."

"That's not going to help me," said Ahvren grimly. "The whole planet has a motive. As to the other two . . . well, the crime hasn't been committed yet, so . . ."

Both antennae lifted. "You have to solve a crime that hasn't been *committed*? No, don't answer, let me think. It's very important to you, and the whole planet has a motive . . . are you trying to find out about those ridiculous rumors of a plot against your emperor?"

Its antennae curled into tight, quivering spirals; its talons, even its limbs, curled and wiggled; its body shook.

"Are you *laughing* at me?" Ahvren demanded.

"Ah, youngling. And I shouldn't, either— if you wagered high on uncovering such a plot, you're in trouble."

"I realize I can't expect you to give up the T'Chin rebels." Ahvren leaned forward. "But if Lessar is assassinated, the retaliation will be terrible. It isn't worth it. Please, believe me. If we could . . . You're laughing again!"

"Sorry. Youngling, I'd gladly sell you the T'Chin rebels for a copper ounce, if they existed."

"You can't mean that," Ahvren protested. "At least . . . do you?"

"It doesn't matter. There is no T'Chin rebellion."

"You don't know that. And what do you mean, it doesn't matter? It has to matter! I agree that no one would go ahead with it now, but if I find out what was planned, I still win the wager. Is there a way to find a plot that no longer exists?"

"Several ways," said the creature cheerfully.

"We'll start with the simplest. If you can find out where this rumor began, that should tell you a great deal."

"How do I do that? Everyone's been talking about it."

"Even a taroch tree starts with a tiny seed. Seek the source, youngling."

"But how? I told you, *everyone's* talking about it."

The antennae drooped and lifted. "Who told you about it?"

"I don't remember. It was days ago."

The mobile antennae shifted back, a gesture that reminded Ahvren of an animal laying back its ears. "Try."

Ahvren thought. "Actually, I think it was Grem who first mentioned it. He never gets upset, so he said it pretty calmly. That's probably why I didn't remember. But I think it was Grem."

"Then find this Grem, ask him who first told him, and you're on your way."

The brass chime sounded. The antennae twitched. "Time's up, youngling." It touched its talons together and reversed the rotating gesture, up to down.

Ahvren rose to his feet. "One more minute.

Why are you helping me? Suppose there *is* a T'Chin rebellion, then what?"

"Nothing." The antennae were relaxed, waving gently. "What I said before was true. Oh, not that I'd sell them for a copper ounce—I wish no one harm. But considerations of mercy aside, if there were a T'Chin rebellion its fate wouldn't matter."

"How can you say that?" Ahvren asked passionately. "It's your home world, and we've conquered it! How can that not matter to you? Are you all such cowards?"

The storm's howl filled the silence. The antennae cocked forward, intent on him. "You're very blunt, youngling. Are all Vivitare so . . . tactless?"

"No, it's a recent problem. I used to lie as well as anyone," said Ahvren. "I think you do mean it, that the rebellion wouldn't matter. You're just a scholar, after all."

"And a scholar, in your culture, is . . . ?"

"A clerk, who wields a pen instead of a sword, serving any man who pays. Are you going to answer my question?"

"No." One of the cocked antennae spiraled softly. "I could, but I'm not going to. For I'm not just a scholar, I'm *the* scholar. The best in K'Moth. And youngling, if you can figure out why the conquest of T'Chin doesn't matter to me, I might consider taking you as my apprentice after all."

"No, thank you." Ahvren unclenched his fists. "Cowardice isn't very hard to figure out, and I've had enough wagers for one day." He turned to go.

"Ah, but it's not a wager. It's a test. Youngling?"

The creature's voice held a demand. Ahvren turned back. It was holding up one small talon again. Whatever that meant.

"What?"

The creature tapped the bowl on its desk. "The barter bowl is one of the few original T'chin customs to survive. One shows respect for the transaction by placing the token currency formally in the bowl."

"Oh. You want your money." Ahvren fished in his pouch for a handful of ounces— the metal didn't matter. He tossed them on the desk, hard, so they'd bounce; so the creature would have to scrabble on the floor to pick them up. He turned and strode out.

# Chapter 4

**A**HVREN'S ONLY THOUGHT was to get out. Sweeping past the small, dark being in the waiting room that looked as if its cracked face had been carved from gnarled wood, he opened the tall outer door and stepped into an inferno of scouring sand. He leapt back into the waiting room and pulled the door shut behind him.

"Shackles," he hissed. He'd have to take the underground train home. He had no idea where the nearest access was—blocks, probably. He was glad he'd listened to Pomo and brought a sand cape.

The rough-skinned being—a woman, Ahvren decided, in spite of her trousers—watched with amused sympathy as he untangled his hair and brushed the sand out of his clothes.

"Do you know where I can find the nearest access to the underground?" he asked her.

*"Jezer om nanin?"* Her voice was deep and gruff, though she smiled as she spoke. Ahvren sighed. She was bald and had very long earlobes, and he had no idea what race she belonged to, which made the language clips in his pouch all but worthless. So how . . .

"Computer?"

The screen on the desk lit. "Working."

"Where is the nearest access to the underground?"

"Nearest from what location, please?"

Ahvren's temper surged. "Here, you stupid slaver-bait," he told it pleasantly, smiling at the woman. "Thirty-three Shakka Street."

"The nearest access to the underground train tunnels is in Norii Court, one street west and two south." A map of the neighborhood appeared on the screen, and Ahvren studied it.

The woman, seeing that he'd solved his problem, went down the corridor to the bibliogoth . . . no, the *scholar's* room. That was all the creature was, for all its bragging. Ahvren only hoped she'd get *her* money's worth.

He tied his headscarf around his neck, then wrapped himself in the sand cape, tightening the drawstrings that snugged it to his body and compressed the mittened sleeves to his arms. Why they called it a cape he'd never understood. The scarf cast a haze over his vision, but it barely hindered his breathing as he stepped out into the storm once more.

The wind bowled down Shakka Street, and Ahvren leaned into it, pushing himself forward. Once he turned south, the buildings offered some protection, though the gusts that buffeted around the corners made him stagger, and sand rained down. The street sweepers would have their work cut out for them tonight.

Ahvren stumbled down the steps to the underground, and the station doors that swished shut on his heels transported him ten centuries into the future. Nothing of the carefully preserved charm of the old town existed down here. Scuffed plastic, grimy steel, and the scent of hot machine oil—the underground train tunnels had all the charm of a cheap freighter. But they worked. After fighting the storm for three blocks of archaic charm, Ahvren was inclined to appreciate that. He pulled off his cape and shook sand out of the folds.

Because of the storm, it was crowded.

Joining the line of beings waiting to be admitted to the multiple levels of the loading platform, Ahvren studied the glowing route listings. Train 4-14 would take him within a block of his house . . . where nothing awaited him but an unresolved wager. It was only half past the fourteenth hour—plenty of time to talk to Grem.

Ahvren bit his lip. He hated to take any advice from that cowardly T'chin, but what it said was true—if he could trace the rumor to its source, he might be able to discover if the emperor was really in danger. And save Sabri and win his bet.

He took the 8-23-5 train. K'Moth's underground transport system was both fast and efficient, but the crush of bodies around him made the back of Ahvren's neck itch. It would be so easy for someone to slide up behind you with a knife . . . *There is no threat*, he told himself as the door closed and the crowded steel tube shot through the encompassing darkness. *This is K'Moth, not Mirmanidan*. The state-of-the-art cooling system worked beautifully, but he was sweating when the doors hissed open and released him only a hundred yards from Grem's arena.

To go above ground, even that short distance, he had to put his cape back on. Grem's door was locked. Bracing himself against the gusts, he peered through the small window; through the veiling of his scarf, he could just make out the words on the note: STORM CLOSED. NEXT DOOR AT BATHS IF NEEDED. GREM.

Ahvren cursed the swordmaster and struggled on up the street, against the wind. But the bathhouse enfolded him in its steamy embrace, and as he sank gratefully into the big round tub beside his old tutor, he took it all back.

"I take it all back," he announced, slouching so the water ran over his stinging shoulders.

"Take all what back?" It was Roi who spoke. Ahvren had winced inwardly when he saw his cousin sitting in the big tub beside Grem—he had been trying to avoid Roi.

"All the things I called Grem when I found out I had to walk another hundred feet in that mess," Ahvren answered lazily. "But I'd forgive anyone anything now. The Bredayma baths are the best thing about this planet. They even make up for the weather."

"Better than the food?" asked Roi. "Better than being richer than we ever dreamed of?"

Grem merely looked amused—and if Ahvren hadn't had years of practice reading his craggy face, he wouldn't even have seen that much. The swordmaster's arms rested on the sides of the tub. The contrast between his hard, battle-scarred muscles and Roi's slender softness was so painful that Ahvren closed his eyes, lest Roi read his thoughts in them. Around Roi, his truth compulsion was silent.

As if thinking of it had awakened it, Ahvren heard his own voice say, "Grem, I told Father about you teaching Sabri."

Ahvren's eyes snapped open and he sat up, splashing. "I'm sorry about it, too. I didn't mean to give you away—it just . . ."

"You just blurted it out, I suppose," said Roi. His perceptive gaze searched Ahvren's face. "What's wrong with you these days? You never used to be so . . . uncontrolled."

"Don't worry about it," Grem interposed. "Your father has a right to know. Teaching her without his consent was a mistake."

There was a pause filled only by lapping water and the distant echoes of other people's conversations.

"I don't know," Roi murmured, once it became clear that Grem had nothing more to say. "When I walked in on you that day, it looked like she was pretty good."

And Roi had kept their secret. Ahvren fought to keep the lash of regret out of his expression. He might be able to help Sabri, but he could do nothing for Roi. "She was, *is*, better than good," Ahvren told him. "Thanks for keeping it quiet."

Roi shrugged.

"I told Father that," Ahvren continued, speaking to Grem. "It's no use. He wouldn't even watch her practice."

A flicker of pain crossed Grem's impassive face, but he said nothing, so Ahvren went on. "There's something else I wanted to ask you. A problem of mine. Father's been assigned to protect Emperor Lessar from that assassination plot people are talking about, and I'm trying to find out where the rumor started."

"That sounds like a tough job," Roi commented. "Everyone's talking about it now."

"I know." Ahvren grimaced. "Grem, where did you hear it?"

Thought creased the swordmaster's brow. "From Mavi. She's one of Lady Rellia's maidservants."

There was a sudden swirl in the water on

**71**

Roi's side of the tub, but when Ahvren looked at him, he slid beneath the surface. He came up a few seconds later, wiping his face with his hands. Of course. Lady Rellia was Dara's mother—and Roi was in love with Dara.

Ahvren turned hastily to Grem. "Could I talk to Mavi?"

"Sure," Roi answered before Grem could speak. "I'll take you there."

So much for avoiding Roi.

There was a sad amusement in Grem's eyes. "No assassin will try anything now," he said. "They'd have to be crazy."

"I know. But if I can find out who they were and what they intended, it will *never* happen."

"Hm. Hard to find them now. Too much time has passed."

But the scholar, Ahvren remembered, had said there were several ways. Finding the source was just the simplest. He frowned. If this didn't work, he would need the creature's help.

A wave washed over him, interrupting his thoughts. Grem levered himself from the tub.

"Good luck," he told Ahvren. Then he turned to Roi. "Tomorrow."

As the swordmaster walked away, Ahvren's eyes were drawn irresistibly to the plastic foot affixed to his left leg. It looked almost like a real foot. It moved almost like a real foot. Almost was the difference between Vivitar and finished man, no matter how highly Grem was regarded . . . and no matter how fit he was genetically. He might marry, though he'd shown no desire to do so, but, being a finished man—that is, one who no longer fought—he couldn't speak out in deliberations, as a warrior could. Would that be Ahvren's fate, if he couldn't overcome his aversion to going to Zodan?

Roi was watching, too, his mouth set in a flat, bitter line.

"Let's go," said Ahvren hastily. "I'd like to talk to this Mavi girl as soon as I can."

The storm had lessened while they were in the baths. They still had to lean into the wind, but now the sand blew around their knees and waists, not in their faces. It was still impossible to talk, though, thank the old ones.

The train was crowded enough to make personal conversation awkward. Ahvren could feel Roi's gaze on him, and it was more than his dislike of the underground that made him hustle his cousin out of the station and into the wind. He was beginning to think they were going to make it to Dara's house in silence when Roi grabbed his arm and pulled him into a covered walkway leading to someone's courtyard gate. The wind shushed past both entrances, but inside there was shelter.

Roi was still holding his arm, a grip that bit into Ahvren's flesh. Then his hand dropped. "We've been friends all our lives, Ahvren. *Viv* Ahvren. Am I beneath your notice already?"

"No, of course not! Roi, it isn't that." He swept off his head scarf, trying to see his cousin's face in the shadows.

Roi released his hood and pulled his own scarf off more slowly. "What is it then, Viv Ahvren? Too busy these days?"

Ahvren winced. "Stop calling me that. I've been avoiding you because I knew you'd ask my help. And I can't help you."

There was a time when he'd have phrased that tactfully—there was a time when he'd have lied, have said he'd try, even though he knew it would do no good.

"You went to him for Sabri. To ask for

an exception. For mercy. Won't you do that for me?"

"I would if I thought it would do any good, but even if Father did petition the emperor, it wouldn't be granted. You know they don't make exceptions on fitness. Ever."

Something crumpled in his cousin's face. He spun abruptly, clumsily, and slammed his fist into the wall. Remembering Sabri's taut grace as she had whirled to face him this morning, Ahvren ached for both of them.

Roi turned back to him, his face under control, though his breathing was still uneven. "It wouldn't be so bad, if I didn't love Dara."

"Maybe it's not so bad anyway." Ahvren struggled to sound calm. "Once you . . . once you've been made safe, you can see her freely. All your lives, you can have that."

"While she bears another man's children." Roi's white face twisted. "Ahvren, you've got to help me. I want to marry her! I want her to have *my* children."

"Work with Grem." Ahvren laid his hands on his cousin's shoulders. "It's four months until you're twenty. Maybe . . ." His voice died. He fought to go on, to tell soothing lies. "Maybe . . ." It was no good. He had known

Roi all his life—he was kind, loyal, decent . . . clumsy and slow. He would never fight well enough to pass the test. "Don't forget the surgery *can* be reversed if you ever . . . if anything changes."

Roi smiled bitterly. "It was simpler when you could lie, wasn't it, Ahvren?" He shook off Ahvren's hands and led the way back to the street.

Dara was one of Sabri's closest friends, though Ahvren had always wondered why, for Dara was everything Sabri was not. Small and very feminine, her plump prettiness verged on true beauty. He watched her as her mother greeted them. Her self-control was formidable; her expression of polite pleasure never wavered. Only someone who was looking for it would see the glow that lit her modestly downcast eyes. But Ahvren wasn't the only one to see it. Lady Rellia's polite expression changed to a worried frown, and she gave Ahvren permission to speak to her servants without a second thought. Ahvren left Roi listening to Dara, who was babbling softly about the gardens under her mother's watchful eyes, and sought out the housekeeper.

Somewhat to his surprise, she was an elderly Vivitare woman—probably a widow with no sons to care for her. She told Ahvren that Mavi was upstairs, overseeing the cleaning of the bedrooms.

Ahvren found her easily—the roaring clanks and thuds of the three cleaning bots she was running could be heard for a hundred yards. Ahvren had to shout before she noticed him and pressed the remote that retracted their tentacle arms into their bodies.

"May I assist you?" Her bored expression lightened. She was Vivitare, too. It was charitable of Lady Rellia to employ displaced Vivitare women, when the T'Chin worked cheaper.

Mavi had heard the rumor from Asssata, a N'Ssser girl who worked for Lady Brendee, who lived at 404 Cressen Street—not the best neighborhood, but Lady Brendee was doing pretty well lately; perhaps she'd found some relation who was helping her out.

Mavi was obviously willing to talk longer, but Ahvren thanked her and left, hearing the bots clatter to life behind him. It was only mid-afternoon—he had plenty of time to call on Lady Brendee.

# Chapter 5

**W**HISPERS OF SAND BLEW around Ahvren's ankles—the storm was passing. He should be able to walk all the way to Lady Brendee's house. Ahvren had gone through the gate and turned onto the street when a hand closed on his arm. It seemed his defensive instincts hadn't softened yet—he freed his arm with a quick twist and spun, putting distance between himself and his attacker. His sword was half drawn before he saw that it was Roi.

"What do you think you're— Don't *do* that! You scared me half to death."

The astonishment in Roi's face made him realize that most people wouldn't be alarmed by someone taking their arm in a quiet, sunlit street. Most people hadn't been on Mirmanidan. But it was too late to call the words back. Ahvren sighed. "What do you want, Roi?"

"You mean what do I want now?" Humiliation shadowed his cousin's expressive eyes.

"I'm sorry, I didn't mean that the way it sounded. I'm just . . . Never mind."

Roi's eyes searched his face, seeing too much for Ahvren's comfort. "Well, you're right. I do want something."

He took Ahvren's arm casually, as if nothing had occurred, and led him down the sidewalk. Count on Roi to know when to let things lie.

"I need your help to get over the wall. It's what, twelve feet high?" Roi looked up at the gray stone wall surrounding Bard Bredan's house and grounds.

"Nearer nine. Why do you want to get over it?"

"I need to talk to Dara."

"You just talked to her."

"Alone. She's going to turn off the surveillance system and wait for me in the garden."

"She . . ." Ahvren dragged his cousin to a stop and faced him. "How do you know that?"

"She told me," said Roi, as if it was obvious.

"When?"

79

"Just now."

"With her mother right there?"

"Oh, Dara's good at getting things across. We've done this before. Except for the wall part. She used to open a gate for me, but they changed the lock code. She hasn't gotten it yet. But there's a place on the back wall where some bushes grow beside it, and I should be able to climb over without being seen. I just need you to help me climb the wall. You're in excellent shape—getting me over a wall should be a snap." Roi turned and led the way, a determined set to his jaw.

"Dara told you all this with her mother *listening*?"

Roi sighed. "It's been almost four months since they stopped leaving us alone together—we've had plenty of practice."

It took only a few minutes to reach the back. In a gap where the ancient street curved and the equally ancient wall didn't, half a dozen bushes clustered, tall enough to screen most of the wall from the street. As he and Roi wiggled behind them, Ahvren was grateful to discover that the thick, scaly needles covering their wind-lashed branches were softer than they looked.

He gazed up at the wall dubiously. The top was only about a foot and a half above his upstretched hands, and the jagged, mortared stones would provide plenty of toeholds, but . . .

"I'm not sure I should help you do this," Ahvren told his cousin. "You could get into lots of trouble."

"Really? What could they do to me? Bredan's too civilized to cut me to ribbons, even if dueling weren't illegal."

"They could cut off your testicles, instead of just sealing the tubes," Ahvren told him bluntly. "That law's still on the books, you know."

Roi paled, but he smiled too. "Sometimes I think it was simpler in the old days, when women were kept enwalled and you met them for the first time at the wedding. We're not lovers yet. Maybe not ever. I won't do anything that could disgrace her."

"If you get caught sneaking in here, she might end up disgraced even if all you do is hold hands."

Roi's gaze was unyielding. "We're always careful. At least, Dara's careful. Are you going to help me?"

"Roi . . ."

"All right then." Roi backed the two short steps the bushes allowed and leapt for the wall; his hands hit four inches from the top and his scrabbling feet found no purchase. He dropped, failed to get his feet under him, and sat heavily in the dusty soil beneath the bushes. He sneezed.

Ahvren winced and tried not to laugh. "Roi, please . . ."

Roi brushed off his clothes and stepped back to try again.

"Wait! I'll help." Roi would get over, eventually, but he'd probably break an ankle doing it. Ahvren could prevent that, at least.

It was so simple for him to leap and grab the capstone, to find a toehold and haul himself up. Straddling the wall, Ahvren was alarmed to discover that the brush wasn't tall enough to conceal him. There was no one on the street right now—he reached for Roi's hands. "Let's do this quick."

The struggle to get his cousin onto the wall left them both gasping. Several beings walked by, but none of them did more than stare for a few seconds. At least no one was likely to assume he and Roi were burglars—

burglars would be more efficient, less visible, and a whole lot quieter.

Finally most of Roi's body was over the wall, shoulders and arms on top, feet dangling. All he had to do was slip down to hang by his hands and drop. Even Roi could do that.

"All right," Ahvren told him. "I've got your wrists; just ease off. Though your lady friend better have the surveillance system shut down."

"She will," Roi assured him, carefully sliding one arm free. "She— Shackles! A patrol!"

A flashing glance over Ahvren's shoulder revealed six men in the familiar scarlet sashes of imperial service, three blocks away and running toward them. Fast.

Ahvren shoved Roi off the wall, ignoring his startled curse. He was between Roi and the patrol, so he doubted they'd seen his cousin. If they had, there was nothing he could do.

He swung his leg over the wall and jumped—five, six feet, not so very far. It was sheer bad luck that one foot lit on a sturdy root, wrenching his ankle sideways. Ahvren clutched the joint, white pain wiping all thought from his mind. It was the patrol leader's distant shout that roused him. They might not have seen Roi, but they'd certainly spotted Ahvren.

At least they weren't close enough to identify him, or to shoot him. Ahvren had to keep it that way.

He lurched to his feet, wincing as his weight came down on his ankle—it hurt, but it held. He set off at a limping run, wind at his back. They were still two blocks behind him.

So much adrenaline pumped through his blood that his sore ankle hardly slowed him. The people he passed stared but offered no hindrance. Ahvren and his pursuers might have been alone on the sun-baked sidewalks.

The high walls that concealed the houses of the wealthy gave way to the shops and offices of the old town, but there still wasn't anyplace Ahvren could lose the patrol.

The stalls of the new market held a thousand crevices where a fugitive might vanish, but the market was almost a mile away. He could make it. He had to.

Ahvren blessed the days he'd spent wandering aimlessly through K'Moth. Both he and the patrol had lost the frantic speed of their first sprint; they were all running steadily now. The patrol leader probably thought they could run him down, but Ahvren dealt with the heat better than most Vivitare, and the stiffness in his ankle was loosening as he ran.

He was drawing away from his pursuers when the crowded stalls of the market appeared at the end of a twisting street. Ahvren skidded around a corner—just a few turns, just a few seconds out of sight were all he needed. He tried to run faster, but his straining legs refused to respond. His strength was almost finished. But when he turned the next corner his goal was in sight—Ahvren ran toward the new market.

The crowd was thicker now, and he slowed to dodge between them, but the patrol would have to do the same and they couldn't shoot through the crowd. Ahvren pulled open his belt pouch and fumbled for his sand cape.

Turning into a small open square, he yanked the sleeves inside out and gazed wildly around for an unoccupied merchant. There, a ceramigoth, sitting on a cushion surrounded by stacks of brightly painted pots. The cushions in front of him were empty.

Ahvren leapt onto one, flinging the sand cape over his shoulders and drawing up the hood. With its sleeves pulled in, it looked like an ordinary short cape, something many species wore, whatever the weather. From the back, Ahvren should look like any other tourist. From the front . . . Ahvren's lungs heaved as he tried to catch his breath. Sweat covered every inch of his skin—it itched. He knew his face was brick red with heat and exertion.

The ceramigoth's coarse hair grew down his back like a Merlon's mane. The tufts of braided hair that grew from the tips of his ears made them look even longer and more pointed than they were. His eyes were wide with astonishment and the beginning of alarm. Ahvren smiled at him. "I'd like to buy a pot."

The ceramigoth was holding out a big blue urn with batlike creatures embossed on the sides and forming the handles when the patrol raced around the corner.

Ahvren could hear them wheezing from where he sat, and his spine prickled. He tried to pay attention to the ceramigoth—if the creature suspected his lack of interest, *he* might give Ahvren's presence away. Listening to them swear, and split up to search in different directions, Ahvren thought he was doing a good job. But when they finally left, the urn the ceramigoth was extolling was orange with black snakes twisting around it.

Ahvren bought it, paying the price asked without haggling, to the merchant's surprised delight. He considered presenting the ugly thing to Roi, with a bill, but carrying it through the streets would make Ahvren conspicuous. It was tourist ware, so he had no qualms about dumping it in a disposal bin as soon as he was out of the ceramigoth's sight.

He left the market by the quickest route. None of the patrol had seen him well enough to identify him, but his sweat-soaked clothes were enough to give him away. He would have to visit a bathhouse, one with laundry facilities, before he went on to Lady Brendee's.

The storm had dropped to a fitful breeze when Ahvren left the bathhouse, and sand crunched beneath his feet. Shutters opened and lights began to appear in the windows. The sky was scarlet, deepening to purple over the sea and brightening to bands of flaming orange and gold where the sun sank over the desert. After two months in K'Moth, the after-sandstorm sunsets still had the power to slow Ahvren's steps.

To walk alone at night on Mirmanidan could cost you your life. How could the bards have gotten it so wrong? It was peace that was glorious. But peace at the price of freedom? Of honor?

He respected the Mirmani because they'd fought to their limit . . . and beyond. They *deserved* to win. And someday they would, just as his own ancestors had defeated the Karg. Didn't anyone else see that the Vivitare had become the Karg? That they were now the villains of all those old songs? He couldn't be a part of that again. But if he wasn't a warrior, what was left for him? If he could no longer fight for what he believed in, whatever that might be, could he even respect himself? Ahvren shook his head. First things first. He had to win his father's wager, keep from being sent to Zodan. Then he could worry about the rest of his life.

Insulting a T'chin who might have helped him probably wasn't a good start. But after the Mirmani's heroism, these soft, safe people . . . irritated him. There were other bibliogoths. Or Ahvren could manage alone, if he had to.

Lady Brendee's house was on the edge of the wealthy quarter—small compared to the one Ahvren's family occupied, but made of stone, not clay or the modern plastics used in the suburbs. Even in the dusk, he could see that the courtyard garden was well tended. A bulky, red-skinned Mafrenz man admitted him and asked him to wait while he discovered if the lady was receiving.

As Ahvren waited, he had time to notice the thick rugs that all but covered the floor—if they weren't Zo work, they were a good imitation. Much of the furniture looked new, and very costly. What had Mavi said? Something about a relation?

The manservant returned. The lady would see him.

Lady Brendee's receiving room was as feminine as she was: soft couches, overstuffed cushions, and trailing draperies. The lady smiled at him. She must have been pretty once, and she was hanging on to the voluptuous remains of her charms.

"Well, Viv Ahvren, what brings a fit young man like you to visit a poor and lonely widow like myself?" Her voice purred.

Ahvren might have panicked had he not seen the bright enjoyment in her eyes. This kind of flirtation was an old game, as patterned as a dance, and as meaningless. The proper reply was "I heard such tales of your beauty, I couldn't deny myself." Ahvren opened his mouth to say it. "Actually, I came to talk to a maidservant of yours. A N'Ssser girl called Asssata." He stopped abruptly, color flooding his cheeks. *That wasn't a lie,* he raged at himself. *It was just a polite game!* "I'm sor—"

"What do you want with Asssata?" Lady Brendee hissed the name like a N'Ssser, glaring at him. Surely his mild rudeness wasn't enough to provoke this reaction? "I warn you, whatever you're going to offer her, it won't work! Asssata is loyal to me, *and* we have a contract. Binding on both of us for the next three years. So whatever bribe you were thinking of, you can just forget it, you young thief!"

Ahvren raised his dangling jaw and swallowed. "Please, Lady Brendee, there seems to be some misunderstanding. I just want to ask the girl a few questions. I have no intention of . . . of . . . of anything." He had no idea what she was accusing him of.

The lady's eyes narrowed. "What sort of questions?"

Bewildered, Ahvren explained about the rumor and his father being placed in charge of the emperor's security. "You have a duty to help protect the emperor," he finished.

"Hm. I've heard about that myself. Very well, you may speak to Asssata, but I will be present the whole time and if you so much as *hint* at anything financial, my manservant will throw you out! Mafrenz are very strong, you know."

She rose and stalked off, leaving Ahvren blinking in astonishment. He barely had time to fit the right clip into his translator bracelet before she returned with a slim N'Ssser girl. At least, Ahvren assumed it was a girl—he found it impossible to determine the lizard people's sex, just like Pomo with the Vivitare. Though he had more excuse than Pomo, for there was no difference in the jewelry that was all the N'Ssser wore . . . at least no difference he could see.

But he didn't find their faces unreadable.

Unlike the N'Ssser he had spoken to in the market, this one's eyes met his easily. There was no hesitation in the soft hisses and hums of her speech, either live or in translation.

Yes, she remembered the rumor he spoke of. Finding it interesting, she had discussed it with many people, Mavi among them. Where had she heard it? Why, from a Brill waiter who worked at the share market.

"Where is this share market?" Ahvren leaned forward. "What's the waiter's name?"

"That's enough!" Lady Brendee cried. Ahvren jumped. "No more questions." The set of her mouth told Ahvren that argument would be useless.

Asssata patted her employer's arm, an intimate gesture for a servant, but it seemed to calm the lady.

"The share market is easy to find," she hissed softly. "Anyone can tell you. As for the waiter—"

"No," Lady Brendee interrupted. "He has no right to know your sources."

"As you will." The girl's head bowed submissively. The amusement in her eyes told a different story, though Ahvren was at a loss to interpret it.

"Can I go to this share market tonight?" He asked the question of both of them.

"No," said Lady Brendee, with some satisfaction. "It closes at the eighteenth hour, and even if it was open you'd need a trader's pass to get in. Good night, Viv Ahvren."

"But how do I get—"

"Good night."

The Mafrenz manservant was holding the door open. The corners of his mouth twitched. Ahvren sighed and departed.

# Chapter 6

**A**HVREN TRUDGED HOMEWARD in the last light of the sunset, thinking. What was this share market? Why didn't Lady Brendee want him to find out? What in the world was a trader's pass and how could he get one?

He turned toward the new market because it was his usual source of information about things T'Chin. A good source of dinner too; his stomach was complaining.

But as Ahvren approached the market, counting the coins in his pouch and thinking of dinner and bribes, it occurred to him that he had another source of information—the bibliogoth, the *scholar*, of 33 Shakka Street.

No. He wanted nothing from that contemptible coward. There were other T'Chin, other sources of information. He wouldn't go back.

It wasn't until a smiling Olopoli pastrygoth handed him a hot meat pie and a plastic bulb of cold tea that it occurred to Ahvren that every T'Chin was a coward. No one had resisted the conquest. Of forty planets, only one had not surrendered. Not a shot fired. Not even anger, at least none that showed. If they were all cowards, it seemed silly to turn down the services of the best bibliogoth in the city. Especially when they were free. The bibliogoth had said he could come back at the nineteenth hour. It was almost that time now, so Ahvren, whose feet were beginning to get tired, turned toward Shakka Street.

The loud clang of the door chime, the waiting room and corridor were the same, but, pushing open the office door, Ahvren noticed something subtly different. The scholar had time to make the touching-talons-rotating-up gesture before he identified it.

"Incense. You're burning incense now."

"I am indeed. We are creatures of scent, we T'chin. If it displeases you, however, I'll put it out. All species react differently to different scents . . . as do individuals within the species, come to think of it."

Ahvren eyed the long antennae it used as a nose and sniffed thoughtfully. It was a pungent scent, like brine or diluted vinegar, but with a spicy undertone. Not something he'd expect from incense, but . . . "I don't mind it."

"Then take a seat, Viv Ahvren, and tell me what luck you've had tracking your rumor."

At least the creature hadn't taken offense at the way he'd left. It sat easily in its cup-chair, its antennae cocked forward, drifting, in what Ahvren thought was its relaxed mode.

He sat and told the scholar about his meeting with Grem and the two servants, finishing with the questions he'd taken away from Lady Brendee's. "So tell me, since she wouldn't, what in the world is a share market?"

It came out more forcefully than he'd intended. One antennae lifted slightly.

"First, am I correct in assuming that the Vivitare do not sell shares in their businesses?"

"What do you mean, sell shares? How can you sell something that's shared?"

"Ah. A share is a portion of the profits. When a business requires capital, it will sell people a 'share.' The more shares an investor buys, the greater his portion of profit. Clear?"

"Yes. And the share market is where

people go to sell these 'shares' of their businesses?"

"I'd say 'more or less,' but it's more less than more." The mechanical voice sounded amused. Ahvren frowned.

"It's primarily through buying the right shares at the right time, then selling them and buying others, that the largest profit is made. Few people make much from their portion of the business's profits, which is comparatively small. Still clear?"

"I think so. I don't know, but does it matter? All I want to do with this share market is find a waiter there . . . Wait a minute. Why would a share market have waiters?"

"You may have noticed, youngling, that business is very important to the T'Chin. Almost a ceremony. We settle our transactions in a civilized manner, showing reverence. The share market, physically, is a great arena filled with tables. As one trades, one takes small refreshments with one's trading partner, or one's opponent, always showing the most exquisite respect."

The creature paused a moment, apparently contemplating this wonder.

"So how do I get a trading pass? I take it that's what you need to enter the market."

An antennae spiraled. "That's what you need to enter the market. To go into the building and look for a waiter, a visitor's pass will suffice. They'll sell you one at the door for a silver bar."

"A bar? Just to go in and talk to someone?"

"It's crowded enough with all the traders. They want to discourage casual spectators."

Ahvren frowned again. "Why would anyone want to watch people buying and selling shares of profits that are too small to care about? I guess I don't understand. I don't understand why anyone would want to do it at all!"

"Perhaps because I neglected to tell you that if you know what you're doing, have sufficient funds to invest, and are very lucky, you can make a fortune in the share market. Or lose one. Even the mightiest sand castle crumbles before the tide."

"It sounds like you don't approve."

The creature turned all its talons outward. "A good share broker is a master craftsman. An amateur . . . Well, let's just say it's not my field."

Ahvren thought this over. "But why wouldn't Lady Brendee tell me this?"

An antennae spiraled. "Now there is a mystery I can solve for you. Asssata is one of the most talented share brokers in the city. Talented enough that when you Vivitare came, her family's fortune was one of the first seized. So she looked around, found a Vivitare with a small amount of capital, and offered to work for her." Both antennae were spiraling when it finished.

"So Asssata is making money for Lady Brendee in the share market? That explains why Lady Brendee is so protective of her, but why does it amuse you?"

"Because the usual broker's fee is seven or eight to twenty percent of the profits. Lady Brendee and Asssata are splitting everything fifty-fifty!"

Its antennae spiraled tighter. Its talons curled and wiggled. Ahvren waited patiently for the fit to pass.

"Ah well, they both profit by it."

"What I really don't understand is why Asssata was willing to help me. She must hate us."

"Why? Oh, because her fortune was seized? The N'Ssser have been part of T'Chin long enough to realize that minor setbacks like that just make the game more challenging. Asssata is probably enjoying herself."

"What game?"

"The game of business, of course."

"I thought you said business was a ceremony, to be treated with reverence!"

"I did." The scholar was holding up one talon again.

Ahvren wished he knew what that meant. He sighed. "Well, none of this helps me find the T'Chin underground. If you tell me where this share market is, I'll talk to the waiter tomorrow."

The talon fell. The antennae drooped, then lifted.

"The share market is just east of the new market—even you couldn't miss it. But it occurs to me, youngling, that perhaps you should take a moment to define your terms, or you'll end up like Om Loppo, looking for something that's under your chin."

"What?"

"It's an Olopoli fable about a man who sets out to find something that's right in front of him through the whole story. But he doesn't see it, because he's looking for the wrong thing. You said you were looking for the T'Chin underground, but if, as I've told you, it doesn't exist . . ."

"Oh. What I'm really looking for is the source of the rumor."

"Much better, youngling."

"So now what?"

"Your pardon?" One antennae arced.

"What do I do differently, now that I'm asking the right question?"

"Nothing at all. Tracking the rumor is still the best course. I just thought you needed to define your terms."

Ahvren gritted his teeth. An antennae spiraled. Nearsighted and nearly deaf, how did the creature perceive his anger? Did his scent change?

"Have patience, youngling. Truth is never cheap."

That struck home. Ahvren sighed.

"And speaking of truth, or at least information, I believe it's my turn now." It paused a moment, antennae still, selecting the first question. "Viv Ahvren, it has been my experience that all societies, even the most primitive, have some philosophical or religious principle that they hold to be the core of who and what they are. Do the Vivitare have such an imperative?"

"Yes, we do."

The antennae lifted, inviting him to continue.

"It's the Law of Life—at least that's what we call it. Do you know about the evolution of species? How those who are fit survive and breed, and the less fit species give way to them?"

"Yes. We call it natural law, but it's the same phenomenon."

"Well, the Law of Life, to be fit to survive, is our guiding principle. If you don't survive, nothing else matters, does it?"

"True enough." The antennae quivered with interest. "But it's a little more . . . stark than most philosophies."

"There's a reason for that." Ahvren's mouth twisted at the irony. "Not very long ago, we were conquered."

"Really? How many year—no, how many *generations* ago was that?"

Ahvren counted back. "Four. My great-grandfather and his father fought the Karg."

"Not very long ago. I take it you won?"

"Yes." Ahvren's head lifted proudly. Let the creature hear how people of courage dealt with conquerors. "It wasn't easy, either. Our technology was primitive, by their standards. We fought with swords and bows, and they had spaceships and energy weapons. Their own planet had become uninhabitable, so they were looking for a new world and there we were, a suitable planet inhabited only by 'savages.' It looked perfect . . . at first."

The antennae twitched insistently.

"They enslaved us. As I said, they had the technology. And they were a big people; a little like the Mafrenz. But none of it helped them in the end. They forgot, you see, that primitive doesn't mean stupid. As their slaves, we learned their technology, at least enough to steal or sabotage it. All their size and strength didn't stop a knife drawn across the throat in sleep, or a sword thrust in the back. Bands of warriors formed. They called themselves Vivitars, which means survivors, because they were determined to survive. They killed the Karg."

The antennae arced. "All of them?"

"Yes. When those left alive saw how it

was going to end, they took their ships, those we hadn't sabotaged, and fled. We pursued them into space and destroyed them. It sounds brutal, but they'd earned it. Believe me."

"I see. That must have had an enormous effect on your culture."

"The Karg made us a people. Before their invasion, we were a collection of warring city-states. After, we were a united planet. Before, we were 'primitive.' After, we had technology we literally didn't know what to do with. But we figured out their technology, repro-duced it, improved on it, and then"—his mouth twisted again—"set out to do some conquering of our own. But we don't enslave those we conquer! We will never enslave anyone. You will be treated as safe men, as protected subjects of the emperor. There's even talk of eventually letting you test to become Vivitars."

"Explain, please, 'safe man' and 'Vivitar.'"

"The Vivitars are warriors. They rule, pro-tect safe men and women, and speak in the council that guides the emperor. And they're the only men allowed to pass on their genes. Men who don't pass the test are made sterile,

surgically. Though the process *is* reversible."
He tried not to think about Roi. "If a safe male
proves his fitness later, he'll be made fertile
again."

"How does one pass this test?"

"It's a simple test of swordsmanship. You
fight three master swordsmen—dull blades—
and if you're good enough, they pass you. It
used to be that a safe male could prove fitness
only by killing a Vivitar in a duel, but too
many people were getting killed, so the
emperor outlawed dueling about sixty . . . in
my grandfather's time. You're right," Ahvren
added thoughtfully. "Generations are a more
meaningful measurement."

"Especially dealing with species with different life spans. So the Vivitars rule, protect,
and pass on their genes. And that's why you
are called *Viv* Ahvren and wear a sword, even
though you have energy weapons, in token of
these things?"

Ahvren looked down at his sword in surprise. It was so much a part of his dress that it
never occurred to him that it might seem odd
to someone else. "Yes, that's right."

"It seems a little . . . inconsistent that a
people who have adopted technology would

prove genetic fitness with a test of swordsmanship."

"Maybe, but the same reflexes that let you wield a sword also help you fly a fightership. And all their technology didn't save the Karg. It seems harsh sometimes, but it's life's law, not ours. We just practice it." Which was all true, so why couldn't *he* practice it anymore? Did that make him unfit? Ahvren suppressed a shiver.

"Hm. The fit do dominate the less fit—natural law, as you say. But the T'Chin leave it up to evolution to decide what is and isn't fit. And in the long run so do you, whether you know it or not. Thinking beings may light a candle, but only a vrishcat can see in a dark room."

Ahvren scowled.

"Tell me," the scholar went on, "how are your women tested for genetic fitness?"

"Well, they aren't tested. If they're deformed or slow-witted, no one marries them."

The antennae lifted. "They too pass on their genes—you must be aware of that!"

"Yes, but women can't be warriors. They're not . . ." It was none of this creature's business, but Ahvren wasn't surprised to hear himself continue. "They're not supposed to be able to be warriors, but I've got a sister, Sabri, who's a better swordsman than I'll ever be. She has the heart of a Vivitar, too. It's a lie, that women can't be warriors."

The antennae twitched toward him. "This distresses you. Surely if you can see the discrepancy, others will, too. If enough coins are cast in a fountain, someday the water will overflow and soak the carpet."

"What's that supposed to . . . Never mind. Do the T'Chin have a philosophical principle that they live by?"

"Of course."

"What is it?"

"Maximize profit."

Ahvren's lip curled in contempt. "That figures."

The antennae spiraled.

# Chapter 7

IN THE FRESH HEAT OF early morning, Ahvren sought the share market. The scholar had kept him for almost two more hours, answering questions about Vivitare culture and history. Ahvren had been reluctant to repeat his rudeness, but he still felt little respect for this strange transaction—and his stupid truth compulsion refused to let him lie with gesture either. He had tossed the silver ounces carelessly into the ancient barter bowl.

As he turned east from the new market, the memory lingered unpleasantly in his mind. But why? He couldn't show respect for the cowardice and greed that ruled the T'Chin. Still . . .

There seemed to be a wall at the end of the street—a curving, buttressed wall. Ahvren picked up his pace, and two blocks later his suspicions were confirmed: It was the side of a huge building. It had to be the share market, and the scholar was right—he couldn't have missed it.

Taking a guess, he started circling to the north. He'd walked several blocks and rounded only a quarter of it when he reached a door. The antechamber was larger than most old-town shops, with desks lining one wall and multispecies furniture scattered over the rug-covered floor. It was filled with beings, but the polyglot babble was quieter than that which assaulted his ears in the new market. Ahvren chose a desk attended by a Vivitare man whose lack of a sword proclaimed his status. Having been warned about the price, he made no protest over being charged a silver brick twenty-five ounces!— for a white plastic tag that gave him a day's admittance, but no access to the market.

Wondering how he could be inside a market and not have access to it, Ahvren walked through the open double doors at the end of the antechamber and into the share market.

It was like stepping into a painting. A wave of brilliant color drew Ahvren's gaze upward—the ceiling was a huge vault of glass, some stained, most simply frosted, pieced together in an intricate pattern that baffled and delighted the eye. It was supported by stone pillars that soared to the ceiling and shattered into arches filled with colored light. It was so beautiful that Ahvren stood and gaped at it, until a polite, incomprehensible murmur behind him reminded him that he was standing in the doorway.

He moved hastily into the room. If it was a painting, it was a painting of a garden. Flowering vines crawled up the pillars; flowering shrubs spilled in graceful curves, watered by feeders from the softly splashing fountains. The air was almost as moist as a bathhouse, sweet with flower scent. A flutter caught Ahvren's bemused eye—*birds* darted among the plants.

Beings of all sorts sat at the tables that covered the floor, and the tables were the only incongruous note in the place. They seemed to have been poured from some dark ceramic. Computer screens were embedded in their glassy tops. Each table carried a silver barter bowl next to a slot. Of course! He had access to the room, but not the *market*, which was an electronic database.

Finding one Brill waiter in this huge arena

was . . . possible, Ahvren assured himself. It would just take longer than he'd thought. He could see several waiters, but none of them had the short, stocky form and bright markings of the Brill.

Ahvren set out, wandering among the tables. At first, only the flow of light through surging water distracted him from his hunt, but soon the attitude of the beings around him began to nag at his mind—they fit this peaceful, spacious place no better than the computer tables. Most were tense, hunched over their access boards with fierce concentration. A few were talking, but the talk wasn't casual. A pallid Cutachan was sitting with some furry creature whose race Ahvren didn't know. Even as he watched, the fur lifted along the creature's spine. It smoothed down immediately, but the Cutachan had seen it, too, and he grinned evilly. Not a pleasant conversation. But why—

"Ahvren, hey Ahvren, over here!" The voice was familiar—looking around he saw Lahr, whom he knew well enough to count as a friend, waving from a table. He sat beside a Tepan woman whose hooded robe almost completely hid her baggy, green skin.

"Hello there! Just visiting, I see," Lahr remarked, looking at the white tag clipped to Ahvren's tunic. Lahr's tag was blue.

"You're not. What are you doing here, Lahr? Last time we spoke, you were trying to get included in the Zodan conquest."

"And getting nowhere." Lahr grimaced. "Every Vivitar on the planet wants a place on one of those ships. I think I'd be willing to go as a janitor, but all those jobs are taken, too. Oh well, if I have to stay here, at least there are compensations. Ahvren, I'd like you to meet Riadeemyea'aria."

Ahvren nodded politely to the woman and she nodded back. Her eyes were downcast, for the Tepani thought it rude to meet someone's gaze, but her long snout wrinkled in their version of a smile. Her loose robe and crumpled, green skin made it impossible to guess her age.

"Riadeemyea'aria is teaching me to trade in shares," Lahr went on. "It's an incredible game, Ahvren—like fighting a battle with numbers."

Ahvren noted the adrenaline shine in his friend's eyes with misgivings. "I've heard you can lose a lot of money here, if you don't know what you're doing."

"So? It hurts less than losing blood. And we all have money now, don't we? At least, our fathers do. What are you—"

Colored numbers flooded across the table screen and the Tepan stiffened. Her short-fingered hand shot out to tap the glass and Lahr cursed, thrust his tag into the access slot, and began working the control panel.

Lahr didn't notice when Ahvren left the table, but the woman's eyes flickered toward him and away. Ahvren wondered uneasily if Lahr had a contract with her, and what it said.

He spent three hours wandering through the vast room. The tension thickened as the day went on, like the scent of blood. Ahvren was thinking of ordering midmeal when a short flash of vivid color caught his eye. A Brill—carrying a tray!

Ahvren stood aside until the waiter deposited his load at a table, where three N'Ssser were so intent on the screen they didn't even notice the food; then he stepped forward. "Excuse me—may I speak with you a moment?"

The Brill looked up. His skin was orange, with symmetrical blue and green stripes that ran into the white, blue, and green feathers of his crest. When he had first seen them, Ahvren had thought the Brill painted themselves, and tastelessly too, but their gaudy pigmentation was natural.

*"Reech prill reempa?"* The bright face smiled.

"Wait." Ahvren offered him a placating smile and dug into his pouch for the language clips. A small, garish hand grasped his wrist and pulled him to the nearest empty table.

"You want to place an order, gent, you've got to take a seat." The translation came from a speaker embedded in the table. "We've got a good catch of meecha in this morning—most Vivitare like them, but if you don't care for fish I recommend—"

"I don't want food," Ahvren interrupted. "I just need to talk to you. At least, I need to talk to a Brill waiter."

"What do you think I am? You don't like the Brill waiter you got, you'll have—"

"No, you're fine. But I'm looking for a specific person—a Brill waiter, who works here and talks to Asssata."

"Then you got the right Brill, 'cause I'm

the only one on the staff just now, but—"

A voice behind Ahvren growled imperiously, and the Brill lifted a hand in acknowledgment and muttered, "Ah, keep your fur on, I'll get there. Some people got no patience. Look, gent, I can't talk now. Sit down, place an order, and I'll come back after the midmeal rush. All right?"

Ahvren sat and ordered whatever the Brill recommended that wasn't fish, and the waiter nodded and rushed off. The only Brill on the staff. No wonder Asssata had been amused— in his own way he was as hard to miss as the share market.

What wasn't fish turned out to be a bowl of unidentifiable seasoned meat, with noodles, nuts, vegetables, and a sweet sauce. It was as delicious as it was expensive. Ahvren paid with credit, wincing, and ate hungrily. He also kept an eye on the Brill as he rushed about, and watched the beings at nearby tables.

The tension seemed to abate as people dined. Conversations became genuinely casual. Ahvren's gaze was caught by a true T'chin, stalking with slow dignity to join another of its kind. As they approached, they made the touching-talons-rotating-up gesture—it must be a greeting. Then they stretched out their antennae and brushed them together, an unnervingly buglike gesture. The T'chin equivalent of a wrist clasp? An embrace? Their antennae were their only organs with a sense of touch.

As meals were finished and dishes removed, the electric intensity returned. Why would anyone care so much about money? Especially if they already had it, and anyone who paid for meals here had to have plenty. Most Vivitare felt that money was only useful if you needed to buy something. Lots of money was unnecessary, unless you wanted something big, like a star cruiser, or . . .

Ahvren's breath hissed between his teeth. Or a rebellion? Rebellions required enormous sums, for weapons, transport, information. The Vivitare had, perforce, done without it—slaves have no money. But on Mirmanidan they had found many of the rebel leaders simply by discovering whose fortune had mysteriously vanished. Ahvren would bet his sword that the first thing any rebel T'Chin would do was amass money. But—

"Here I am, ready to talk." The Brill waiter reached out a bare foot, its prehensile toes as

brightly striped as the rest of him, and lowered a chair. He sank into it with a sigh of
relief. "The pay's so-so, but the education you
get around this place makes it all worthwhile.
Good thing the T'chin are so stuck on tradi-
tion. Any other planet, they'd replace me
with a bot! So what do you want to know,
gent?"

"I'm trying to trace the rumor you told
Asssata about, that someone was going to
assassinate the emperor."

Blue feathered brows rose. "I wish you
luck! Everybody's talking about it."

"Do you remember where you heard it
first?"

"Hm." The striped forehead creased.
"Yeah, I think I do. It was over a week ago,
mind, but there were three Vivitare all excited
about it when I brought their dinner."

"Who were they?" Ahvren leaned forward.

The brightly feathered crest lifted and fell.
A shrug? "No idea. They all had day passes,
like you. Never seen 'em before or since."

"What! But . . . Does the market keep a
record of passes?"

"Nope. What for? As soon as credit is

transferred, all records are erased. Sorry, gent."

Ahvren felt numb, as if he'd had the breath knocked out of him but the pain hadn't set in yet. "It's all right. Or at least it's not your fault. How much do I owe you?"

The Brill frowned. "I don't seem to have done you much good. I prefer to get information in exchange for information; I'm always willing to take a tip from Asssata, say. But you . . . Tell you what, I'll just let you owe me a very small favor. There might be a time I could use a favor from a Vivitar, even a small one. Or if you'd rather, toss a couple of copper ounces in the bowl. Whichever."

Ahvren stared at him. "I thought all T'Chin expected to be paid for everything."

"So? I'd rather be paid in favors. Money is the cheapest form of tender."

Ahvren frowned. The Brill shrugged. "You can forget the whole thing if you want—I'm not so needy I can't give a stranger a few minutes for free."

"It's not that. I'd be glad to owe you a favor. But what you said about money being cheap, I've heard it before."

"Not surprised. It's a T'chin proverb."

"T'Chin, or T'chin? Ahvren asked. "I mean—"

"Yep," said the Brill.

"Yes what?"

"It's T'chin."

"But which . . ."

The Brill began to laugh. "Sorry, gent. It's a word game we play, to see how long we can keep that conversation going. I'm told the record is over an hour, but I'm not sure I believe it. It's T'chin with a small *c*. The proverb, I mean. The guys with the long antennae."

Ahvren rubbed his forehead. "You people are crazy."

"Which people? The T'chin, or the T'Chin?"

Ahvren groaned. The Brill laughed again and rose to his feet. "Much as I like playing with you, I'd better get back to work. What's your name, Vivitar-who-owes-me-a-favor?"

"Ahvren. How did you know I was a Vivitar?"

"Wearing a sword, aren't you? For what it's worth, the Vivitare I got the rumor from were all safe males."

It probably meant nothing, but . . .

**119**

"Thanks. Say, what's your name?"

"Reecheep Crraveel Barrcrreem Ramrra Remacree. But Reecheep is enough for most people." He grinned and hurried back to work, leaving Ahvren deep in thought. The rumor trail had come to an end, but perhaps there were other ways. There was one thing every rebellion needed, even more than money.

When Ahvren left the share market, he went to Grem's arena and asked him to find out if anyone in K'Moth was buying large amounts of weaponry.

# Chapter 8

"IT DIDN'T WORK!" Ahvren pushed open the scholar's door and froze in his tracks, staring at the mound of greenery that sat on a platter on the scholar's desk.

"You're early," the scholar observed mildly. It laid a pair of tongs on the platter and made the rotating-up gesture.

"What are you doing?" Ahvren asked. The incense tonight smelled of plants, like a damp meadow.

"I am conducting an advanced experiment in the conversion of vegetable matter into kinetic energy."

"Really?"

The antennae twitched. "I'm eating dinner, youngling."

"All that?"

"My body mass is greater than yours." The scholar picked up the tongs, dipped a leaf in a sauce bowl, and tucked it daintily into its small mouth. "And the energy contained in vegetable matter is less easily converted. We are an herbivorous species, in case you were wondering." Its chewing had no effect on its speech, since its synthavode worked on secreted pheromones instead of a voice. The alienness of it unnerved Ahvren and he swallowed.

"Would you like some?" The scholar pushed the platter forward but didn't offer the tongs—using fingers must be acceptable.

"Uh, sure, why not?"

The tray held some sort of sliced tuber as well, and long grassy stalks. Ahvren selected a leaf—how bad could it be?—dipped it in the sauce, and popped it into his mouth. The sauce coated his tongue, sweet to the point of bitterness. His glands responded with a rush of saliva and he swallowed again, trying not to gag. If the leaf had any flavor, he couldn't taste it.

"It's so sweet!"

"Well, if you find that sweet I won't offer you anything to drink." The creature gestured at a bulb with a straw. Was one of its antennae spiraling, just a little? "We T'chin have a passion for sweet things." It continued to eat as it spoke, going through the greenery on the platter at an astonishing rate. "But tell me, what didn't work?"

"What . . . oh!" Ahvren had been distracted from the day's frustrations, but now they returned in a rush. "Tracing the rumor to its source. Reecheep, the Brill waiter, just overheard some strangers discussing it. He had no idea who they were."

The antennae were focused on him. "You seem more excited than disappointed. May I know why?"

"Because I've got an idea." Ahvren began to pace before the desk. "If someone wanted to start a rebellion, they'd have to have lots of money, right? Money we didn't know they had, so we wouldn't notice when it was spent on weapons and so on, right?"

"I know little about rebellions, but that sounds logical."

"If someone was trying to conceal a fortune, how would they do it? Could you trace it electronically? Find their names?"

"Youngling, you've forgotten how you defined your goal. To find the source of the rumor, remember? Not a dubiously extant rebellion."

"I'm changing the goal. Someone planned an assassination. They must have had other steps in mind—things to do after the emperor was killed. Things they'd need money for."

"Hm. With a little patience, you could try tracing the rumor again. No? Well, it's your investigation."

"Can you find out for me?"

"Let me think. Hidden funds. Financial transactions *are* confidential, but people talk about unusual sales . . . and companies' records of who holds their shares are available to other shareholders . . . Yes, I think I can find out who is trying to conceal the extent of their wealth. But you should consider that there might be more than one reason to do that, and more than a few people doing it. Will you investigate them all?"

"If I must," said Ahvren. "I'm not going to worry about that until I have to. Just get me a list."

"Very well, but it will take several days— you're talking about gathering and analyzing a *large* amount of data, and a computer can take you only so far." It finished the last leaf and pushed the platter aside.

"I know. But in the share market this

morning I realized that a T'Chin rebellion would *have* to start with money."

The antennae lifted. "That's an astute observation, youngling." It held up one small talon.

"Thank you," said Ahvren. This was the first time the scholar had praised him. "In the market, I could feel how important the money was. As if it was the lifeblood of your people, and the share market was the heart that pumped it."

"The share market has often been called the heart of K'Moth." But the talon had fallen, and the antennae drooped in what Ahvren was almost certain was the equivalent of a sigh. "We are, after all, a trading port. First sea, then air, then space, but always a city of trade. I just hope that if your idea works, it works out for you. You've never told me what this wager of yours entails."

Ahvren frowned. No compulsion forced his tongue, but for some reason he wanted to reply. "My father thinks I should go to Zodan with the shield fleet, but I don't want to. If I win, he'll give me a year to find another career. If I lose . . ." The bleak anguish of Mirmanidan surfaced in his memory, and sweat pricked his skin. "I can't afford to lose."

The agile antennae swept out to hover over him, but this time Ahvren managed not to flinch.

"You feel very strongly about this," said the scholar. "Was this war so terrible?"

Ahvren shrugged. "It was war. You know . . . You don't know." It astonished him, but of course none of the people on this world had any idea what war was like. Even most of the Vivitare, who served on the ships of the shield fleet, hadn't experienced a ground war. A guerrilla war, like Ahvren had fought on Mirmanidan. Loneliness wrapped around him, and he shivered.

The antennae quivered. His scent must have changed.

"No, we know nothing of war," said the scholar. "I'd heard that your people gloried in it, but I see this isn't so."

"Not for me," said Ahvren. For some reason it was easy to say it to that expressionless, alien face. "I don't think anyone who was actually there gloried in it. Though most of them seem to have coped better than I have. The thing is . . ."

But he wasn't certain what the thing was.

The scholar waited. Even its restless antennae were still.

"There was a girl," said Ahvren.

The antennae quirked.

"Not a girl like that. A little girl. Not more than ten years old, I think." The memory rose in a vivid wave, as it did in his nightmares.

"What happened?" The voice from the synthavode was amazingly soft.

"She poisoned a senior officer. Viv Garren. He was a good man. I knew him pretty well." Well enough that his throat still ached when he said the man's name. "She posed as a servant. She just walked into the briefing room, handed him a cup of poisoned tea, and walked out, as if . . . as if it was nothing. I met her eyes as she passed me and she smiled."

The antennae lifted. "You were there?"

"Oh, yes. I and several dozen other officers. It was a general briefing for all junior and senior staff in the region. I was there to present my commander's report on terrorist activity in his sector."

He'd been wondering, even then, if the Karg had referred to the Vivitare resistance as "terrorist activity."

"It acted very fast, the poison. She hadn't

been gone more than a minute before he began to choke. And she was the first Mirmani servant to smile at me in all the time I'd been there."

"So you pursued her?"

Ahvren nodded, the familiar cold already numbing him. "I caught up with her in the kitchen. One of the cooks had delayed her there. She started for the door but I yelled to alert the guard, so she ran down into the cellar instead. There was no way out of the cellar." His mouth was dry. She'd been very small, a tiny heap of dusty fabric and twisted limbs. "She had a disrupter hidden there. She shot herself."

The silence stretched. He hadn't been able to tell that story to anyone. Not even Roi or Sabri.

"Terrible indeed," said the scholar quietly. "I don't claim to know how you must feel, though I see why it's so important for you to win your wager. But doesn't your father understand this?"

"No. Not really. He thinks it's just war weariness. And maybe that's part of it, but it's not all. Though I'm sorry I can't . . ." Be what he wants. ". . . do as he asks."

"Now that I do understand," said the scholar. "It's no light thing to disappoint a parent."

"He will be disappointed," Ahvren admitted. He only prayed he could find some way out of this mess that wouldn't shame his father as well. "But going to Zodan is something I can't do. I just . . . can't."

The antennae drooped almost to the desk. "That, too, I understand. The K'va seed travels farthest in a strong wind."

"K'va seed? No, never mind. What do you mean, you understand?"

Antennae twitched back. "I understand because I too have a parent whom I disappointed. That's why I'm warning you that it's no light thing. But I also *had* to. Yes, I understand."

"*You* had a parent?"

"Did you think I was formed full grown from desert rock? Of course I have a parent. It's still alive, and we still quarrel about my career whenever we meet."

The voice was exasperated, but there was a spiral curve in one antennae so Ahvren felt free to ask, "Why did you . . . Wait a minute. Parent? *It?*"

"Certainly. Didn't you know we T'chin are hermaphroditic?"

"You mean you're not a male?" He had assumed . . .

"Actually, I am *both* male and female. Does this disturb you? It troubles many of the multisexed species when we first encounter them."

"Well," said Ahvren, "I guess I don't care. Why should I? But I can't say how other Vivitare will react. It seems . . . odd."

"As do many of your attitudes to me. A turtle encountering a rock thinks it a very slow creature."

Whatever that was supposed to mean. Ahvren eyed the antennae closely, but there wasn't a trace of a spiral. Ignore it. "So you have only one biological parent?"

"What did you say!" The antennae whipped back and flattened over its skull. Joints and talons pointed outward, and a bubbling hiss came from its synthavode.

"What?" The T'chin might be slow moving, but those chitin-covered talons would make formidable claws. Only the fact that Vivitars weren't supposed to retreat kept Ahvren in his chair. "What did I say?"

There was a long pause. A curl of smoke rose from the incense burner. Then the bibliogoth's limbs relaxed and its antennae crept forward. "I apologize, youngling. You couldn't know, but the severest insult you can offer a T'chin is to tell it, 'Your parent bred with itself.' Not only is this utterly forbidden, it is biologically impossible. Though it is possible with . . . artificial assistance."

Ahvren decided he didn't want to know. "So you actually have two parents. Why do you keep saying 'parent'?"

"Because among the T'chin, only the progenitor who gives birth to you is considered your parent. It's the one who raises the child. It is, after all, the only one you can be certain *is* your parent, barring genetic analysis."

"Then the T'chin don't marry?"

"Not as you think of it. One sometimes has a companion, with whom one lives, and who assists with the rearing of the young they've bred, but nothing binds them. Some companionships last only until the young are grown, some less than that, and some endure throughout the lives of both participants."

"Then you don't have families?"

"Of course we do! My family is my parent,

131

my children, and their children. In a few cases, my children's children's children. I have a huge family."

"But no one living with you."

"No. All my children are grown and I have no companion, currently."

The face, as always, was expressionless, but there was something in the voice . . .

"It sounds like a lonely way to live, between companions," said Ahvren cautiously.

"Ah, but there's more than one form of companionship." An antennae reached out to stroke one of the antique books. "A faceted gem sees everything from a different angle."

"Books are good," Ahvren agreed. "But not the same."

"No," the scholar admitted. "They aren't. Though should I find a companion, it would become part of my family, for a time. As would an apprentice, if I took one on. No recipe turns out exactly the same twice. But tell me of your families, youngling. How are they ordered? How do they work?"

So Ahvren told it about his father, who had taken no other wives even though his mother bore only one child, and how his father had takcn in his best friend's daughter when her parents died in a flitter crash. He went on to speak of other families he knew, and how those with no family fared. It was very late when the scholar made the rotating-down gesture of farewell.

Ahvren managed to put the silver ounces into the barter bowl carelessly, as if he weren't thinking about it. It was his first successful lie in a long time.

# Chapter 9

"P LEASE BE AWAKING, Viv Ahvren. Your father is wanting to speak to you."

"Go 'way, Pomo." Ahvren pulled the covers over his head.

"A mem/ser has come from the emperor. You are summoned to be attending him. Right now!"

That brought him out of the blankets. His bleary eyes found Pomo's earnest face. "But it's . . . it's barely light! Even if it's urgent, surely he only wants Father."

"Your father was told to be bringing you. He gave an order to be waking you, and you are awake. Now it's your problem." He grinned and waddled off.

His problem indeed. Ahvren grimaced. He had avoided the emperor since Mirmanidan. Not anymore.

From the air the emperor's "palace" looked like every other house in the wealthy quarter.

Ahvren sighed and sank back in the flitter's passenger seat. He'd heard that Dravik had insisted that there *had* to be a palace some-where, and had been furious when they finally convinced him there wasn't. When Dravik was younger, if anything wasn't just as he wanted it, he either changed it or destroyed it. Unfortunately, he hadn't matured much. And Ahvren had promised to try to talk him out of marrying Sabri. Oh, joy.

They'd all been astonished to learn that the mighty T'Chin Confederation had no leader. It was Emperor Lessar who made K'Moth the capital city, because it had the largest spaceport on the planet. There was no ruler or ruling body, unless you counted the assorted trade councils and guilds. Perhaps that was why they had surrendered so easily—no one was empowered to defy their conquerors. But all the Vivitare leaders were dead or enslaved by the time the Vivitars destroyed the Karg. No, only cow-ardice accounted for it. A pity. Ahvren sighed again.

"Stop that," his father snapped, his edgy voice contrasting with his hands, steady on the controls. "I don't know why they wanted to see you, but it is *always* an honor for a Vivitar to attend the emperor. So show a proper respect and keep that loose tongue of yours between your teeth. In fact, let me do the talking. I don't like this come-immediately-no-explanation nonsense. It smells like an ambush."

Ahvren sat up straighter. "Ambush?"

"Political ambush. Which can be the most deadly kind, so do what I say."

"I'll try," said Ahvren gloomily. He prayed that his absurd compulsion would let him.

The honor guard in the corridor, in their gold-trimmed sashes, looked unusually alert. Ahvren and his father hurried past the great hall, which Ahvren thought had once been a dancing room, and stopped at a door that led to the antechamber of the smaller court, which Ahvren thought was once some rich merchant's private office. He wondered where the being that had owned this house was now. Then he wondered what had happened to the people who'd lived in the house his father occupied.

His father touched a blank, upright monitor screen on the small table beside the door, and it flared to life.

"Hello, Wythan. Myself and my son, to see the emperor." He rotated the screen—a vid pickup, Ahvren realized—so whoever was on the viewing end could see the whole corridor.

"Come in, Viv Saiden. You're expected."

Heavy bolts snicked and the door opened. The small chamber (once a receiving/waiting room) held four guards and an array of electronic equipment that barely left room for the people.

His father nodded briskly to all of them, smiled at one, and headed for the inner door. The man he'd smiled at—Wythan?—reached it first. "Excuse me, Saiden, but your orders were to scan *everyone* who goes in. That includes you."

Ahvren's jaw dropped. Viv Saiden grinned. "If you'd let me through, I'd have nailed your hide above that door. And then replaced you."

Wythan laughed.

They scanned Ahvren and his father for metal, energy sources, and chemical reactions, then patted down their clothing and took their swords. Ahvren was staring at his father with surprised respect when the door finally opened—he'd never seen security this tight. Generally the emperor's only protection was his honor guard. He was, after all, a Vivitar, and Vivitars were supposed to take care of themselves.

*Even when they're old?* Emperor Lessar sat on a throne at the back of the room. His heavy gold bracelets didn't conceal the thin muscles of old age. His spine, beneath the rich fabric of his tunic, was still straight, but his hair had gone from gray to white since Ahvren had seen him last, and the skin of his face was crumpled and sere. The grave, steady gaze was the same, but it couldn't conceal the truth: Lessar was almost finished. Would he even be fit to command the shield fleet at Zodan? A leader must lead. If Lessar was judged unfit, Dravik would become emperor. Ahvren hadn't realized it might come so soon.

Lessar's children flanked him on the dais, his daughter Jennah standing a little behind him on his left, plain and solemn as a hider owl, and Dravik sprawling in the heir's low chair at his father's right hand. If his sister was an owl, Dravik's gold-embroidered, scarlet tunic made him a flara bird. A sleepy, sulky flara bird, perhaps a little hungover.

Ahvren's lips tightened. His father climbed the three steps of the dais and clasped Lessar's bony wrists. All Ahvren had to do was keep his mouth shut.

"Old friend." The emperor smiled, changing the whole cast of his somber face. "It was good of you to come so early, asking no questions."

"Oh, I have plenty of questions. But I thought I'd ask you, instead of badgering the messenger. What is this, Lessar?"

A voice rose in angry protest behind the antechamber's closed door. The emperor's smile faded. "I'm afraid you're about to find out."

Ahvren's father looked baffled but stood aside, prepared to wait if that was what Lessar wanted. Dravik sat up straighter, a gleam of interest entering his eyes.

Viv Redahd burst through the door, blocky and revved as an engine on overdrive. "It's an insult to me and every Vivitar in your service to subject them to that . . . that craven indignity!"

"It is a necessary security precaution." The flash in Viv Saiden's eyes was like the sun on a drawn blade. "All who care about the emperor's safety have submitted without protest."

"*I* will protect the emperor by finding and destroying his enemies, not by stripping every man who steps into his presence."

"When you have done so, we will all rejoice and abandon these tiresome precautions, but until that happy time—"

"Until then, I demand to pursue my investigation without interference! How dare you set your whelp to fumble after me and get in my way?"

There was a moment's startled silence.

"Is *that* what this is about?" A smile tugged at Ahvren's father's lips. "I'm afraid I don't see your problem, Viv Redahd, for Ahvren can only get in your way if he's in *front* of you. And that, surely, is impossible."

Dravik laughed aloud. He didn't care who was right, Ahvren judged; he simply liked conflict. *Keep your mouth shut.*

"Stop this, both of you," said Lessar in a voice that held no trace of frailty. "My person is not something to squabble over, like jacca over a bone. Viv Saiden, why did you set your son on the task I had assigned to Viv Redahd?"

"He has connections among the T'Chin, Lessar. I saw no harm in letting him ask a few questions, and if he discovers something, so much the better. Surely the important thing is to find these assassins, if they exist, not who does it."

"Oh, they exist." There was a note of triumph in Redahd's voice. "Hasn't your little spy learned even that? I discovered a servant they'd bribed for information about your security precautions and the imperial household's schedule over the next few weeks. So it's not only real, it's soon."

A chill raced over Ahvren's nerves—the plot was still active! He could save Lessar's life in truth—*deserve* the boon of Sabri's freedom. But how had Redahd known . . .

"If you found a man they bribed, then you've got the beginning of the trail!" His father's voice was crisp—all enmity cast aside. "Do you have any names? Or descriptions? Even knowing the assassin's species would be useful."

The emperor was expressionless, but Jennah's mouth tightened and Dravik grinned. Redahd flushed with rage and embarrassment.

"I would have, but the shackling coward was so fragile, he died under the questioning!"

"You were torturing him?" The anger in Viv Saiden's face was not only for the incompetence of it. "Why in blazes didn't you use truth drugs?"

"He was a Norii. Our drugs didn't work on him."

Not only barbaric—stupid, too.

"That's stupid as well as barbaric," Ahvren heard his own voice say.

Redahd turned toward him, his hand going to his hip, where his sword hilt should have been. "What do you know about it, slaver-bait? I doubt you'd have the stomach to question a spy at all, much less find out anything useful. *You* didn't even know the plot was real!"

"Maybe not, but I know that T'Chin medigoths can treat most of the species in the Confederation. You could have bought a truth drug that would work on a Norii for a few gold ounces, if you didn't prefer killing to thinking!"

There was a moment of silence as the truth of it sank in.

The anger in Redahd's eyes was so hot

that Ahvrcn looked away. His father's eyes were closed—he shook his head, slowly, resignedly. Jennah's eyes were wide, and Dravik's sparkled with malicious amusement. The emperor's were grave and rather sad.

"I see what you mean, Saiden. He is useful."

Redahd protested, but the emperor held up a hand for silencc. "Have you discovered anything yet, Viv Ahvren?"

"No. Nothing yet."

"Well, I see no harm in your continuing." He glanced at Jennah, and she nodded judiciously.

"Sir, may I ask a question? How did Viv Redahd know I was investigating?"

All eyes turned to Redahd, who shrugged. "There was an anonymous message on my comm-unit yesterday—who cares? The insult—"

"I fail to see how Viv Ahvren's investigations could be construed as an insult." The emperor might be old, but the strength in his voice could have cowed a dozen younger men. "You will not regard them as such."

Redahd glared, but he nodded in submission, and Lessar turned to Ahvren. "I hear you're a good swordsman."

"Only fair," said Ahvren compulsively.

Lessar's lips twitched. "As a Vivitar, you should be able to take care of yourself. But if you discover anything, you will tell your father, and *he* will share the information with Viv Redahd. Now I need to talk with both of them, privately. Dravik, you and Jennah see to Viv Ahvren's comfort, will you?"

Jennah nodded. Dravik shrugged and strolled down the dais steps and out the door, not looking to see if Ahvren followed.

They retrieved their swords from the guardsmen in silence. In the corridor, Jennah turned to him. "Will you come with me, Viv Ahvren? If you haven't had breakfast, I can see you served."

"No, thank you, I'm fine. But I need to speak with Dravik." Who was escaping down the corridor right now. "Excuse me, Lady. Viv Dravik! Dravik, wait, I want to talk to you."

Dravik stopped, somewhat to Ahvren's surprise, and waited until Ahvren reached him. "So talk."

Ahvren glanced at the interested faces of the honor guard. "It's private. Can we go somewhere?"

"Why not?" A gleam replaced the boredom in Dravik's eyes. "Since I'm marrying your lovely sister so soon. At least, her hair is lovely. The rest of her . . ."

Ahvren followed Dravik to his suite, listening in teeth-gritted silence to his lazy speculations about Sabri's body. This had to be deliberate provocation, but why? He grimaced ruefully; this was Dravik. The next emperor. Ahvren shuddered. He was here to plead for Sabri. Be tactful. Keep your stupid mouth shut!

". . . but soon I'll know just what her thighs are like," Dravik finished, pushing open the door. "As well as the rest of her." A woman turned from the window and came toward them, smiling. She was young and pretty—except for the yellowing bruise that distorted one side of her jaw.

All thought of tact vanished. "It's a Vivitar's duty to *protect* the defenseless—only a coward beats women."

Another man would have reached for his sword. Dravik just grinned. "A man must discipline his household, or he is no man. Surely you've discovered that with your own women . . . or have you?"

The woman took one look at Ahvren's face and fled. Ahvren felt as if he was strangling, but smashing his fist into Dravik's smile would only result in a call for the guards. It wouldn't help Sabri. Curse it, the bastard wanted him to lose his temper. Giving in to him was, as the T'Chin would say, unprofitable. *So don't.*

He dragged a deep breath into his lungs. Another. He discovered that his hand was clenched on his sword hilt, and he pried his fingers off it. The room was pleasant, almost feminine, full of rich fabrics and soft cushions. It suited flara bird Dravik. It would suit Sabri like bunting on a fightership.

"Sabri doesn't want to marry you." His voice grated, in spite of his effort to sound calm.

Dravik grinned. "I know. It lends a certain . . . excitement to the prospect, don't you think?"

"You don't know Sabri." The thought was richly satisfying. Sabri could break this pretty bully without half trying. He'd never have to see bruises on his sister's face—thanks to Grem. Perhaps all women should be taught to fight before they married.

"I don't know her well, but I've seen her, and with your sister that's enough." Dravik looked puzzled as he scanned Ahvren's face. Good. Let him wonder. "But women are much the same, especially in the dark. Or wouldn't you know about that?"

This time the barb didn't bite. "I'm almost glad you're marrying my sister. I'd hate to think of another woman in your hands, but Sabri . . ." Ahvren let a smile curve his mouth. "May your marriage bring you all you deserve, Dravik."

He strode out, leaving Dravik scowling behind him.

Ahvren waited for his father at the flitter, his satisfaction at the thought of Sabri beating Dravik to a pulp slowly growing cold. Not that it wasn't a real possibility—Sabri would trounce the fool the moment he laid a hand on her. But she deserved more from life than marriage to Dravik. Though there might be compensations. Lessar was almost finished. In the past, strong women with weak husbands had ruled kingdoms in all but name. Even now, if the emperor had no male heir, his daughter, advised by the council and her

147

husband, ruled after him until her sons were old enough. But Dravik . . . no. Ahvren had to uncover the plot before the wedding—just five days hence. With Redahd on his heels. Lovely.

Who in the world had told Redahd he was tracking down that rumor? Not even a T'Chin would help Redahd, no matter how much he was paid. And Redahd hadn't mentioned paying for the information, but he must have. Who knew Ahvren was investigating? The bibliogoth, Mavi, Asssata. Lady Brendee. Reecheep. His family, Grem, and Roi. The bathhouse attendants, or the waiters at the share market. Dozens of possibilities. Oh well, what mattered was finding the rebels in time, not who had given his name to Redahd.

At least he'd gotten through both interviews without betraying his reluctance to fight on Zodan. When he thought of what he might have said to the emperor, had the conversation taken a different path, his blood ran cold. He had to do something about that, but what? There were no healers for the mind, and even if they'd existed, Ahvren wouldn't dare go to one. This bizarre cowardice of his was something he couldn't reveal to anyone, or he might be decreed unfit. There had to be some way to get out of going to Zodan that left his reputation, his honor, intact. But Ahvren couldn't see it.

Viv Saiden returned to the flitter, looking almost as subdued as Ahvren felt. They were in the air and halfway home before he spoke. "I don't like this. If I'd thought there really was a plot, I'd never have involved you."

Ahvren snorted. "You'd send me into battle without a qualm, but you're worried about my asking a few questions?"

"Not without a qualm," his father protested. "But in battle you know who your enemies are, and hopefully where they are, and you have allies to fight beside you. This . . . You're groping in the dark for a fist-ful of vipers, and if they become aware of you before you find them . . . Redahd isn't above making trouble for you, either. I don't suppose you want to concede our wager?"

"And go to Zodan? No, thank you. Will *you* concede?"

"Giving you a year to waste?" There was an unsettled pause. "Shackles, I'm almost tempted."

"Really?" Ahvren stared at his father's

worried face in astonishment. This might be his chance. But it wouldn't help Sabri. And if the plot was still active . . . "Don't concede. If there really are assassins, you need someone besides that idiot Redahd hunting for them. If you think it's that serious, I'll be doubly careful. I promise."

"It's serious, all right." Viv Saiden's hands tightened on the controls. "I got the details after you left. Someone bribed that servant for a complete description of all my security precautions and the household's schedule for the next month. They got them, too—the creature delivered his information before he was captured. It's real. And if they succeed, Dravik will become emperor now. The council isn't ready for that, Ahvren. We need more time. More controls on him."

"I see," said Ahvren, chilled. "Is Sabri one of your 'controls'?"

His father's mouth tightened. He didn't answer. He didn't have to.

Ahvren found Sabri in the garden at sunset. The day's heat still radiated from the stone wall and walkway, but the air was cooling. Ahvren had spent the afternoon prowling the city, thinking, and resisting the temptation to go ask Grem and the scholar how they were doing. Grem would send word as soon as he had something. The scholar had said it would take several days. Pestering them would only slow them down. But the waiting was hard.

Now, watching Sabri pace through the sweet-scented flowers like a caged cat, he wondered if she too found waiting hard.

She caught sight of him and smiled. "Congratulations. I hear you insulted that slaver-bait Redahd so effectively, he almost skewered you on the spot. Why didn't you go for Dravik while you were at it?"

"I insulted him later, but he just laughed. You're right about him, Sabri, he's . . . he's unfit, whether he can use a sword or not." Not the best thing to say to the woman who had to marry him, but his truth compulsion was stirring, like a sea monster in the depths. Sabri deserved truth. "There must be something wrong with his mother's genes; he doesn't get it from Lessar."

"I don't know. Lessar got only two children from seven wives, and one was Dravik."

"There's nothing wrong with Jennah. I

wish she could be emperor."

Sabri's face was luminous in the growing dusk. "Everyone who knows them wishes that. Even Lessar."

The glow in her face was gone now. A trick of the light. Or perhaps he'd imagined it. "Sabri, *you* could be the next emperor, in all but name. Dravik may not be simpleminded, but he's a fool. And he doesn't care. With a little subtlety, a little tact, you could rule the whole Vivitare Empire."

Sabri snorted. "Ahvren, have you ever heard anyone, even Mother, describe me as subtle and tactful?"

Ahvren grinned in spite of himself. "Your touch. Well maybe you won't have to. I've got a plan . . ."

Sabri listened intently as he told her about trying to trace the rumor, and his new idea about tracing financial records. When he finished, she nodded. "I think tracing the money might work. Certainly better than trying to find the source of a rumor. But heart-sib, watch out for Redahd—he's dangerous, whatever Lessar told him." Her eyes were serious. "I couldn't bear it if he harmed you because you were trying to help me."

"I'm trying to help myself, as well," Ahvren reminded her. "And if these crazy assassins have decided to go through with it, they have to be stopped for everyone's sake, not just ours. I'll be careful. *I'm* the careful, tactful one, remember?"

Sabri snorted. "Careful, maybe, but tactful? Ahvren, what happened on Mirmanidan? When you first got here, you were so depressed . . . That got better, but you've changed. You used to be discreet—now you blurt out things I wouldn't dream of saying."

"Everything I say is true." Ahvren felt the compulsion rise, helpless to stop it. "It was the things I saw during the Mirmani revolt. The bards sing about courage and honor and glory, but war's not like that. War is never walking anywhere alone because anyone—the old woman selling fruit, the boy with the dogs, the mother with two toddlers at her skirts—might have a hidden knife. It's realizing that we are, to them, what the Karg were to us, but having to fight anyway because they'll kill you if you don't. They didn't steal our technology before rebelling, so they didn't stand a chance. Next time, they might. It's all lies, Sabri, what the bards say."

Her strong-boned face was filled with love and sympathy . . . and no comprehension at all.

"We don't enslave them, Ahvren. We've never treated anyone like the Karg treated us. Besides, you've missed the point. It's not about honor and glory, it's about being the survivor. About being so fit that no one can ever conquer us again."

"I know that." Ahvren turned to pace, as she had, among the flowers. It was almost dark now, and the glittering cobweb of stars began to appear. "You're right and Father's right, but I can't be part of it."

"Then what do you want to do?"

"Father asked me that. I told him I wanted to serve with my wits and my sword. In a clean fight. He said there was no such thing."

"Maybe not," said Sabri. "But if anyone can find one, it will be you. *I'd* wager on that."

"Don't," said Ahvren. "One wager is enough. I only hope I can get you what you want. But Sabri, very few people find love in their marriages. That doesn't mean they don't find love, or happiness. Truly." The irony of that final assurance twisted the corners of his mouth, but it was too dark for them to read each other's faces.

"Ah, but I wasn't looking for love. I wanted something far more impossible than that." There was a strangely light note in her voice.

"To be a warrior? If I fail, as an emperor you'll have all the battles you can fight."

"Good guess, but wrong. I wanted something no emperor ever has. I wanted freedom. And if I can't have that, the rest doesn't matter."

The lamplight gleamed on her fiery hair as she passed through the doorway, leaving him alone in the dark garden.

# Chapter 10

THE NEXT DAY WAS A scorcher, light and heat pouring from the sky. No word from Grem yet, but Ahvren could go to the scholar this evening. It had said several days—two was several, wasn't it?

The fourth time he prowled past his father's office, Viv Saiden looked up. "If you've nothing better to do than stalk the house like a hunting mirka, there's something you can do for me."

If he left the house, he might miss a message from Grem or the scholar. If he didn't leave the house, he might go crazy.

"What is it?"

"There's a cargo ship I've been asked to invest in. It sounds good, but between increasing the emperor's security, my normal council duties, and your mother turning up every ten minutes with another problem in the marriage plans, there's no way I can get out to meet the captain and inspect the ship."

"I'm not an engineer. It could be about to fall apart and I wouldn't know."

"Perhaps not, but you've been on ships before. You can tell if the crew is competent and disciplined or if they're slaver-bait. Or a bunch of pirates. Just *go*, will you?"

So Ahvren flew out to the spaceport. There were more patrols than in other parts of the city, but the T'Chin didn't seem to be intimidated. At the entry gate, he saw a red-sashed squad exchanging laughing comments with a stout Cutachan pastrygoth. They were probably off duty for midmeal, but even so . . . Ahvren was glad the emperor's guard wasn't so carefree.

The furry Werada captain seemed pleased to see him and perfectly willing to submit to a surprise inspection. It was strange to return to a world of synthetics after three months in K'Moth—Ahvren jumped the first time a door whooshed open in front of him. The ship was clean and seemed to be efficiently loaded, and the crew seemed relaxed and competent. Ahvren went home and reported to his father, adding that it all *seemed* fine to him. His father snarled and sent him to run errands for his mother, who kept him busy until it was too late to go to the scholar, who hadn't sent a message anyway. That evening, Sabri asked if he'd learned anything. Ahvren hated having to say no.

The message from Grem came the next morning, just as Ahvren finished breakfast. He ran up to his room to grab his belt pouch and sword and was almost out the front door when he heard Pomo calling, "Viv Ahvren, Viv Ahvren! You should be taking a cape! The sand will be coming this afternoon."

The little Olopoli waddled rapidly down the hallway, a sand cape trailing from his arms. Ahvren snatched it. "Thanks for the warning."

Pomo beamed. "You are not always remembering to check the weather forecast, but you are always remembering to thank."

Ahvren nodded and began to move away. He liked Pomo, but he was in no mood to be delayed by his chatter.

"Much pleasure to work for you is here." Pomo laid his hand on his heart. "But are you remembering . . ."

Ahvren closed the door, cutting off the

rest of the lecture. Even in the morning freshness, it was too hot to wear the cape, so he tucked it under his sword belt, where it soon made a sweaty patch against his skin. It was also too hot to walk as fast as he was walking, but Grem had seen him sweat before.

"What did you find out?" he demanded as the swordmaster opened the door.

"Not much." The cool stone corridor was almost invisible after the bright light outside. Grem led him down to a workroom where he was repairing plastic practice blades. Ahvren had never seen the room before, but the equipment was utterly familiar.

"Beginners' class coming up?"

Grem removed a cracked blade from its hilt with the deftness of a lifetime's practice. "Everybody starts somewhere."

Ahvren hefted one of the practice swords. The worn grip fit his palm as if he'd used it yesterday. "How much is not much?"

"Nobody's buying weapons that I can find. Though that may just mean I haven't found them. But someone did purchase five thousand pounds of weapons-grade boridium about a month ago."

"Five *thousand* pounds? That'd power

disrupters for a small army! Maybe even a large one."

Grem shrugged. "It's used for many other things, too, but this was weapons grade. Thought you'd be interested."

"I am. Who bought it? Did you get his name?"

"Yes."

Ahvren knew better than to interrupt Grem's thinking pauses, but he was fidgeting before the swordmaster spoke again. "This is a strange place. Or rather, a strange people. Most of them were perfectly willing to talk to me. No anger."

"I know. A whole race of cowards."

One iron-gray brow lifted. "*Forty* races of cowards? Besides, cowards are usually the first to hate."

"So maybe it's a culture of cowards. Maybe they're raised not to fight. That would account for it, wouldn't it?"

"Hm."

Ahvren couldn't stand it anymore. "Grem, the name?"

"Oh. Maffatti. A Mafrenz with an office at the crossing of Dockside and K Street. A purchasing agent, they said."

"Dockside. Isn't that in the old port?"

Grem nodded. "Ever been there? You'll be all right with a sword in the daylight. You're a fair fighter. But if you go there at night, forget symbolism and take a disrupter. Rough part of town. Patrols don't go there much."

How did Grem know that? The ironic gleam in his eyes told Ahvren that his old teacher was perfectly aware of his curiosity and had no intention of satisfying it. At least Ahvren had the name.

Leaving Grem's arena, Ahvren walked briskly until he reached the steps that led down to the underground station. It was a two-hour walk to the old port, but the train would get him there in ten minutes. The backlash of sunlight off the sidewalk was hot enough to roast a scorpion. The train would be cool . . . and crowded. Ahvren decided to walk. He thought better when he walked.

At the edge of the wealthy quarter, the high stone walls vanished and ruins took their place. The buildings lining the Afaz River were even older than the new market, and without protective coatings sprayed over their walls, they were slowly crumbling back into the desert clay from which they'd come. Most of the walls were between knee- and waist-high, but where roofs had survived, whole rooms remained intact. Ahvren had been told that people lived here, addicts, lunatics, and a few very unsuccessful criminals. Ahvren saw no one and heard nothing but the wind.

On the other side of the bridge that carried a trickle of ground traffic between city and spaceport, the ruins had been razed to make room for warehouses. Ahvren turned east and followed the river to the sea, where Dockside, which ran the length of the old K'Moth seaport, began.

This part of town had been inhabited as long as the ruins but the area was neither completely leveled nor preserved. Buildings were torn down and replaced whenever there was need. Rusty prefab tin from two centuries ago stood beside modern prefab plastic, both looking equally tacky and impermanent.

The late-morning streets were almost empty—a few ships' crewfolk, a handful of warehousers taking an early midmeal—nothing alarming, though Ahvren thought that if he ever came back at night, he'd take Grem's advice.

There was only one building at Dockside

and K that wasn't a tavern. It had what Ahvren assumed was a listing of occupants beside the door—translator bracelets were no help with the written word. He pushed the door open and went in.

How could a building made of yellow plastic look dingy? There were two shops on this floor; one sold recreational drugs, the other, Ahvren guessed from the posters of gaudily decorated beings that adorned its windows, was some sort of body-painting or tattoo studio. At least, he hoped that was what it was.

He stuck his head through the door of the drug shop and the proprietor turned its body toward him, since its thick carapace didn't allow its neck to bend much. *"Amsa?"*

The clip in Ahvren's translator bracelet was for Mafrenz, and he saw no need to change it. "Maffatti. Where?"

A ropy tentacle indicated the barter bowl and Ahvren sighed, reached for his belt pouch, and froze. He'd forgotten to see if he had enough money before coming out this morning. That was probably what Pomo had tried to tell him. Fortunately he had some change left; he sorted through a handful of metal shapes and threw two copper ounces into the bowl.

The proprietor scooped the coins into a fleshy pouch on its belly and pointed upward with three tentacles, one after the other. Third floor.

Eyeing the rickety stairs, Ahvren chose to take the lift and regretted it when he heard the mechanism squeal as it rose with archaic slowness. He took advantage of the delay to count his money—just enough for midmeal, if he didn't spend much on bribes. Just enough to buy some information, if he took the time to go home to eat, and get more money. If he went home, his mother would probably draw him into the increasingly frantic preparations for the marriage—she had found him "very useful" yesterday. If Ahvren was going to stop that wedding, just three days away, he had no time to waste.

The lift shuddered to a halt and wheezed open. There were two doors off the hall, and the plaques beside them had no pictures. Wonderful. No, wait. One of the plaques had a comm-speaker beside it. Ahvren pressed the button and heard a distant buzz.

"Who comes?" His translator reproduced

the syllables from the speaker. A female voice?

"My name is Ahvren. Viv Ahvren. I want to talk to Maffatti about a purchase."

"Enter, friend Viv, enter." The language was now slightly accented Vivitare, so Ahvren's translator was mute. The door's lock clicked, and Ahvren pushed it open and went in.

The outer office wasn't as cheap as the rest of the building had led him to expect. The inner office, into which a big, bald Mafrenz woman beckoned him, looked almost respectable.

But the woman's beaming smile reminded him of the gragii lizard, which gave its victims a joyous grin when it pulled back its lips for the poisoned bite. Her dark-red arms bulged with muscle. Ahvren hoped she wouldn't mind his questions—he'd hate to make her mad, unarmed female or not . . . and he wouldn't bet a cracked copper that she was unarmed. He resolved not to come to the point of his visit immediately. To feel his way, gradually, carefully. Good idea. He smiled back and went into the office, taking the chair she indicated.

"So you wish to discuss a purchase? Have you something in mind and require a discreet agent? No one is discreeter than Maffatti! Or do you need investment advice? I can put you on to some very sweet ventures. A trifle of risk, perhaps, but the greater the risk, the greater the profit! Whatever you seek, just ask Maffatti!"

Gradually. Carefully. "Actually, I'm looking for some information about a purchase you made for someone else. Five thousand pounds of boridium. I need to know who you bought it for."

Her smile vanished as if it had been amputated. Ahvren froze his own smile into place with an effort. What in blazes made his stupid compulsion think *she* deserved the truth?

"But young Viv, Maffatti is discreet! Did I not just tell you that? Even a poor woman like myself has some honor!"

"I didn't mean to insult you. Isn't there some way you can put me in touch with your client without compromising your honor?"

"If it becomes known I have violated a client's confidentiality, I will have no more clients! I'm a poor woman, young Viv. I have an office to rent, a family to feed. Poor

Maffatti's reputation is her only treasure. Surely you aren't asking me to *give* it away?" It was her glare that finally clued him in. Most T'Chin parted with information so easily, Ahvren had almost forgotten what it was like to be asked for a real bribe. He hoped she'd take credit.

"I'm sure your reputation is—" He intended to say "valuable," but managed to cut off the sentence before the words "for sale" popped out. She might be a crook, but he still didn't want to make her mad. Perhaps if he kept it very, very simple.

"How much?"

Her eyes narrowed, but she was a businesswoman. "Two gold bricks. I risk ruin to help you, young Viv. If this gets out . . ." She let the threat hang in the air between them, emphasized only by the look in her eyes. It was enough.

"I won't tell anyone, but I won't pay two gold bricks, either. A good data pilot could eviscerate your dubious computer security for half that. But I'm in a hurry. Two gold bars."

She settled on four gold bars, credit, with a speed that left Ahvren convinced he'd been robbed. But he left her office with the name and address of her client: Loba Amm, a Zo merchant whose shop was east of the share market.

The wind was beginning to stir. As he crossed the bridge, Ahvren looked upriver—he could just make out the low brown cloud over the desert. He probably had several hours before it moved in, but suppose this Amm closed his shop early? Sabri's marriage was in three days. Ahvren took the underground train back.

On his way through the new market he bought a pie and a bulb of fruit juice from a vendor who was just folding down his shutters. Most of the shops were still open, but the crowd was beginning to thin as the rushing breezes gave their warning.

He crossed into the old town and was only a few blocks from his destination when he caught sight of the sword in the display window and froze in his tracks.

From the tip of its curving blade to the elegant knot where the flaring guard joined the pommel, it sang of power and balance. Looking at it just sitting there, with the sun gleaming on the watermark that rippled down its blade, was like watching Sabri fight. For all his cynicism about war, Ahvren could no more stop responding to the sword's beauty than he could stop his heartbeat. It had to be Nisol work. Before conquering the T'Chin, the Vivitare had decorated their swords, chasing the blades with gold, studding the hilts with gems—why not? Once they'd gained energy weapons, swords were only symbols. Then they saw the plain steel Nisol blades, and almost overnight the gaudy ornamentation vanished, as those not fortunate enough to be able to buy a Nisol sword sought to imitate them.

Buy or steal. In the heady rush of conquest, hundreds of the swords had been looted from Nisol shops. Even from their forges. Ahvren's father said that was dishonorable, that a stolen sword never served its master well. Then the Nisol swordsmiths sought out the most influential Vivitars and offered to make them a sword or two in exchange for protection, and the looting stopped. Ahvren's father deeply regretted that he hadn't been on the planet when the Nisol smiths were seeking patrons. When the Nisol discovered their swords' value to the Vivitare, the price novaed. Most Nisol swords were sold before they were made—but here was one of them, sitting in a window, for sale. Ahvren could never afford it, but his father might—

A sudden gust made him stagger, reminding him of where he was and what he was supposed to be doing. It would take only a few minutes to go in and put a deposit on that sword . . . and in those few minutes Loba Amm could close his shop and go home. No. Ahvren turned and strode down the street. If the sword was sold to someone else, so be it. But the exquisite curve of the blade still haunted him, as he thrust open Loba Amm's door and stumbled in from the windy street . . .

. . . to stare at the shop in surprise. The Zo were as famous for their textiles as the Nisol were for swords—not surprising since the rhee-silk forest was the dominant ecosystem on Zodan. But this Zo sold electronic sound systems and communication gear.

The lights flashed blue as the door opened, and the man behind the counter looked up, his polite smile freezing when he saw Ahvren. He was a typical Zo, blue skinned, his skeletal thinness accentuated by almost seven feet of height. His white hair was coiled neatly at the crown of his head, and the sleeves of his caftan, no more than three feet long, indicated moderate wealth for all their silver embroidery. Although, Ahvren remembered, it was allowable for a wealthy Zo to wear shorter sleeves; it was considered lying only if you wore longer sleeves than you were entitled to.

"You need something, Vivitar?" Ahvren had changed the clip in his translator bracelet as he walked, but it wasn't necessary. Perhaps it was just the difficulty of speaking an alien language that made the merchant sound so curt. Or perhaps not. The shield fleet would be leaving to conquer Zodan soon.

"I'm looking for Loba Amm. Is that you?"

The Zo hesitated before answering. "Yes. What do you want of me?" His face was closed, wary.

The back of Ahvren's neck prickled. His voice was very casual as he said, "I need to ask a few questions about a purchase you made. Five thousand pounds of boridium?"

"Ah, yes. I bought that for a supplier of mine. Boridium powers much of the equipment he sells."

Weapons-grade boridium? Right. Ahvren summoned a smile as false as the Zo's own.

"Why did he use you as a purchaser? Why not buy it himself?"

The Zo shrugged. "The seller was trying to raise his price. My supplier knew if he refused to buy, the seller would be forced to sell cheaper to Maffatti. It's not an uncommon practice."

Ahvren suffered a moment of doubt. It sounded plausible, but he knew so little of business. If it was true . . .

"Then you won't mind telling me who you purchased it for and how I could contact him?"

"Not at all. Wait here a moment and I'll check my records." He vanished into the back of the shop.

Ahvren paced, gazing blankly at the glowing buttons of the sound systems. *That was too easy.* Of course, it wasn't over yet. Why would Amm go to the trouble of hiring Maffatti to preserve his client's anonymity and then give his name to a stranger? The barter bowl on the counter caught his eye. Without asking even a token payment. Why—

The lights flashed blue. Ahvren spun toward the door, reaching instinctively for his sword, but there was no one there. The door

172

hadn't opened. Why had the lights flashed? *Because there was another door in the building attached to the same warning system!*

Ahvren raced through the back of the shop, past open cartons and a cluttered repair bench. There was the door. He had to brace his feet to shove it open against the force of the wind, but the sand wasn't blowing yet. Good thing, too; he didn't have time to put on his cape—Loba Amm's silver-embroidered caftan was disappearing around the corner, almost a block away. Ahvren ran.

The wind was behind him; it threw his balance off, though it added to his speed. He skidded around the corner and saw Amm walking hastily, like everyone else on the street, toward the entrance of the underground. His height made him visible. Alarm leaped over his face as he looked back and saw Ahvren. He began to run, shoving through the crowd at the top of the stairs. Ahvren followed, ignoring the incomprehensible curses of the beings he shouldered aside.

Down the stairs, through the door. Amm was running for the nearest loading platform, caftan flapping with each long stride. But there was no train there. Ahvren had him trapped.

The Zo realized it and skidded to a stop, staring wildly about. There was no way out of this underground cage except back past Ahvren, unless . . . He spun to the right and dashed into the tunnel, running on the concrete that supported the triple bars of the track. Several beings cried out, warning clear in their voices. A few started after him. Ahvren pushed past them.

He was in the tunnel, a dozen strides beyond the light. The darkness fell over him like a smothering velvet cape. Ahvren's pumping legs faltered. People were calling behind him, incomprehensible shrieks that undoubtedly translated as "you idiots, come back here."

But he also heard the rapid slap of Loba Amm's feet, running into the earth . . . getting away. Ahvren dragged air into his lungs and plunged into the tunnel.

It wasn't completely dark. About every twenty feet, green glow bars were laid into the center track, shedding just enough light to touch the curving ceiling and walls. Enough light to show the rectangular niches cut into the walls on either side of the tracks; a niche at every light bar, thank the old ones. Those niches were his only hope if a train came. When a train came.

It was supposed to be the safest fast transport ever designed—if you were in the train. If the runners left the rails (which was, of course, impossible) a repulser field would spring from the tunnel walls, forcing the train back into position. But for the field to generate enough force to control a speeding train, the walls had to be close to the train's surface. Five inches close. Too close for a fool who chased another fool into the tunnels to survive, unless he reached a niche in time.

Which direction did the trains in this tunnel run?

Ahvren glanced over his shoulder—nothing but a shrinking circle of light. Looking ahead he saw the shiver of green light over silver thread as the Zo ran past a light bar. He was six light bars ahead, neither gaining nor losing distance as far as Ahvren could tell. Once, Ahvren caught sight of his face as he turned to look back—for Ahvren or a train or both? No way to know, but surprise slowed him for a few precious seconds when Ahvren passed a light bar. He probably hadn't thought Ahvren would be brave enough to follow him into the tunnel . . . stupid enough to follow him? *Too bad, merchant—you guessed wrong.*

Ahvren was settling into his stride, muscles warm, lungs working in quick, easy rhythm. Then he heard it, behind him, a rattling moan that rolled down the tunnel. Three long, panicked strides brought him to a niche and he plunged into its shadows.

The niche was about four feet deep. The sound grew louder. Ahvren found himself counting the seconds, as he would count the seconds between lightning and thunder. One and again. Two and again. Three and again. It would be useful to know how many seconds he had to reach a niche. Six and again. Seven and again. The rattling moan became a roaring scream. The rough concrete vibrated beneath his hands. Eight and again. Nine and again. Ten and again. Ahvren huddled in the farthest corner of the niche, his hands over his ears. Thirteen and again. Fourt—

The train crashed past, slipstream buffeting him against the concrete. Its roar was a solid wall of sound, its windows a chain of blurred gold ovals. Then it was gone.

Ahvren sagged against the wall, his knees so limp they almost dumped him on the floor. His back was slick with sweat. He pried his hands away from his ears and heard the train rattling into the distance. His hoarse panting echoed. He heard the Zo's footsteps stumble and begin to run, unsteadily, down the tunnel. Amm sounded as wobbly as Ahvren felt. *Curse* the shackling bastard. Ahvren pulled himself off the wall and ran.

He concentrated on the light bars and his quarry, relying on his straining ears to warn him. Fourteen seconds from the time he had heard the train until it reached him. Ahvren timed the seconds between light bars, trying not to chant in rhythm with his stride. In fourteen seconds he could run almost three sections. When the next train came he could run another full section before he had to find a niche. If the Zo went to safety immediately, he'd gain on him. Probably. He was breathing harder now, but it seemed to him that his quarry was slowing, too, in spite of his longer legs. Yes. The Zo was only five sections ahead now. *You should have spent more time working out with a sword and less standing behind a counter, my friend. My enemy. The fit always prevail. It's the Law of Life.*

Another section had closed between them when Ahvren heard the next train. Amm heard it too and darted into a niche. Ahvren roused himself to sprint, despite his laboring lungs. *Quick, quick*—the roar of the train was growing louder, but still not too close . . . he'd made almost three sections when he timed it.

He made his decision and passed a niche, running full out as his mind screamed second thoughts. Too late now. The train was fast, faster than he was, the cry of its passage roaring down on him like a waterfall, taking the air from his straining lungs. *Don't dare look back, don't look, don't*—

Leaping into a niche, he felt the slipstream pluck his tunic as the train raced by. The concrete floor shook beneath him, or perhaps it was his body shaking. Stupid, stupid, *stupid*. Too shackling close. *So don't waste it!*

He staggered to his feet, clutching the wall, getting ready. He stumbled from the niche the moment the train was past and gained another half section before the Zo darted from his own niche and looked back. Ahvren was close enough to see the alarm that flashed over his face, and he smiled grimly.

The Zo ran. Ahvren listened to his footsteps between the light bars. Three more sections—the Zo was stumbling now, almost exhausted. Then the footsteps stopped. Ambush. Did he have a weapon? To reach him, Ahvren had to pass the light bar—an easy shot. So make it harder!

His dark-adapted eyes could just make out the tracks. Without breaking stride Ahvren crossed them and sprinted through the light, on the other side of the tunnel, crouching low. The hiss of a stifled curse; the buzz of a stunner beam. He felt the nimbus prickle along his back. Wild shot. The unfit fool.

Out of the light, dodge across the tracks just in time to avoid the second shot—there he was, stunner aimed. Ahvren dove and rolled into a low, flying tackle it had taken almost a month with Grem to perfect.

The Zo went down beneath him in a tangle of silken cloth and writhing muscle. He still had the stunner. Small, close-range, a hunting weapon, but enough to paralyze Ahvren's body and leave it lying helpless on the tracks. Dread vibrating through his nerves, Ahvren slithered up the Zo's long body, grabbed his right wrist with both hands, and slammed the hand holding the stunner against the track with all his strength.

The Zo's left hand shot for his eyes and Ahvren shut them, shaking his head to avoid the gouging fingers, smashing the Zo's right hand against the track again and again until the skitter of plastic across concrete told him he'd succeeded.

He grabbed the clawing hand from his eyes, but he couldn't force it down. They hung a moment, suspended, muscles locked, breathing each other's panting breath.

He felt it before he heard it, a subtle vibration in the track beneath the Zo's pinned wrist. Amm's eyes flared wide, flashing back down the tunnel. There was nothing visible, but Ahvren heard the now-familiar sound of the speeding train. The Zo writhed, twisting frantically, trying to gain some purchase, but Ahvren hung on. *This was madness!* But he hated to give up. He *wouldn't* give up! The cry of the train grew louder. His grip tightened.

The Zo's muscles slackened, yielding. "There is no profit in dying!"

"You're right!"

As one, still clutching each other, they

scrambled up and dove for the niche. But Ahvren was the one who kept his hold as they came down, who got an armlock on the long, twisting limbs as the train raced past, and was finally able to draw his sword with his free hand and force the Zo's surrender.

# Chapter 11

SILENCE RETURNED TO the tunnel. Loba Amm knelt before Ahvren, arm locked behind his back, Ahvren's sword at his throat. He had him . . . so now what? Ahvren would have to put down the sword to tie him up, and once he let go of the sword . . . Maybe the man really had surrendered. "What did you buy the boridium for?"

"I told you, I bought it for a supplier. I'd promised not to reveal his name, so I left. You chased me, so I ran."

Ahvren's lips tightened. "You're lying."

The Zo twisted around and smiled unpleasantly. "And if I am, Vivitar, what are you going to do about it? Torture me?"

"No," said Ahvren thoughtfully. "Is that pendant around your neck a credit identifier?"

Puzzlement in the hostile eyes. "Yes."

Slowly, sword ready to cut, Ahvren let go

of the Zo's arm and lifted the pendant. "Now it's in my pouch." He stepped back, on guard, but Loba Amm showed no sign of attacking. "I'm investigating the plot to assassinate the emperor."

Amm blinked, an expression that looked like honest surprise crossing his face. Then he smiled and shrugged. "I know nothing of that, so you can torture me forever and it will do you no good. Whoever it is, I wish them luck."

The man evidently realized Ahvren wasn't the torturing type. No matter. "I don't need to torture you—we have truth drugs. You'll tell us everything you know."

"I hope you waste days on me."

Ahvren would have sworn the man's smile was genuine. "Oh, I won't be doing it. I have orders to turn anything I discover over to Viv Redahd."

The blue skin paled. Amm stepped forward, and Ahvren warded him off with a twitch of his sword. "But he . . . I have a family! You can't . . ." He swallowed convulsively. "What do you want?"

Ahvren felt no triumph. He hated using Redahd's reputation—but if it kept new victims out of Redahd's hands, he'd use it for all it was worth. "Why did you buy the boridium?"

The Zo was silent, then his bony shoulders slumped. "I bought it for my uncle, Odan Mo. I can take you to him."

"Yes." Anticipation hissed in Ahvren's voice, despite his effort to sound calm. "I'd like that."

They took the underground out to the suburbs, for the storm had come in. Standing in the station doorway, Ahvren watched Loba Amm fuss with his sand cape. He'd sheathed his sword as they left the tunnel—people had stared enough as it was. His real hold on his captive was the credit identifier—it would give Redahd all the information he'd need, but Amm had made no move to take it from him. He even looked to see if Ahvren was ready before leading him up to the street.

"It's only a few blocks," he shouted over the wind.

Ahvren gestured for him to go on. Even with the scarf over his face, it was hard to breathe. Amm leaned into the wind at an impossible angle, his long legs propelling him forward. Ahvren had to struggle to keep up.

Like the houses of the wealthy quarter, these houses were protected by high walls. But through wrought-metal gates, through the haze of the scarf and sheets of blown sand, Ahvren caught glimpses of the homes they passed. Poured of modern plastics, they seemed to be formed of crescent curves—the angles, peaks, and arches unlike anything he'd seen in K'Moth. This must be one of the Zo ghettos. He'd heard that the Zo preferred to live among their own species.

They reached the corner and Amm turned through a gate and into a garden, heading toward a house whose strange, spiked angles rose four stories. A native bush, its ropy stalks blowing almost flat to the ground, tangled Ahvren's feet and he fell, the wind rolling him until he flattened himself against the earth. He tensed as Amm's hand closed on his elbow, but the Zo simply hauled him to his feet and led him, staggering, to the house.

There was a plaque outside the door, covered with a column of some elegantly curled writing. That was all Ahvren had time to notice before the doors whisked open—automatic doors in this part of town—and then closed behind him, sealing out the wind.

They took off their sand capes and shook them over the ribbed catching mat. Judging by the tiled expanse of the entry hall, this place was a mansion to equal any in the wealthy quarter, suburbs or no. But it had an impersonal atmosphere, and the furniture wasn't rich enough to match the room.

There were plaques beside several of the doors—one slid open a crack and a single, blue-lidded eye appeared, about four feet above the floor. A Vivitare child that tall would be nine or ten—the Zo child was probably much younger. The blue fingers wrapped around the door frame were thin as spiders' legs. Ahvren smiled at it and the eye widened and vanished, but he knew it would reappear as soon as its owner thought he wasn't looking.

"Come with me. I'll take you to Uncle Odan's rooms."

"His rooms? He doesn't own this house?"

"Oh, he still owns it, though now it's more a building than a house. My uncle rents suites to a dozen families. I live here myself—as you'll find out." He glanced ironically at the pouch that held his credit ID pendant. Ahvren shrugged. His neck and back were tight with a strangely familiar discomfort.

Uncle Odan's rooms were at the rear of the house. Amm ran his fingernails lightly over the door and called, "Uncle? I've brought someone to see you."

The door whisked open. "Loba! I was beginning to . . . worry about you."

The man staring at Ahvren was plump for a Zo, which made him look normal to a Vivitare. The skin around his eyes crumpled with the lines that, in a humanoid, almost always came from smiling. His sleeves were only six inches long.

"Come in, both of you. And tell me what this is about."

"He came to my shop this afternoon . . ." Loba Amm told the story with crisp accuracy, while Ahvren looked around. The furniture had been expensive but was now comfortably worn. The hiss of blowing sand outside the plasteel windows would have made the room feel cozy, if it hadn't been for the edge in Amm's voice.

Odan Mo listened in attentive silence until Amm told him how they had run into the tunnel. "You young fools! Fool," he amended, glancing at Ahvren. "No, fools. You could easily have been killed, both of you!"

Amm visibly decided not to go into detail. "Anyway, he captured me, took my credifier, and threatened to go to Viv Redahd, so I brought him here. He suspects us of being part of that plot to kill the emperor that people are talking about." His face was full of ironic amusement.

"He what? But surely that's just a rumor. Even if someone wanted to kill the man, and I can't think why anyone would, with all the talk, they'd have to be mad to do it now."

It sounded so honest, so sincere, but . . . "I can think of reasons why someone might want to kill the Vivitare emperor," said Ahvren softly. "Especially if his fortune was seized when we invaded."

There was a moment of silence; then Odan Mo sighed. "Go home, Loba. You've done well, except for the stupidity in the tunnel. I'll deal with it."

"Uncle—"

"No. Go."

Amm nodded deeply, almost a bow, and left.

"Come, Viv Ahvren, and let me explain." He led the way to a small kitchen. A spouted pot, Cutachan ware, chipped but still lovely, sat on the warmer. Odan poured two cups and passed one to Ahvren. Some sort of herb tea, fruity, not too tart.

"It's true that I lost part of my fortune to your invasion, but it was so small a part that I almost don't begrudge it." The irony in his face was tinged with humor.

The tension in Ahvren's back diminished. "I find that hard to believe."

"Yes, well, I'd be angrier if it wasn't my own fault. I made several bad investments— oh, not bad, but risky, and I lost on them. But I was too proud, too foolish, to admit I had woven such a tangle. And truly, it's harder to bargain when your adversary knows you're in need. I was still trying to conceal the extent of my loss when you people came and took what was left. In a way, I'm grateful to you—it gives me an excuse for my poverty that keeps me from looking like a fool. Of course, I intend to start investing again, more carefully, as soon as I amass a little capital. I don't suppose you have any funds you'd care to invest?"

Ahvren smiled in spite of himself. But . . . "But what about the boridium?"

"Ah, that was an attempt to recoup some

funds—it misfired badly. I told the seller I couldn't afford to buy at the price we'd originally agreed on—and that was true enough! I hired Maffatti to buy it cheaper. Unfortunately, my buyers were also trying to retrench. They couldn't afford to buy that boridium, even at cost! Finally I gave it to a ship captain, to sell on consignment on other planets. Surely someone, somewhere can pay for it! But when I'll see a profit from it, only the Allmother knows."

"I see." And he did see, all of it; the chaos the invasion had caused in the planet's business community, the fear that had led to desperate gambles. He would ask the scholar to check on the story, but he was almost certain it was true. Yet there was no anger, no hatred, in the white-lashed eyes. What was it with these people? This man had enough pride to shrink from exposing his business failures; why not pride enough to fight?

"Viv Ahvren, if you wish to tell that . . . Viv Redahd about me, I can't stop you. But Loba was only acting as my agent, and there are twelve families living in this house. Even if he only uses truth drugs, the children will—"

"No." Ahvren didn't want to be begged for

mercy, even this quiet, civilized plea. "I believe you, and I see no reason to tell Redahd anything. It's only"—his lips twisted bitterly—"another dead end."

Odan kept him there for several hours, insisting he stay until the storm's fury lessened. It was Odan Mo who steered the conversation, asking what Ahvren had seen in K'Moth, what he found valuable in the rich variety of T'Chin culture. What other Vivitare might value . . . Even knowing that he was being pumped for information, Ahvren enjoyed himself so much that he almost forgot to return Loba Amm's credit identifier before he left.

"I thank you, Viv Ahvren. For everything." The front door opened and Odan gazed out. Sand whipped over the ground in skittering wisps, and the sunset coated the world with glowing copper. "It's still light and the underground is only a block away," Odan muttered, half to himself. "You'll be all right."

"Of course I will. Thanks for letting me wait out the storm."

Odan bowed. "My pleasure, Viv Ahvren. Truly."

● ● ●

The sand blowing around his ankles was only a nuisance. The cool wind was glorious after the sullen heat of the day. Ahvren started into the underground and almost tripped over the chair in the middle of the entryway. A neatly printed sign taped to its back said, ACCESS IS NONFUNCTIONAL. PLEASE USE HULMAR ACCESS. The arrow beneath the message pointed into a side street.

Ahvren sighed, but walking down the quiet street the sign had indicated, he decided he didn't really mind.

*Another dead end.*

There were fewer pedestrians here, and Ahvren barely noticed the sidelong glances of the Zo who walked past him. He reached up and rubbed his tense neck muscles.

*Another shackling dead end.* The wedding was three days off, and the assassins would strike within the month, according to Redahd. But perhaps the scholar would have something for him. It had been three days. And Grem had said he'd keep looking. It was ridiculous to expect to find the rebellion at the end of the first trail he followed.

Ahvren scowled. The sky to the east was

darkening, scattered stars beginning to appear. Here in the Zo ghetto there were no streetlights, only lamps beside the gates, whose warm glow did nothing to dim the night's beauty. But that beauty was only a distant tug at the edge of his grim thoughts. He rubbed his neck again.

Redahd's reputation had already spread through the city, angering people, frightening them. Couldn't the idiot see—couldn't *Lessar* see—that if they became angry and fearful enough, even the T'Chin might fight back? Still, this strange cowardice seemed to be deeply rooted in their culture. But as the scholar had said, they knew nothing of war. Could you even call it cowardice if they knew no alternative? If you were raised not to fight, was it your fault that you grew as you were raised? Ahvren sighed, rubbed his neck again, and froze. He hadn't rubbed his neck this way, felt this tension coiling up the muscles beside his spine, since he had left Mirmanidan.

The Mirmani buildings were square, the Zo's curved. Mirmanidan was covered with mist-filled forest; K'Moth was in a desert. But the sullen resentment in Loba Amm's eyes was the same. The wary, hidden glances of the people he'd passed in the street were the same. And the following footsteps that stopped when he did were the same as they'd been on the night Breal had died and Ahvren had acquired an eight-inch scar along his ribs.

He started walking again and the footsteps resumed behind him—about half a block back, more than one pursuer. The sunset was dying with the wind, and there was no one in sight. Where were the patrols when you needed one? He had to reach the underground station, a public building, a crowded street.

A hand-written sign. Written in *Vivitare*, in a Zo neighborhood. There was no underground access down this street. They were herding him. Ahvren swore silently. *How could he have been such a fool?* Just two months in friendly, peaceful K'Moth had spoiled him— relaxed the instincts the Mirmani had ground into him. He'd never have been caught this way on Mirmanidan.

They were making no effort to close the distance. As long as they didn't know he knew, he might reach safety before they made their move. Had Odan known? Probably. Set him up for this? No. Odan Mo had all but told him to take the underground. He'd been warned, and he hadn't even realized it. Fool.

Two Zo came around a corner ahead of him, walking toward him. Strangers . . . help? Darkness shrouded them, but as they passed a gate lamp, Ahvren could see they carried long sticks, too thick for walking sticks. Clubs. The same reach as his sword. At least they didn't have stunners or, worse yet, disrupters.

Two ahead and more behind him; they'd have him boxed in in minutes if he didn't get off the street. There was a side street coming up on his left—narrow, dark, but better than being trapped. He started to cross it, as if he was still unaware, then darted down it, sprinting full out, adrenaline-propelled.

He grinned at their startled shouts. He had a lead and was scared enough to outrun a train at this point! He could—

Four dark shapes stepped away from the alley wall, blocking his path. Ahvren skidded to a stop and spun. Four in front, four behind, high walls on either side, no gates, no lights—this was where they'd wanted him! They were closing in. *One chance.*

He crossed the street in a burst of speed that took him halfway up the wall, textured plastic slipping under his scrabbling shoes. His fingers clamped on its top. Ahvren swung one leg up and started to slither over. A blue hand grabbed his tunic, dragging him back into the trap. The Zo were tall, curse them.

As he fell, he drew his sword. He was only a fair fighter, but he was a Vivitar, a survivor. They'd learn what that meant before they took him down. He slashed out, felt the shock of connection in the bones of his wrist, and slashed again, missing.

They fell back at the sound of their comrade's scream, a half-circle around him. At least he had the wall at his back. Only seven now, as one stumbled and fell, moaning and clutching the stained cloth over his belly. Another ran to kneel beside him, crying in Zo, "Moz, are you—" He heard Ahvren's translator render it into Vivitare and fell silent. Ahvren grinned, and the others exchanged looks over the sand scarves that concealed the lower halves of their faces. He had one name—and only six of them surrounded him now. Amateurs. Perhaps he had a chance.

He lunged and another Zo cried out, clutching his bleeding arm, his club skidding down the street. Again! His sword lashed out, but now, *finally*, they were on guard. The man jumped away and a club crashed down on Ahvren's shoulder—missing his head—clumsy, clumsy. It throbbed dully, but he ignored it. It wouldn't slow him down.

They were moving in on him. *Figured out you have me outnumbered, cowards?* The clubs swung. He jumped into them, left arm lifted to protect his head, and slashed open a wrist. Blood splattered. One more out of it.

Then a club hit his leg, just missing his knee, hard enough to break the joint had it found its mark. Ahvren staggered, a cry of pain escaping him.

It encouraged them. The clubs fell again, slamming him against the wall. His left arm hurt horribly—it had taken many blows. It shook. Soon it would fall, useless. He lashed out blindly, driving them back, and a club came down on his right wrist, numbing it—broken? Hardly mattered, for his sword had fallen, clattering, to the pavement.

Run! He leapt at them, breaking the circle, but the end of a club caught the side of his head, making it spin . . . slowing him. Another club struck his ankle and he fell. He tried to roll, to leap to his feet, but his bruised knee gave, and the blow that found his ribs took him down again. They were playing with him now, he realized dizzily. They had him. *His own stupid fault.* He'd never have been so careless on Mirmanidan.

But no more blows fell. Was that shrilling just his ringing ears? Cautiously, Ahvren pulled his arms away from his head and looked around. The Zo were running, running away, carrying their wounded with them. What . . .

He looked in the other direction. A slim four-footed being ran toward him with long, springy strides. The shrieking whistle came from an alarm box on its belt. A watchman. Ahvren wasn't sure if the sound he made was a laugh or a sob.

The watchman skidded to a stop beside him, glaring after the fleeing Zo, his tufted ears swiveling furiously. The Grishik were the least humanoid of the furred races; cats, with all a big cat's grace and power. His rumbling growl would have doubled the Zo's speed if they'd heard it. This one had the facial stripes of a male. His tail lashed twice. Then he sighed. The sharp quills that rose with his hackles sank slowly into the rest of his pelt, and he settled upright on his haunches beside Ahvren. *"Greesht raa mau proo?"*

Grishik mouths were unsuited for any language but their own. Ahvren tried to open his pouch, but his arms throbbed, and neither of his hands was working very well. Stubby, velvet-backed fingers pushed his gently aside. The Grishik extended his claws and unlatched Ahvren's pouch. Claws that, instead of being filed blunt, were tipped with rubber caps. Sharpened claws. Ahvren gazed with interest into the whiskered face of the first Mirall he'd met. Their Grishik servant had waxed eloquent about these masters of the martial arts.

The Grishik fished out the packet of translator clips. His slit-pupiled eyes narrowed, and he hissed something.

Vivitare writing would be meaningless to him.

Ahvren fumbled out the correct clip and tried to insert it in his bracelet, until the Grishik took it from his hands and did it for him. "There! Are you . . . No, I know you're not all right. How badly are you hurt, young sir?"

"Not bad," said Ahvren, despite the fact that every muscle in his body throbbed and the pain was making his stomach turn in slow, heaving rolls. "I'm very, *very* grateful you showed up when you did." He took slow, deep breaths, trying not to move—trying not to stir the nausea.

"It's my job." The Grishik examined him as he spoke, running his hands along his bones with slow care. He tipped up Ahvren's sagging head and peered at his eyes. "How many of me do you see? Just one? Excellent." His fingers moved softly over Ahvren's skull, feeling more carefully when Ahvren's breath hissed, as he found the place the club had struck. "I think you're right—no bones broken, and your color's coming back to what I believe is normal for your kind. Even so, there's a medigoth who lives about two blocks from here. Shall I take you there?"

"No." The dizziness and nausea were receding. Ahvren moved his hands and arms carefully. Then his legs. Everything hurt but worked. "No, I don't need a doctor."

"Then where do you want me to take you? My flitter is parked three blocks from here, if you can make it that far. If you can't, I'll call for someone to come and pick us up."

Ahvren rose to his knees with slow care,

then, with the Grishik's help, to his feet. When the Grishik sank down to walk, his shoulder was as high as Ahvren's hip. "I can make it."

He did make it, limping and leaning against his rescuer, though it took all his concentration. So he still hadn't thought of an answer when the Grishik, who had settled upright on his haunches to drive, leaned over to buckle the safety harness around Ahvren and asked, "Where do I take you, young sir?"

Home? Ahvren gazed at his reflection in the dark window. Except for the faint bruises and scratches Loba Amm's struggle had left around his eyes, his face was unmarked. But even if the bruises on his arms, now changing from red to purple, weren't visible, one look at the way he moved would tell his father everything. And he'd decide that the investigation was too dangerous and put a stop to it. Not home. Ahvren needed time to come up with some arguments. Life had been simpler when he'd been able to lie. "Umradi and Pahast. My cousin Roi has rooms there."

"Very well." The flitter lifted with a quiet hum and accelerated. The field of lights below was brighter than the stars.

"Thank you. Though that's inadequate. You saved my life . . . I don't even know your name."

"Wurrul. And they may have intended only a beating. But as I said, it's my job."

"It's not your job to cart me around the city."

"On the contrary." Was that lift of the lip a Grishik smile? "I'm employed by the people of this neighborhood to keep the peace. You are clearly a disruptive influence. Therefore, it's my duty to remove you."

"*I'm* a disruptive influence? What about the Zo who attacked me?"

"As I said, I'm employed by the people of the neighborhood. And you, young sir, should not come back. At least not alone, at night. The Zo are new to T'Chin; many of them fear and resent the Vivitare."

"You don't. You couldn't be so kind if you did."

"Ah, but the Grishik have been part of T'Chin for a long time now."

"What difference does that make? You're a Mirall, aren't you?"

"How did you know that?"

"The rubber tips. Your claws are sharp.

You're a *fighter*. How can you be so . . . so . . ."

Wurrul was making the hissing whuff that served Grishik for laughter.

"I'm sorry." Ahvren slumped in his seat. "I have no right to question you."

"You poor cub—you sound so baffled! Never mind. It doesn't matter."

"Because you're a part of T'Chin? That keeps the conquest of your planet from *mattering*?"

"Precisely." He was laughing again. Almost soundlessly.

Ahvren let his aching head fall against the seat back. "I don't understand you people at all."

"That also doesn't matter."

Ahvren sighed and let his eyes drift closed in defeat.

# Chapter 12

**"I** MUST KNOW SOMETHING, or they wouldn't have attacked me." Early-morning sunlight flowed through the thin draperies as Ahvren paced, limping, across Roi's main room. Roi's suite was smaller, more modern, and far less prestigious than the mansion Ahvren lived in, yet Ahvren envied his cousin every time he saw it.

Roi had taken him in, treated his bruises, and called his home and told several small, reassuring lies. Now Ahvren was stiff and sore, but aside from that he felt . . . frustrated. "It's infuriating to know you know something and not know what it is!"

Roi, still wrapped in a rumpled night robe, regarded him seriously. "Did you go there to trace the source of the rumor?"

"No, that didn't work out. This was something else." He explained, briefly, about the boridium, and Roi nodded.

"I thought tracing a rumor that's been circulating for almost a month would be a waste of time. But there could be other reasons to attack you. This Odan Mo delayed you for several hours."

"I told you, he tried to warn me. If they hadn't sidetracked me, I'd have come home on the train, surrounded by people."

"If he warned you, he *must* have known about the attack."

"No." Ahvren's pacing slowed. "It wasn't that kind of warning, just a hint that the neighborhood might be dangerous for Vivitare."

"Then maybe they attacked you because you're Vivitare."

"No, they were stalking me. Besides, no other Vivitare have been attacked anywhere in K'Moth—on all T'Chin, I think. I must know something!" And knowing that gave him his first real hope—there were only three days left till Sabri married.

Roi grinned. "Perhaps they just think you know something, and you really don't."

"Thank you, Cousin. I suppose it's possible. But since they attacked me, I do know something. I know that one of them is named Moz, and that several of them have been treated for sword cuts. Surely that's enough for me to trace them!"

"You mean for Redahd to trace them. Or do you?"

Trust Roi to hear the subtle implications. Ahvren's pacing slowed. *There are twelve families living in this building . . . Even if he only uses truth drugs, the children . . .* "No. I'll tell Redahd when I'm sure. He . . . well, I need to be sure."

Roi nodded. "I know what you mean. That man is"—his lips twisted with the irony—"unfit."

In four months they would judge honorable, decent, clumsy Roi for fitness—and find him wanting, while a man like Redahd passed. Intolerable. "Roi, I'll talk to Father for you. I don't think it will do any good, but I'll try."

"Don't bother. I went to him myself, after I talked to you the other day. You were right. He won't help."

"There's probably nothing he could do. Roi . . ."

A dozen soothing lies rose to his lips and froze there, leaving him mute.

"Forget it." Roi smiled wearily. "You're

going to have your own problems. What are you going to tell him about this?"

After careful thought, Ahvren decided that his only hope was to say as little as possible. After all, he didn't really *know* anything. And if worst came to worst and he found himself blurting out the whole thing, well, it shouldn't be too hard to talk his father out of going to Redahd.

Actually, it was easier than he expected. His father took in everything, from his slight limp to the bruises around his eyes, in one comprehensive glance and fired off a string of questions.

Was he all right?

Fine, except for a little stiffness.

What happened?

A band of Zo attacked him in the Zo ghetto.

What was he doing there?

Pursuing a lead, but it turned out to be a dead end.

Could he identify any of his attackers?

Not if they were standing in front of him right now; they were all masked.

Was he all right?

His father was the one who suggested that since there seemed to be no connection between the attack and the plot, there was no need to report it to Redahd.

Clenching his teeth over surging words, Ahvren told his father about the Nisol sword, which distracted him nicely. Ahvren listened to his astonishment, smiled, nodded, and left the room sweating as hard as if he'd been working out with Grem.

He went to his room to find his lightest long-sleeved tunic. Explaining to his father was one thing; explaining to his mother was something else. But when he reached his room, all thought of tunics went right out of his head. On his comm pad was a message from the bibliogoth of Shakka Street, asking him to meet it tonight at the usual time.

Ahvren spent the rest of the morning in a Bredayma bathhouse and the other half of the day trying not to jitter too obviously as he ran errands for his mother. All the wedding preparations fell to her, since Dravik's mother was dead and Lessar's other wives detested Dravik. The rehearsal was tomorrow, the wedding the day after that, and Ahvren's mother was so busy, she had time to fuss over his bruises only every half hour or so.

Sabri did her part with an air of serene resignation, as if she'd given up all hope. She'd asked anxiously about her brother's bruises, though she'd been relieved when he'd assured her Viv Redahd wasn't behind the attack. Ahvren's heart bled for Sabri, but he didn't dare try to encourage her. His clues were too tenuous, and the time was too short.

Thus it was that he banged open the scholar's office door in no mood to take any more harassment from anyone.

No incense burned tonight, but the light gleamed warmly on the shelves of books and artifacts. The chair Ahvren preferred sat before the desk, ready for him.

"Enter, youngling." The bibliogoth started the gesture of greeting but froze in mid-rotation. Its antennae quirked toward Ahvren; then the bibliogoth rose and leaned forward, using its eyes to examine him. "Forgive me, but are you supposed to have those dark blotches? I don't remember them being there before."

"No." Ahvren's lips twitched. "They're bruises. I've been busy lately." And perhaps the scholar could figure out his attackers' motive. He sank into his chair and launched into the tale. The need to be methodical, the familiar room, the scholar's listening presence slowly relaxed Ahvren, diminishing his sense of urgency. "So I spent most of today in the Bredayma baths, though they weren't run by a Bredayma. In fact, I've never even seen a Bredayma."

"You won't, either." The synthavode voice sounded abstracted. The scholar was clicking two talons together, very softly—a nervous habit Ahvren had never seen before. "A single cup of water, poured onto a perfectly flat plane, will spread farther than the eye can see."

"What? What does that mean?"

"Hm? Oh. You won't ever see a Bredayma. They came to T'Chin a long time ago and discovered that, with a little genetic manipulation, they could interbreed with another race. Their descendants call themselves the Aj'Amadii."

"A cup of water." Ahvren shook his head blankly. He had resolved not to get drawn into this, but . . . "But wouldn't the surface tension, even on a perfectly flat plane, keep it from spreading out of sight?"

"That depends on how far you can see."

The antennae were curled in tight spirals. Ahvren swore silently. "All that is left of the Bredayma is part of a rich cultural heritage— and the name we give to the best thing they brought to us."

The impertinent question loomed in Ahvren's mind. He shouldn't ask— "Do you bathe?" Color surged into his cheeks. "I'm sorry. I know I shouldn't ask personal questions, but—"

"Don't be embarrassed. To ask questions, all questions, is essential to the bibliogoth's craft." But one antennae still spiraled softly. "The answer is, yes and no. We don't immerse ourselves in water as you do, but we smooth the rough spots on our chitin with pumice stone and polish it with a soft wax."

"I see." Ahvren's fascinated gaze ran over the gleaming curves of the bibliogoth's exoskeleton. "Thank you."

"Not at all. In the past chitin painting has been fashionable, but now a more natural, austere look is preferred."

The images in Ahvren's mind were so startling, it took him several moments to pull his thoughts back to the topic. "Do you see anything in what I told you that I'm missing?

They must have had some reason for attacking me."

"Yes. They must." But the scholar added nothing more.

"And what did *you* learn? You must have discovered something, or you wouldn't have sent for me."

The silence grew, and Ahvren's suspicion began to grow with it. He had almost been distracted earlier. Was that deliberate? Why . . . "Why aren't you answering?"

The antennae drooped and rose. "Great risks should result in great profits," the scholar murmured. "Or you shouldn't take them. Youngling, the most dangerous thing in the world is not a disrupter beam or a virus, it is knowledge. Because bibliogoths deal in knowledge, we, unlike informagoths, take responsibility for what we do. Before I give you this information, I want your promise, in whatever form has meaning to your people, that you will think"—one talon rotated up—"before you act on it."

"All right," said Ahvren impatiently. "I give you my word as a Vivitar that I'll think before I act on this information. What information?"

The scholar hesitated a moment more,

then pulled a small stack of flimsy, plastic printouts off a shelf and handed it to Ahvren. Names and addresses. Several hundred names. Ahvren scanned the list. If he had to investigate all of them, he'd—

One name caught Ahvren's eye and he froze, staring. Odan Mo. Odan Mo wasn't poor, had made no unfortunate investments—he was *concealing* his wealth. He had lied. He had lied, and was purchasing weapons-grade boridium, and had probably had Ahvren attacked, and Ahvren had *believed* him and defended the shackling, treacherous bastard when even Roi had seen the truth.

"He lied!" Ahvren leaped to his feet, starting for the door.

*"Stop!"* All the scholar's talons crashed on the desk. The voice from its synthavode was so loud that, for the first time, it sounded mechanical. "You swore to me that you would think—I hold you to that oath. If you don't fulfill it, all transactions between us are at an end, and I will destroy the credit of your character throughout K'Moth! Throughout the Confederation if necessary! Stop and think!" It rose from its cup-chair and towered over Ahvren, antennae flattened back. Its anger

was formidable—Ahvren wondered why he wasn't frightened.

"I'll keep my word. You don't have to threaten to . . . destroy the credit of my character?"

"Would you choose to deal with a man who defaulted on a moral debt?" The scholar sank back, its antennae relaxing again.

Ahvren returned to his chair. "No, I guess I wouldn't."

"Nor would any honest being. No one deals with those who have no moral credit except, oh, Maffatti and her like."

"I see. What is it you want me to think about?"

"Youngling, you're the one who promised to think. Only a kapuka would feed another's young before its own."

Ahvren glared at the scholar but refused to be distracted again. Odan Mo had lied. Odan Mo had had him attacked . . . but also warned him. That didn't make sense. But if the merchant wasn't part of the rebellion, the plot, then what . . . "What other reason could Odan Mo have to buy boridium and secretly amass money?"

The scholar's spiky limbs relaxed. Ahvren

hadn't realized the creature had been so tense until it settled. "I don't know. But the Zo are the second-most-recent species to come to T'Chin. They still dwell together in their own neighborhoods, though more and more of their young are moving into the main current of our culture. Almost half the names on that list are Zo . . . but more than half are not."

"You're trying to tell me that there might be other reasons for Odan Mo to conceal his wealth? But what about the boridium? Wait . . . Do you know of anything else he bought?"

"Not in detail. I know he's purchased large amounts of many raw materials, including gold and some iridana."

"The stuff of which money is made. They must intend to do some counterfeiting."

"That's a very sweeping assumption, youngling. Investing in currency is generally regarded as a risky venture."

"Why?" Ahvren frowned. "Gold and iridana will always have value."

"As long as you're dealing with Vivitare perhaps, but before you came, our currency consisted of colored stones."

"Yes, I've seen them. I thought it was odd.

I mean, they were just stones—no intrinsic value."

One antennae spiraled. "The form of currency has never mattered to the T'Chin. It's the transaction that has value. A cloud shaped like a peeka mouse can still flood your grain field. But as long as you keep the questions in your mind, and seek answers instead of victory, that's all I ask."

The scholar's talons came together and rotated down, ending the interview.

Ahvren rose. "You have my word."

"Youngling?" One small talon lifted. Ahvren stared at the scholar blankly. The antennae twitched in irritation. "My fee, forgetful one." It tapped the barter bowl.

"Oh!" Ahvren groped in his pouch for three silver ounces. It wasn't too late yet. If he hurried, he could return to Odan Mo's house tonight. Though why he should care if he got the shackling liar out of bed . . . Ahvren placed the silver squares in the bowl with careful haste and turned to go.

"Youngling?"

"Now what?"

"You should also give thought to protecting yourself. I still have many questions to ask about your culture—I hate to lose an information source before I've finished with it."

"Don't worry." Ahvren found himself smiling. "I'll be careful. I promise."

Ahvren took the scholar's advice, so it was late when the flitter whirred down to land in the garden in front of Odan Mo's mansion— his father's flitter, which was shielded against anything a handheld weapon could throw.

"You're sure you don't want me to go in, while you wait here?" Grem asked, as he shut down the engine.

"No," said Ahvren. "As long as you're out here, I'll be safe. I'm sure of it." Most of the windows were dark, but some of the arches that still glowed held shadowy silhouettes.

"Lots of the Vivitars I've seen end up dead were sure they'd be safe," Grem told him dryly. "Half an hour, boy, or I'm off to your father and the emperor."

"I won't forget."

Grem snorted. "Make sure they don't forget."

"Right." Ahvren slid from the flitter and closed the door, rendering the machine almost invulnerable; a turtle shell protecting his old teacher. Nothing protected Ahvren but the disrupter he wore instead of a sword, and his spine prickled as he strode across the dark garden. The door whisked open when he stepped onto the porch, and he flinched like a nervous gaza stag. No searing beams ripped the darkness. Odan Mo stood there, smiling sadly as he saw the disrupter at Ahvren's side. His robe was made of dark vellatin, rich, but worn to comfortable softness, like the furniture he seemed to prefer. His sleeves were so long they almost brushed the floor.

A bitter smile curved Ahvren's mouth at the sight.

Odan Mo sighed. "Come in. I've been expecting you."

"If I don't come out in half an hour, my friend will go straight to Viv Redahd and tell him all I know."

"I'm surprised that you haven't done just that already." To Ahvren's surprise, the merchant was leading him to the same rooms they had gone to before. "You have nothing to fear from anyone in my house, and you may leave in half an hour, or anytime you choose. I don't blame you for doubting it, but I'm not responsible for that attack. Indeed, I was sorry when I heard of it . . . and for more reasons than the obvious one."

Odan led him through the sitting room and into the homey kitchen, where he filled a pot and set it on the warmer. The long sleeves weren't as impractical as they looked—when he reached for something, the edge of the counter swept them out of his way.

"Which reason do you think is obvious?" asked Ahvren dryly, taking a seat. He found nothing obvious about this man.

"That it roused and redoubled the suspicions I had succeeded in lulling," said the merchant, setting a tea sieve in the pot. "I was furious when I found out about it."

"Furious with who?"

Odan Mo hesitated, then smiled ruefully. "No use trying to hide it, I suppose. It was Loba, who is well intentioned but sometimes very foolish. I'd say he's young, but there's a degree of stupidity even youth doesn't excuse, and sometimes he . . . Well, he won't do anything like that again, I assure you."

"Why? Was it just anger, because I caught him in the tunnels? Because of the conquest?"

"Allmother, no! He's angry, but not that

angry. He thought you still had his credifier in your pouch and was going to get it back. Though what good he thought it would do to get the credifier when you could identify him, I don't know."

"Then he didn't intend to kill me?"

Odan Mo's eyes dropped for the first time. "He told me he didn't, and in truth, I can't believe even Loba would be that stupid. I don't know. *He* may not have known, not really. He panicked when he saw you leave the house and thought I'd failed."

"You hadn't failed. I believed every lie. So why should I believe one word you're saying now?"

A timer on the warmer cheeped and Odan Mo poured tea. Two cups. "You have a point. The traditional fate of liars is to be disbelieved when they tell the truth. But if *I* wanted you dead, then Wurrul—who works for me, not the neighborhood—would have finished you off and disposed of your body with his usual competence. But here you are. Is that proof enough?"

"Wurrul lied, too? You sent him to find me?"

"As soon as Loba told me he'd arranged

the attack. Though why you didn't take the underground home, I can't imagine. I did warn you."

"So you did." A chill crept over Ahvren. He was grateful for the warm cup in his hands. "Loba may not be as foolish as you think. If I'd been killed, no one would have suspected there was anything but general hatred for the Vivitare behind it. No one would ever have questioned you. So why did you stop them?"

Odan Mo gazed down at his cup. For once his mouth held no lurking twist of humor. "I may not be T'Chin enough to regard the loss of all I've earned as . . . as a setback in some cosmic game. But I am T'Chin enough to know that currency is the cheapest form of tender. To save my fortune at the cost of an innocent life would be a very poor bargain. And I really do like you . . . believe it or not."

Ahvren smiled bitterly. "The liar's fate. But you're smart enough to have let me die if you were involved in a rebellion, so I suppose . . . Why did you lie to me?"

"Because money may be the cheapest form of tender, but it isn't always cheap." The merchant paced the small room, and for the first time, Ahvren saw anger in the white-lashed eyes. Anger and pride. "I was born on Zodan, in a threader's hut. I've worked all my life to get what I have today—enough wealth to never fear want, to take my family and friends into my home in times of risk and need, enough . . ." He noticed Ahvren's expression, and the smile crept back to his mouth, dispelling the startling passion. "Enough to tempt any conqueror. But I thought, with a little cleverness, I could protect it. I bought huge amounts of raw materials, and shipped them off the planet, in ships I still own no matter whose name is on the records. I bought shares for a lower price than was reported, so it looked like a loss when I sold them. I did everything I could to make my wealth invisible when your collectors came snooping through our data banks. But that's all I've done, and all I intend to do. Do you believe me? Or are you going to Viv Redahd?"

"Oh, I believe you. You're very believable. But I have no idea if you're telling the truth . . . So I'm not going to Viv Redahd." Whose reputation, it seemed, was a two-edged sword. "Because I wouldn't turn a crazed jacca over to that man unless I was certain. I don't think I'll ever be certain about you." He would have sworn the regret in the merchant's face was genuine.

Odan Mo's mouth twisted. "The fate of liars. So be it. But I'll remember this, Viv Ahvren—if you ever need my help, you have only to ask. I'm honest enough to pay my debts, at least."

"So you *say*," said Ahvren wearily, turning to go back to the waiting flitter before Grem could start worrying. Before the situation became clouded with more silken lies.

# Chapter 13

To Ahvren's mother's visible relief, the marriage rehearsal went off without a hitch—after a fashion. Dara came with Sabri. It was traditional for the bride's best friend to help her dress and lend moral support, though Sabri hardly seemed to need it. She was quiet, her eyes properly downcast in perfect feminine modesty—behavior so unusual that Ahvren was seriously worried.

He had failed her. She hadn't blamed him when he told her that the last of his leads had evaporated, and that made Ahvren feel even worse than he had before. He would investigate the others on the scholar's list, but he knew it would take days at the least. He might save Lessar, and himself, but it was too late for Sabri. And judging by the way she acted, she knew it.

His parents didn't seem concerned, but they were both intensely busy, his mother with the ceremony, his father with the emperor's security. The wedding would take place in the great hall, where all the important Vivitars would gather to see the heir married. Ahvren's father interrupted the rehearsal half a dozen times, demanding the installment of electronic surveillance in the servers' corridor, another guard by that window, another by this door, until Ahvren began to fear there would be no room for the guests.

Dravik, of course, noticed nothing. Watching him eyeing Dara's soft loveliness as Viv Saiden and Lessar glossed through the ceremony that bound Sabri to him for life, Ahvren was grateful that at least it was Sabri, and not someone defenseless, who would fall into his hands. Her physical safety was in no doubt—it was only her chance for happiness that would be lost.

The two fathers finally finished their parts—*now I say this, you say that, and then we both say*—and tied Dravik and Sabri's wrists together with a soft scarf, which would promptly be untied so they could go to separate rooms to change into less restrictive clothing for the dancing that would follow the feast. At this point, Dravik left—he'd promised to meet some friends, and all he had to do for the rest of the ceremony was sit.

So Sabri sat alone between Saiden and Lessar until Jennah came to occupy her brother's empty chair, her expression full of grave sympathy. Dara sat across from Ahvren. After one startled question about his bruises, she showed no desire to talk, though her gaze wandered alertly around the shadowy hall, dropping only when she met Ahvren's eyes.

Parades of servants carried in tables, mimed their duties, and whisked away, following Ahvren's mother's instructions: *Now the first course is served, then the wheat is presented.* Symbolizing prosperity. *Now the second course, then the cups are presented.* Symbolizing joy. *Now the third course, then the sword and cradle . . .* Ahvren realized he'd forgotten to ask his father if he'd succeeded in purchasing the Nisol sword. It would be a splendid gesture to give it to Dravik (symbolizing his duty, as the cradle symbolized Sabri's) but Ahvren hoped his father wouldn't do it. Dravik was the last person to deserve such a weapon. He deserved Sabri even less.

Ahvren was bitterly depressed when he entered the scholar's study that evening.

The incense tonight smelled like fresh-cut wood, with an underlying fruity scent. Could incense be to the T'chin what music was to more aural beings? Ahvren dropped into his waiting chair as the scholar's talons rotated up.

"So, youngling, what happened between you and Odan Mo?"

"Nothing much. You told me once that your name would mean nothing to me because it's just a scent, but I'd like to . . . may I smell your name?"

"I'm not sure you're, ah, equipped"—the antennae wagged—"to do so. Perhaps if I 'shouted.'" It reached down and lifted the synthavode off its thorax. After a moment Ahvren became aware of another scent in the room, acrid and spicy.

"Yes." He sniffed. "I can smell that. Thank you."

The scholar resettled the synthavode. "Did you say something, youngling?"

"Uh, yes. I smelled it. Thank you." He was blushing—he knew the scholar couldn't understand him without the synthavode.

"Don't be embarrassed. I still remember how I felt when I realized that the globs of sound I detected when dealing with speaking beings were rich with meaning to them, and nothing to me."

"How did you feel?"

"Deprived. Alien. A little lonely."

"Yes. That's it exactly."

"Yet here we are, talking together. So tell me—"

"What happened when the T'chin first encountered a vocal race? I mean, how did you communicate?"

"With great difficulty. The first aliens to come to T'Chin were a vocal race—the M'richt Tha'ad Ban. And different modes of communication weren't the only problem. We T'chin are a social people—you'll never meet a T'chin hermit. We are community dwellers, and the more beings in the community, the better. The M'richt came as conquerors. By the time we learned to communicate enough to, well, communicate, it was too late. For both of us! But tell me—"

"So why haven't I seen any M'richt, or heard of M'richt woodwork or some such thing?"

"Youngling, that was a *long* time ago.

Spoken T'Chin is basically the M'richt language, so we still have the best thing they brought to us. But—"

"Then 'T'Chin' is a M'richt word? What—"

*"What happened between you and Odan Mo?"*

The antennae curved softly at Ahvren's startled expression . . . or scent. "Forgive me, but I've been indecently curious all day. And don't think you can fob me off with 'nothing much,' either!"

Ahvren laughed. "Nothing much happened." He described the encounter. "So it's another dead end, and I have nothing to go on but a list of several hundred names, people whose reasons for concealing their wealth are probably as innocent as Odan Mo's."

"You're sure he was telling the truth?"

"I'm not sure of anything that man says, but if he'd been part of a rebellion, he'd have had me killed instead of rescuing me. Unless that's what he wanted me to think, and . . . no. It would be too dangerous to let me live. He's not a fool, whatever else he is. But now"—he spread his hands helplessly—"I'm stuck."

"Well, you've already rejected my advice, so—"

"No, I haven't . . . What advice?"

"Think about it." The scholar held up one small talon.

Ahvren thought. "Tracing the rumor? That didn't work."

The antennae twitched back. "Are all softlings so impatient, or just the young ones? The dekka bird builds its nest one twig at a time."

"You think I should try to trace the rumor again?"

"That's up to you."

"But it's been circulating for weeks! Roi said . . ." The idea didn't explode in his mind, it crept in, like a trickle of water undermining the foundation of a house—fragments of conversation, vague impressions.

He was silent so long the scholar's patience gave out. Its antennae cocked toward him. "Well?"

"Roi said the rumor has been circulating for almost a month," said Ahvren slowly. "But I heard it only a couple of weeks ago. Perhaps less than that. The others I talked to heard it just a little before I did. I think Roi heard it long before. So he's probably closer to the source of the rumor, right?"

"That seems logical."

"I'll ask Roi where he heard it. Tonight . . . no, tomorrow. He'll be more willing to think about it if I don't wake him up." The marriage was in the evening—tracking the rumor would give him an excuse to avoid the preparations until he had to go to the ceremony. Was it cowardly to want to avoid watching a catastrophe you couldn't do anything to stop? Probably.

"When we first met, you said you'd take me as your apprentice, if I could figure out why you didn't resist our invasion. This . . . pacifism is part of your culture, isn't it?"

"It is part of our culture, our philosophy, if you will, but that's not the answer. And I'd hate to take an apprentice who defines his terms so sloppily. That's *not* what I said."

Ahvren struggled to remember. "You said you would consider taking me as an apprentice, if I could figure out why our conquest didn't matter to you . . . Isn't that the same thing?"

The scholar held up one small talon. It didn't reply.

Ahvren sighed. "I'd better go. I want to see Roi early tomorrow." He dropped three silver ounces in the barter bowl and rose, then hesitated. "You never did tell me what T'chin means." He thought of the M'richt encountering this species for the first time. Big bugs. "Insectlike?"

"In a sense." Its talons rotated down in farewell. Both antennae curved in tight spirals. "It means 'crushable.'"

Ahvren departed, wondering why that made the scholar laugh.

Next morning he awakened and set out early. He hoped to catch Roi at breakfast, but when he reached his cousin's rooms, Roi had already left. Roi's manservant, a reserved safe male, was immune to bribes, but he'd known Ahvren since childhood, so it wasn't hard to persuade him to reveal Roi's whereabouts.

Roi and Grem fenced down the practice floor. It was only at times like this that the effect of Grem's prosthetic ankle showed, in the slight deliberation with which Grem placed that foot. It scarcely marred his fluid grace, especially now, when he was fighting at half speed to give Roi a chance.

His cousin had developed some muscle lately. Ahvren's throat tightened as he realized how hard Roi had worked, for it was obviously futile. Even though Grem was fighting slowly, Roi barely managed to parry his strokes, and his feet were never quite where they should be. When one of Grem's lazy swings sent the practice sword clattering over the floor, none of them was surprised. Sweat rolled down Roi's face like tears, but his expression held only resignation as he went to pick up his sword.

"Hello," Ahvren called softly. He was trying not to startle them, but Roi jumped and spun around.

Grem, who had his back to Ahvren, simply nodded before turning. "I haven't found anything else for you. There are a few more places I can try, but they're long shots."

"Thank you. Actually, I want to talk to Roi for a moment."

"I'll be finished soon," said Roi, wiping his face.

"You're finished now, lad. Go on. There's a class coming."

Roi looked as if he wanted to protest, but students never argued with Grem. Ahvren followed him to the changing room.

"So, Cousin." Roi went to the hook where his clothes hung. "Why aren't you busy with marriage preparations? I suppose it's too much to hope that the whole thing's been called off."

Ahvren grimaced. "I'm afraid so. Roi, how do you know Sabri doesn't want this marriage?"

Roi snorted. "I'm her cousin and I'm in love with her best friend, but even if I weren't, I know Dravik, and Sabri isn't crazy. Oh well. At least she can outfight him."

"There is that. But I wanted to ask you something else. When did you first hear the rumor about the assassination?"

"Are you still messing with that? I thought you were tracing money trails or something." Roi pulled off his tunic and wiped his damp torso with it before reaching for a clean one.

"That didn't work out. When did you hear it?"

"I don't know." The clean tunic had somehow become twisted, and the fabric muffled Roi's voice. Ahvren untwisted it and yanked it down. "It was a long time ago and I didn't take it seriously. I mean, my father told me that on Mirmanidan there were rumors like that once a month."

"How *long* ago?"

"I said I don't remember. Three or four weeks, I guess."

"That's good enough." Ahvren took a deep breath. "Roi, who did you hear it from?"

"From Lahno, my manservant. Are you trying to trace the source again?"

"Yes. Shackles, I saw the man not ten minutes ago. Do you mind if I go back and talk with him?"

"I'll save you the trouble, I know where he heard it." Why was Roi grinning? "This should frustrate you, Cousin. He got it from your own servants. He said your whole staff was gossiping about it, because the little Olopoli—Pomo?—had just told them."

Ahvren fought off an impulse to grab his cousin's collar and shake him. "Why didn't you tell me this before?"

"You didn't ask me, and I didn't know it mattered. Does . . ."

Ahvren was out of the room before Roi finished his question.

# Chapter 14

**A**HVREN'S MOTHER DIDN'T KNOW where Pomo was—the housekeeper might—but she needed him to . . . Ahvren told her he had urgent business to attend to, and she shrugged and quite obviously forgot him within seconds of turning to the next urgent task.

The housekeeper certainly did know where Pomo was—Viv Saiden had sent him out to pick up some silly package, just when every hand was needed. She didn't know what he'd been sent for, but she had the address; it was the shop with the Nisol sword in the window. Ahvren was delighted his father had bought it, until he realized that his father probably meant to give it to Dravik.

The housekeeper told him that Pomo had left ten minutes ago. With the household so busy, he would have taken the underground to save time—Ahvren took it for the same reason. It was too late to help Sabri. There was no reason to feel this pressing urgency, but Ahvren fought an impulse to run as he climbed into the sunshine and set off for the shop.

It was almost noon, and heat was beginning to accumulate in the walls and pavement. The stillness of the air promised a sandstorm, though when Ahvren looked west he saw no trace of the boiling, brown cloud. Too early yet.

He was reaching for the shop door when it opened and Pomo stepped out, almost bumping into him. The little Olopoli smiled apologetically, squinting as the sunlight struck his round, dark eyes. "Please be pardoning, mem/ser. You were not being visible, and . . . Viv Ahvren? What are you doing here?"

The sword box probably wasn't heavy, but it was taller than Pomo, and he clasped it awkwardly as he struggled through the doorway.

"Here, give me that. Pomo, about the rumor that someone is going to assassinate the emperor, where did you hear it?"

Pomo shut the door quickly and raised troubled eyes to Ahvren's face. "Wondering there has been, if someone would be asking about that. Much worry was here"—he laid a hand over his heart—"for knowledge of what should be done is not here. But do you want to be discussing it now?" He glanced at the beings walking briskly past them.

"Why not? I mean . . . Is there any reason we shouldn't?"

"There may be." The grim expression sat oddly on Pomo's round face. "Be coming, Viv Ahvren. There is a place nearby where there can be talking without being overheard."

At this point, Ahvren didn't care if the whole world overheard, but Pomo sounded so serious that Ahvren followed him down the street without comment. Pomo, for once, was silent, his face grave and thoughtful. Ahvren, who had never seen him other than cheerful, realized that he had thought of Pomo as a childlike creature, though surely no simple race would prosper for long in the competitive world of T'Chin business. He tried to remember what the Olopoli had brought to the Confederation, but nothing came to mind except someone saying something was complicated. That was it—as complicated as Olopoli math. Math?

"Pomo, what did you do before you became our servant? For a living, I mean."

The round eyes had to look up to meet his, but they were startlingly shrewd. "A chemist was here, Viv Ahvren, and still is, though currently an enforced vacation is being taken." His voice was cheerful again. "When your people invaded, the labs were closed, for your emperor was fearing that something would be invented to defeat you. This was foolish, for you are not mattering to us, but your emperor isn't knowing this."

"But that's . . . Pomo, you went from chemist to servant. How can that not matter to you? How can it? You people don't make sense!"

Pomo's eyebrows lifted at his vehemence. "It is being regarded as an opportunity. When working for Machemka, their projects had to be pursued. Now working for love in spare time is here, and interesting prospects are being discovered. When the labs open, the formulas will be selling for great profit. Besides, working for your family is not minded, for you are liked, and much love for each other is there." His face went serious. "That is being the problem. But arriving is here."

Pomo had led him to a small square surrounding a fountain. Thin-leafed desert trees, with benches beneath them, were scattered about, but the square's only occupants were a band of grubby urchins. Their wildly mixed species didn't seem to hinder their enjoyment of the game they played, with two balls and an insanely complex web of string that twined back and forth between the trees. Ahvren, remembering the expensive, high-tech toys he had seen in the shops, smiled.

Pomo wove his way to a bench and sat in the sun. He glanced at Ahvren for permission, then dropped the robe from his shoulders, baring his torso. His skin darkened quickly and he turned his face to the sun, which was the Olopoli's god, and murmured something in his own language.

Ahvren found a seat in the shade and waited till the brief prayer was finished before asking, "Well?"

"It will be one month ago tomorrow, exactly." Pomo's gaze dropped to the darting children. "The plants in the long corridor were being fed. You know how high those windows are being?"

Ahvren nodded. The corridor that ran

along the north side of the house was lined with windows looking out on the garden—if you were as tall as a T'chin. Ahvren had to stand on tiptoe to see through them. Pomo couldn't have done so.

"It was dusk, and the windows were being open. Voices in the garden were there. They were walking beside the wall, and following them was here." One small, square palm touched his heart. "One of them said, 'If you are committed to this, all the aspects must be considered carefully. To be killing a member of the emperor's house is something for which there will be no mercy—they will be hunting . . . they will hunt down and destroy everyone involved. If we are to be surviving . . . to survive success, we'll have to be more than careful.' Then the other one said, 'That's not likely to be being . . . to be my problem.' And the first one said, 'Are you certain this is what you are wanting? They might . . .' and then something was being said about other approaches, but they were walking on and the corridor was ending. The only door to the outside is being at the other end. By the time the garden was being reached, they had gone—seeing them was not here. Sorrow for that is here, Viv Ahvren, for—"

"But that's impossible! Pomo, no one would be mad enough to plot such a thing in my father's garden! Unless . . ."

"Unless they were being members of the household." Pomo sighed. "This was realized shortly after talking to the staff. That was being careless, but there was much need to discover who it was in the garden, and there was hope someone had seen them. That's why there has been silence here, for there is no wish to be harming your family, but there is also no wish to see someone killed. Hearing the rumors has been hard."

"Of course, *you* are the source. But you said a member of the emperor's house? Not the emperor?"

"That's what they were saying, and it was seeming a strange turn of phrase, but many of your phrases are seeming strange. It changed almost immediately in the telling, but it couldn't be corrected without suspicion being caused to fall on your family."

"My father would never do such a thing, unless . . . unless the council fears Dravik becoming emperor so much . . . No, I don't believe it. My father is a Vivitar, not an assassin. Besides, hc *wanted* me to investigate. It must be one of the servants."

"That may be possible, for recognition of alien voices is not here. But they were speaking Vivitare, and all of your staff are being T'Chin. They are not speaking Vivitare unless they're talking to one of you. It's a puzzle, and not being simple like chemistry. Much relief is here, to leave it in the hands of someone who is knowing what to do." He rose, took the box that held the sword, and threaded his way out of the string game, leaving Ahvren staring blankly after him. He had no idea what to do.

Wind eddied between the buildings. Ahvren knew he must have seen the streets he'd walked through during the last few hours, but now, standing in front of 33 Shakka Street, he had no idea how he'd gotten there. Or more important, *why* he'd come.

Because he needed help. The realization broke the trapped looping of his thoughts. The scholar didn't expect him this evening, but with the sandstorm coming . . . He should have brought a sand cloak. He was surprised Pomo hadn't mentioned it. Pomo . . . A chemist working as a servant. But doing a good job and, from what he'd said, working on chemistry projects, too. They were hard workers, the T'Chin. They seemed to be able to land on their feet and build anew, no matter what happened to them. The Vivitare had overcome the Karg, yes, but what had they built? Ahvren shivered, for reasons that had nothing to do with the changing temperature, and opened the door. The familiar chime welcomed him, but at this time of day the computer secretary was on.

"Vivitare," Ahvren cut through its introductory babble. "I don't have an appointment. Has anyone canceled yet?"

"There is a cancellation in forty-five minutes. Do you wish to make an appointment for that time?"

"Yes." Ahvren told it his name, and the screen thanked him and winked out. He paced the empty room. He wasn't used to waiting to see the scholar. This room was too small, too quiet.

He went out into the street. It was almost as empty as the waiting room, but the muttering, gusting wind gave him something to struggle against . . . something he could defeat, unlike this mess. He paced across the sidewalk in front of the scholar's house dozens of times before the roaring hiss of approaching sand sent him running for the door. Inside, he leaned against it, the clang of the chime echoing in the silence.

"If you are Viv Ahvren, you may go in. The bibliogoth's last client has gone," the computer informed him.

"Thank you." But he waited, counting off the seconds, until the wind slammed into the building. Then he roused himself and went down the hall to the scholar's room.

"I'm sorry to come unexpectedly like this, but I need your help."

The scholar's antennae arced in surprise.

Ahvren frowned. "I told your computer I was here."

Evidently the scholar hadn't consulted its schedule; it held out all of its hands, talons pointed down. Silence? Wait? Using two of its hands, it changed the clip in its synthavode, while Ahvren fidgeted. No incense burning today—perhaps the previous client didn't like it. The artificial light that seemed so warm at night blended oddly with the brown storm-glow that leaked around the shutters.

"Youngling, what are you doing here? Your scent . . . is something wrong?"

"Yes," said Ahvren. "And I don't know what to do about it. I need someone . . . to help me organize my facts in a manner in which I can use them, and then figure out how to put them to use. An informagoth is very inferior, isn't it?"

"What have you discovered?" The scholar gestured to Ahvren's favorite chair, but he was too restless to sit.

"I found the source of the rumor." The story poured out, facts, opinions, and his appalled astonishment all jumbled together. "If they intended to kill Lessar, surely they would have said 'the emperor' not 'a member of the emperor's house,'" he concluded. It was a problem he'd been wrestling with for hours. "So the victim must be Dravik. And half the men in the city might want him dead—shackles, I wouldn't mind it myself! But I can't believe anyone would plot such a thing in my father's garden unless my father was part of it."

"Does your father have a motive?"

"Sort of. He's part of the council, and they don't want Dravik to be emperor—no one does! But this method . . . I don't know. It's hard to believe, especially since he asked me to investigate, but it's the only answer that makes sense. He's in charge of security—it would be easy for him to leave a hole for an assassin. It might even be his way of protecting Sabri. Or perhaps he agreed to the marriage to keep people from suspecting him. It all fits, it's just . . . I could believe it of Viv Redahd, but it's not like my father. Unless I'm not seeing him as he really is, and in that case . . . I don't know what to do."

"I see your dilemma. Yet there are a few gaps in your logic. Is this Dravik the only member of the emperor's house?"

"The only one who counts, the rest are women."

Ahvren went on pacing. The scholar was holding up one small talon, a gesture he was beginning to recognize. Think about it. About what? "What?"

"Just a few possibilities. Does no one ever kill women?"

"Murder in a fit of anger, yes. A scorned lover, a betrayed husband. But no one plots to assassinate them; they don't have that kind of power."

"Well, it's your culture, you should know. The other possibility is that someone chose your home to plot in, precisely because no one would suspect a gathering there. They're probably people your family knows, but they might be plotting without their hosts' knowledge. Or perhaps they came to trick your father out of some information about the emperor's security, and what your servant overheard was their discussion of what they had learned."

"That could be . . . no. My father wasn't given the task of assuring the emperor's security until after the rumors began, and this conversation was the *start* of the rumor."

"You assume your father was given that task because of the rumor, you don't know it."

"But . . . You're right! It was about a week ago that Father told me he was assigned to security, but I have no idea *when* he was assigned to it. I have to find out!" He started for the door.

"Youngling, to let impatience rule you in this strikes me as extremely unprofitable. The more I hear of it, the more dangerous it sounds."

"Don't worry, I'll be careful. I'm just going to talk to my father, hopefully before . . . Shackles, what time is it? I have to catch him before the wedding!"

# Chapter 15

**E**VEN THE SLIGHT DELAY involved in borrowing a sand cloak from the scholar itched on Ahvren's nerves. He took the underground home, and it wasn't until he emerged onto the wind-whipped street that he realized he had forgotten to pay the scholar for this session . . . and the T'chin had forgotten to remind him. Ahvren smiled, warmed by the scholar's concern. Was his urgency necessary? Surely he could wait till after the ceremony to speak to his father. His mind believed it; his twisting gut wanted his feet to go faster.

He struggled through the lashing gusts, burst through his own front door, and grabbed the servant on duty there, the Grishik Prram. "Is my father still here?"

"No, Viv Ahvren." The slit-pupiled eyes blinked in astonishment. "The storm was going to ground everything, so they had to leave early. In fact, they left before it hit."

"Shackles!" Ahvren spun for the door and heard the soft growl that was the Grishik equivalent of "ahem."

"Your mother told us to remind you that the ceremony is formal; anyone who is improperly dressed won't be admitted."

"Shackles." Ahvren took a deep breath and thought. He could argue his way past the guards, but it would probably take longer than changing his clothes. He strode down the hall, almost running. Why was he in such a hurry? Whoever the conspirators were, they could do nothing during the ceremony, for Dravik would be surrounded by people. It was only when he and Sabri went to his rooms, and the servants retired, that Dravik would be in danger. And so would Sabri.

Ahvren cursed his father for permitting this marriage—whatever his motives! But during the feast, the dancing, he'd have plenty of time to drag his father off to some private room and confront him. There was no need to tear off his sand cape and tunic as if they were scorching him . . . but he did it anyway.

An eternity later—the underground was packed and the wind fought him every inch of the way—Ahvren staggered up the steps to the emperor's mansion.

He felt a little calmer, perhaps because he was finally here, or perhaps all that racing around had exhausted his panic. The guards who scanned him, searched him, and took his sword soothed him further—surely if his father was involved, he wouldn't have made security so tight. But then, the security was centered on Lessar. Dravik had been running all over town these last few weeks, easy prey for anyone who wanted to kill him. And no one had. Had the plot been abandoned when the rumors started flying? The servant who sold the information had been tortured—he would have said anything. The whole thing might come to nothing . . . but Ahvren didn't believe it. *Talk to Father, now.*

He pushed open the doors to the great hall, saw a wall of well-dressed backs, and heard his father's voice rolling out: ". . . coming together to create new life, that the chain may continue unbroken."

The ceremony had begun.

The audience's chanted reply rumbled around him. "May your marriage be fruitful, may your children be fit."

Ahvren opened his mouth to say the ancient words with them and found his truth compulsion blocking his tongue. So be it—he'd be slaved if he'd wish success to this marriage! His mother was standing on a low window ledge so she could observe the room. Ahvren avoided her accusing glare and looked around.

The former dancing room was too small for the full court. Men and women were crammed into the corners, leaving the center of the hall clear. How was his mother going to seat them all? Ahvren squirmed unobtrusively through the crowd, trying to see the main participants.

"Your lives will pass, but in your children you go on," said Lessar.

"May your marriage be fruitful, may your children be fit."

Most of the ceremony, except for the addition of fitness to the chorus, predated the Karg. It hadn't changed much, not even when references to the "chain" of life and "binding" had developed unpleasant connotations.

There, he could see them. His father's expression was formal and a little abstracted. Lessar looked tired. Dravik and Sabri had their backs to him. Dravik wore a sword, the only man in the room allowed to do so. Sabri's head was modestly bowed, but even so she was several inches taller than Dravik. It was especially apparent as they were both dressed in shimmering cloth of gold—his long-sleeved tunic and her long-sleeved gown were almost identical from the back.

"So we, whose blood you carry, bind you together," the two older men intoned. "That you may send our blood into the future."

Dravik and Sabri crossed wrists on the cue, his down, hers up, pulse to pulse, and Viv Saiden and Lessar tied them deftly together. "In your children, you two will be one. May your marriage be fruitful, may your children be fit."

The audience chanted the response in a cheerful roar that probably had more to do with the imminent serving of food than genuine goodwill—at least in Dravik's case.

Dravik faced the crowd, pulling Sabri around a little faster than she could manage in the confining gown. He held up their bound wrists for all to see, grinning smugly at the cheers.

Sabri's eyes were lowered, but Ahvren

knew her as a swordsman as well as a sister. Her still face looked as it had in the darkened garden, alight with . . . exhilaration? Fear? Exaltation? It was an expression he sometimes saw when she swept a sword from his hand or launched a killing stroke, and it chilled Ahvren to the marrow of his bones.

Sabri had more reason to want Dravik dead than anyone.

Surely not. She was a woman! Women were . . .

She was Sabri. She had the skills of a Vivitar. He and Grem had taught her.

The wild light faded from her face—had he imagined it? She and Dravik were walking, together perforce, to the rooms where they would change clothes—separate rooms, thank the old gods, and Dara would be in the room with Sabri to help her change and Dravik was armed and she wasn't. No, this was ridiculous! Surely even Sabri wouldn't . . .

Sabri was one of the few people who might be forced to do her plotting in his father's garden. An unmarried woman had little privacy except in her home, and after her escape attempts she'd never been allowed out without a guard. For Sabri this would be an honorable battle—especially since Dravik would probably be armed and she wouldn't. The only duel a woman warrior could fight. And Sabri was one of the people who'd known Ahvren was investigating and might have tipped off Redahd to try to stop him. Her accomplices could be any of the dozens of people who feared or hated Dravik. But not Ahvren's father. To plan this would be as wrong for him as it was right—yes, ah gods, the old gods help them—right for Sabri, who had not only the skills of a Vivitar, but also the heart.

Ahvren started toward his father, who was taking his seat beside Lessar at the high table. But the clear space in the center of the room was now full of servants setting up tables—every time he dodged around one, another materialized in his path. Now that the ceremony had ended, the roar of conversation was deafening.

Sabri and Dravik would be separated while they changed, and surrounded by people all evening. Even if Ahvren was right, Sabri could do nothing until they were alone tonight . . . and she would have an excuse for killing him. In fact, if she cried and told enough lies, they might let her live. Ahvren frowned—he couldn't imagine Sabri being that subtle. But it was hard to imagine her being subtle enough to bribe a servant for information. The people she was working with—being used by?—must have influenced her. A weird mixture of fury and gratitude shook him. If she followed her natural inclination—grabbed the nearest weapon and killed him—she wouldn't stand a chance.

Ahvren slid through a gap between the tables and hurried behind the high table to where his father and Lessar sat. "Father, I have to talk to you." He had to speak in a half shout to make himself heard.

"Ahvren." His father turned to him, smiling. "It went off well, don't you— Is something wrong?"

"Yes. At least I think so. I have to talk to you."

His father glanced around—there was no one nearby except Lessar, Jennah, and the guard at Lessar's back, but since Ahvren had to raise his voice, they might well be overheard.

"What is it?"

"It's . . . it's private. I need to see you alone. Now!"

"Ahvren, I can't leave now—they're going to start serving. Surely it can wait until the dancing starts."

By all his reasoning it could wait, couldn't it? Ahvren bit his lip, his screaming nerves warring with his brain. "No, it can't. Father, please—"

The hoarse cry barely penetrated the din, but the shock in it sent him spinning in search of the sound. A manservant backed from the open door of the room where Dravik was changing, his eyes wide with horror. *But they were in separate rooms! He had a sword and she—* The sizzle of a disrupter beam outside reached his ears, and his heart began to pound sickly.

A slim figure in a dark tunic and breeches, the lower half of her face (surely *her* face; please, gods, not her!) covered with a scarf, her hair concealed by the tunic's hood, darted past the servant and into the room.

The cry, the sizzle, were heard by only those who stood nearby, and they had no time to react. She darted between them, leaped the first table like a gaza stag, and was halfway across the room before the shouts rang out.

There was a sword in her hand, Dravik's sword, the only sword in the room. She ran, not for the doors where guards with nerve disrupters struggled to get a clear shot, but to the windows, where only unarmed guests blocked her escape. But the men were beginning to shift toward her.

Ahvren's father grabbed a guard's disrupter and climbed onto the table, trying, like the others, for a clear shot.

"No!" Ahvren grabbed his arm and pulled him back.

"Are you mad?" his father howled, struggling in his grasp.

She had reached the windows. Half a dozen men had moved fast enough to intercept her, all Vivitars, even if they were unarmed. But she had the sword. Her first slash would have decapitated the closest one, but he flung up his arm, and his bracelet served its ancient purpose and kept the blade from severing his wrist. As her sword arced down, she pivoted on one foot, an accurate stomach kick sending another man staggering into the path of a third. The next slash almost took the throat of the man who stood between her and the window, but he leaped back and someone grabbed her sword arm from behind.

She spun and broke his nose with the heel of her free hand, pulling away from his slackened grip, but another man grabbed her and kicked her knee, destroying her balance. Then they were on her, a pack of wolven bringing the stag down, ripping the sword from her hand as they pummeled her, stunning blows that weakened her until they could bind her hands.

Ahvren stood in paralyzed dismay as they dragged her across the floor, barely aware of his father twisting furiously out of his clutch. It was Sabri; that first slashing pivot kick had identified her as clearly as if she'd screamed her name.

Lessar had gone into the small chamber Dravik had occupied. Now he emerged, his white face set like stone, and Ahvren heard the murmurs sweeping through the crowd. Strangled . . . strangled with a woman's belt cord . . . assassin came through the window . . . strangled . . . why the guard outside didn't . . .

The guard wouldn't have seen her until she tried to escape. She must have climbed from her window over to Dravik's; there was a ledge, Ahvren remembered dimly. It was when she tried to climb down that the guard would have seen her and fired. Ahvren understood it all now . . . too late.

They shoved her to her knees before the emperor whose son she'd slain and ripped off the hood and scarf. Ahvren's father choked as her flaming hair tumbled free.

Her bruised face was stiff with hard-held courage.

Astonishment fractured Lessar's calm. His voice shook as he demanded, "Why? Why did you kill my son?"

Sabri lifted her head. "Because he was unfit. Whether he could wield a sword or not, he was unfit. I would not have my children sired by such a man."

Shocked gasps hissed through the room. To Ahvren it sounded . . . rehearsed. But why would she lie? The lines in Lessar's face looked as if they'd been carved with a chisel. Jennah stepped up to stand beside him, tears streaking her pale cheeks.

Lessar drew a shuddering breath. "By your own words you are condemned. Since you chose to take a man's part, you will take a man's punishment. Put her hand on the table."

Ahvren knew what would happen, and bile rose from his stomach. He didn't realize he'd stepped forward until his father grabbed his arm.

The restraining grip woke an overwhelming impulse to struggle, to grab a knife and throw himself at the men who held her, fight until they took him down. If he died, he wouldn't be forced to watch the rest of it, five days from now, when they tortured and dismembered her. A true Vivitar's response. In his place, Sabri would have done just that. Ahvren snorted. True Vivitar, but *not* profitable. So think! But he couldn't think; he could only watch, unable even to close his eyes, as someone handed Lessar Dravik's sword.

They held her right arm flat on the table and she didn't struggle. He saw her lips press tight in determination; she would not make a sound.

The room was utterly silent as the sword lifted, hovered, and swept down, embedding itself with a thunk in the wood of the table. If Sabri cried out, the sound was lost in the sudden, shattering reverberation of his mother's screams.

Ahvren had forgotten she was there. Several women held her, stroking her, quieting her screams to frantic sobbing.

Sabri sagged in her captors' grip, barely conscious, as they clamped their hands around the spurting stump and wrapped cords around it, tighter and tighter. They didn't want her to bleed to death before her execution.

"Ahvren." His father sounded as if he were strangling. "Take your mother home. I'll see that a surgeon is sent to her cell. I'll . . . I'll attend things here. Take your mother home. Now. I'll come when I can."

# Chapter 16

**A**HVREN TOOK HIS MOTHER home and summoned a healer to sedate her—her grief had become hysteria when she realized what was to come.

When she finally slept, he paced the corridors, waiting for his father to return so they could start planning. Five days until Sabri's execution. Ahvren flinched. *Don't think about how she'll be killed; concentrate on the time limit.*

Traditionally, a condemned prisoner had five days to wrap up personal affairs. Even Redahd couldn't touch her during those five days of sanctuary. Five days of suspense, of anticipation. Ahvren wondered if those five days were a mercy or a cruelty.

"You must be eating, Viv Ahvren. Going hungry will be serving no one, and you cannot afford to be weakened."

Ahvren jumped; he hadn't heard Pomo approach. "I'm not hungry. Thank you."

He paced on, but Pomo scuttled around him and stood firmly in his path. "You must be eating. Dinner is prepared—you will be needing your strength."

What Pomo said made sense, but it was the grief that twisted his round face that tipped the balance. They served Ahvren in the smaller dining room, not far from the kitchen. Ahvren didn't think he could eat, but when the food was in front of him, he realized he'd had nothing since breakfast. Pomo served him, and it was some time before Ahvren came out of his own grim thoughts enough to notice the Olopoli's uncharacteristic silence.

"It's not your fault, Pomo. Even if you'd recognized Sabri's voice, there was nothing you could have done."

"That knowledge is here"—he touched his breast softly—"but it isn't being of help. She was . . ." His voice shook and he turned away, sweeping a serving cloth over the perfectly clean table. "She is much liked. If recognizing her voice was here—"

"Pomo, I just had a thought. I should . . ." *Don't give it all away, don't say, "talk to the people she was working with."* ". . . talk to the people she was working with," Ahvren heard his own voice say. He felt only resigned disgust. Pomo wouldn't betray him. "Would you talk to the maidservants and find out who Sabri met frequently over the last few months? Discreetly?"

Pomo nodded and withdrew. The more Ahvren thought about it, the more necessary it seemed. Suppose the conspirators had some plan to rescue her and Ahvren fouled them up? But could he reveal their names to his father? Viv Saiden had given his loyalty to Lessar before Ahvren and Sabri were born. Sabri was his daughter, but perhaps this was something Ahvren needed to do on his own. It would have to depend on his father's plans.

Forgetting the remains of his meal, Ahvren rose to pace until Pomo returned. The name the Olopoli gave him astonished Ahvren so much he could hardly believe it, unless . . .

"But you can't be attending to that now, for your father is home. He went to his office, and is asking not to be disturbed—"

Ahvren walked out before Pomo finished the sentence. He burst through his father's office door. "Well?"

Viv Saiden sat behind his desk. The Nisol

sword shimmered in an open box in front of him. The eyes he lifted to Ahvren were red-rimmed, dry, and infinitely tired. "What do you want me to say? The surgeon took care of her arm. She doesn't want to see anyone, including us, though she did send a message to Dara, to apologize for knocking her out."

"That fig—"

His father went on as if he hadn't spoken. "There's nothing left but the waiting—and damage control, if I can manage it."

"Damage control? What do you mean, *damage* control?"

"I mean trying to . . . negate the political damage this has done to our family. It may not be possible, but I—"

The foundations of Ahvren's world cracked. "Political damage? Sabri's going to die and you're worried about *politics*?"

His father's fists slammed on the desk. "There is nothing I can do!" He was standing now, glaring at Ahvren, panting with suppressed emotion. "She disgraced our house. She killed her own husband, the emperor's heir! She never gave a thought to . . . to . . ." He seemed to deflate, sinking back into his chair. He rubbed his eyes. "I can't save her. All the power I've amassed . . . I can't save her. So I'm going to save what I can, because you and your mother *are* alive, and—"

"So is Sabri!"

"Not really," said his father, with the calm of despair. "Not in any way that matters."

His father had given up. Fear seeped icily into Ahvren's bones. Viv Saiden had no plan for saving Sabri. He wasn't going to do anything. And she would die. "I see," Ahvren whispered, and got out of the room before his unruly tongue could betray him.

Viv Saiden had given up. The thought made Ahvren's heart clench in panic. All his life, his father had been the strong one. If he surrendered . . . then Ahvren would have to fight in his place. Ahvren drew a shuddering breath. So be it. And his first move must be to talk to Sabri's confederates. Soon.

"Lady Dara will see you." The manservant sounded surprised, though he must have had several minutes to get used to the idea.

It had taken Ahvren ten minutes to talk them into giving Dara his message. It was too late to call on a lady; she had retired, asking not to be disturbed. They gave up only when

Ahvren made it clear he wasn't leaving until they did as he asked.

She received him in the ladies' parlor; the silken hangings and cushions were a perfect setting for her soft loveliness. Like Ahvren's father's eyes, Dara's were red-rimmed . . . and dry.

"Leave us, Vahana," she told her chaperon. "This is my friend's brother—I want to speak to him alone."

It was an outrageous order from an unmarried girl, but knowing what he did, Ahvren wasn't surprised to see the woman depart with no more protest than a disapproving glance.

"I'm so sorry, Ahvren," she began gently. "If I'd only—"

"If you're so sorry, why didn't you stop her?"

The dark eyes widened in hurt innocence. "But she knocked me unconscious! I—"

"I don't mean that, and you know it. It was a good idea to have her knock you out— I doubt that anyone will wonder how she did it before you could make a sound, and no one will ever suspect you. Was it her idea or yours?"

Dara's gaze met Ahvren's, possibly for the first time in their acquaintance, and her eyes were not soft—they blazed with ironic intelligence. She lifted her chin and said nothing.

"You didn't want to stop her, did you? You used her, like a sacrifice, a weapon to be broken and thrown out. No wonder she's in trouble, if the rest of her friends are like you." His hands twisted into fists; he tried to relax them, then thought better of it. He couldn't wrap clenched fists around her throat.

She glared at him, but her voice was calm. "You seem to be implying I'm part of some sort of conspiracy, Viv Ahvren. I deny it, and will go on denying it, so unless you have proof? I thought not." Her mouth twisted in mockery and . . . pain? "But you're wrong about Sabri and me. If I'd created this plot, I wouldn't have let her throw her life away. Think about it. Over the next few months there would have been a dozen, a hundred ways she could have killed Dravik and made it look like an accident. Which would have been a far more discreet way to handle the matter, don't you think? It's not as if she was in any danger from him. If she'd lis—if she'd confided in me, it would have turned out very differently."

"But I thought . . . Why wouldn't she listen to you?"

Her mouth drooped, her dwindling anger leaving her drained, resigned. "*If* I had known about it, I'd guess it was Sabri who insisted on this plan. I'd think she'd have found a subtler scheme dishonorable; she'd say she was a Vivitar, not a murderer to kill in stealth, giving her opponent no chance to defend himself. She thought of herself that way—as a Vivitar, I mean."

Tears tracked her plump cheeks and she wiped them away impatiently. "If she had confided in me, I'd have argued and argued. But I don't think she'd have listened."

Ahvren's fury evaporated, too, leaving only weariness. "That sounds like her. So what are you going to do? I want to help."

"What are . . . You think I'm planning some sort of rescue? Ahvren, she's being held in the tightest security. Even if I were a man, I couldn't free her."

"All right, *suppose* you were . . . the leader?—one of the leaders?—of a conspiracy. Suppose you had people, and information, and weapons. Would you be planning something then?"

He was pacing again, uncontrollably, but she was still, no longer weeping. Something in her expressive eyes (no wonder she kept them lowered!) reminded him of his father. A chill touched his heart, even before she spoke.

"No, I wouldn't, for I could do nothing without risking this supposed organization. As a leader, if I were a leader, I couldn't do that. No matter how much I grieve for Sabri." Her ironic smile widened. "But I'm not a rebel leader, just a young woman, and such a thing is impossible. For now."

"What do you mean?"

It was her turn to pace. "Sabri told me that you've explored this city, spoken to its people. Have you noticed that among the T'Chin, gender doesn't matter any more than species? Their women can be merchants, artisans, soldiers—anything. And they marry when and whom they choose."

"But we've conquered the T'Chin! And we don't let women do those things."

"Even with a female emperor? With a woman emperor, in this new world, I think a great deal might change, someday."

"Is that what this is about? To make Jennah . . . Does she know about . . . No, don't tell me—I don't want to know."

"Since there is no plot, it hardly matters," she agreed. "But if there were such a plot, I'd keep Jennah out of it. She's too honorable for that kind of thing. If there were such a plot, and it succeeded, then someday bards, women bards, would sing of Sabri as a great hero . . . and a martyr."

Bards again. Glory. Ahvren had to unlock his clenched teeth to speak. "Oh no, they won't. Not if I have anything to say about it."

Turning on his heel, he left her in the soft room that suited her rosy prettiness so well and her ruthless intelligence so badly. Did Roi have any idea what the woman he loved was really like? Roi, the perceptive one. Of course he knew. It was probably *why* he loved her, and the old gods help him if he ever got her! Did Roi know about the plot? No. Roi, like Jennah, was too honorable to be let in on such a secret. But thinking of Roi reminded Ahvren of another source of help. To organize a prison break, he'd need men, weapons, and all the help he could get.

The streets were almost empty as he hurried toward Grem's arena, for it was after midnight. He should have taken the underground, but he needed the time to order his tumbling thoughts. He was so tired that the dark patches between streetlights seemed to stretch as he passed through them.

The arena was closed, of course, but light shone from one of the windows on the third floor, where Grem lived. Ahvren found the discreetly camouflaged comm-button and leaned on it.

"Grem, I want to talk to you. It's Ahvren. Grem?" He tried talking for several minutes. Then he tried shouting. He had drawn his sword and was pounding on the door with the hilt when it finally opened. Ahvren lost his balance and would have fallen into the room if Grem hadn't shoved him back. "Grem?"

He was crying—something Ahvren had never thought to see—and the scent of alcohol reached out like an invisible hand.

"Grem? I need to talk to you. Can I come in?"

"What for?" He pronounced the words with the careful exactness of the very drunk.

"You want to hate me for it, you can do it out there."

"Hate you for . . . Grem, it's not your fault. Sabri was—"

"No?" He released his hold on the door to gesture and almost fell. "Who taught her t' fight? Who else was it taught her t' react and think and *feel* like a free man, a warrior, and then . . . then patted her on the head an' said, 'Go be a girl now.' Huh? Who else was it?"

"Well, I have as much responsibility as you do for teaching her to fight, and Father's the one who forced the wedding, and frankly, I blame Sabri for taking the most . . . unprofitable way out. She could have . . ."

Have what? She'd tried to run. Her only choices had been to endure marriage to Dravik or kill him. Though she could have taken Dara's advice, and . . . No, *she* couldn't. To challenge an armed man, with nothing but her bare hands, was probably the only way Sabri could kill anyone. She had always been a Vivitar at heart.

Ahvren took a deep breath. "Blame doesn't matter now. What matters is getting her out. We need to raise a strike force, and . . . Are you listening?"

He wasn't. "It was because she was good, I did it," he muttered. "Kind of student comes once in a lifetime. Once if you're *lucky*. M'self, whole again. My shackling fault, all of it." Tears streamed down his face; he started to close the door.

"Grem wait, I need— Grem!" Ahvren tried to push his way in, but even drunk, Grem was a match for him. He let Ahvren in, got a lock on his arm, spun him around, and shoved him back into the street before Ahvren could gather his balance to resist. "Wait!" he cried. Even as he said it, the latch clicked shut.

He walked home slowly; there was nothing left to hurry for. All the people he'd counted on had failed him. Despair, it seemed, was a stronger opponent than the emperor's guards—it had defeated them before they even tried, and at this point Ahvren was almost tired enough to give up, too. He stumbled as he climbed the steps, thinking only of bed. When the door opened, he looked up to thank the servant for waiting up for him, but the words died on his lips. Viv Redahd was holding the door.

"What are you doing here?" Adrenaline

coursed though Ahvren's exhausted body; his nerves tightened.

"Waiting to talk to you. Your father retired after we finished our discussion. I believe he thought I was leaving. And of course your poor mother is insensible. But I couldn't go without talking to my . . . fellow investigator."

Panic welled in Ahvren's heart. He didn't care much about Dara at the moment, but if his stupid truth compulsion overcame him now, how many other women would she take down with her? Did he even care? Should he care? They had plotted to assassinate the emperor's heir, and they had left Sabri to take the blame. No. No one deserved what would befall them at Redahd's hands. He *had* to keep silent, keep off the subject. Maybe if he told some of the truth.

"Surely even you must realize that if I'd known anything, I'd have prevented what happened today." Ahvren pushed past him into the hall and started to unbuckle his sword belt, but there was no servant present to take it. Where were the servants? "How is Sabri?"

"Maimed." Redahd smiled. "She asked to

be alone, so I can't speak to her . . . for the next five days. Then I'll learn all I need to know."

"So what are you doing here?"

"I was thinking about why she said she killed Dravik—because she didn't want to bear his children."

A spate of words rose in Ahvren's throat and he clenched his teeth against them. Redahd waited until it was clear he wasn't going to speak and then went on. "It struck me that methods for preventing conception abound on this planet. If all she wanted was to keep from bearing Dravik's children, she could easily have accomplished it without killing him."

Redahd paused. Ahvren said nothing.

"So I thought she might have another motive, and it might be worth my while to find out what it is . . . before her accomplice who bribed the servant has time to cover his tracks. It wasn't your sister. No large sums have been charged on her credit account."

Stupid! How could Dara have been so foolish? He had to say something, put a stop to this before he blurted out the truth. Fortunately there were truths that he wanted to say, and Redahd's temper was notorious. If he could distract him . . .

"I'm surprised you're trying to get that information now—if you succeed, you won't have any excuse to torture Sabri before executing her. Of course, just killing her would be enough for most men, but I'm surprised it would satisfy you."

An ugly flush rose in Redahd's face but he still smiled. Push harder.

"Viv Ahvren, you—"

Ahvren talked right over him. "But then, you usually torture helpless men—safe men, T'Chin pacifists, prisoners who can't fight back. I bet you're really looking forward to torturing a woman."

The smile was fading; Redahd's hand clenched on the hilt of his sword. "Listen you soft, young—"

"A young, lovely, helpless girl . . . or do you prefer the men after all? I'd—"

Redahd's sword flashed out and toward him in a single gesture, but Ahvren was ready. He leaped back and drew his own sword just in time to block the second slash, and the third.

The buzz of a stunner stopped them both

279

in their tracks. Ahvren dared not take his eyes off Redahd. He backed away until he could see the rest of the hall without opening himself to a sudden thrust. The missing servants crowded into the doorways, lining the stair rail, filling the landing. Several of them had stunners and one held a nerve disrupter. All the weapons were pointed at Redahd.

Redahd looked around and the wild rage faded from his face, to be replaced by calculation. He sheathed his sword. Warily, Ahvren did the same.

"Does this mean, Viv Ahvren, that you don't want to talk to me? Then I suppose I'll have to ask your sister about it. In five days. You could spare her a great deal by changing your mind."

A hiss of indrawn breath came from the watching servants. Ahvren said nothing.

"Very well. But remember, *you* could have spared her."

Redahd stalked out of the house and into the night. Prram closed the door behind him as Ahvren's knees gave way—he sank to the floor and buried his face in his shaking hands.

# Chapter 17

**A**HVREN AWOKE THE NEXT morning and lay still for a while, watching the sunlight creep slowly down the other side of the slatted shutters. He needed help. He needed to organize his thoughts, his efforts, instead of running frantically from option to option. And he needed to leave the house before his parents woke up. Who knew what he might blurt out if his father questioned him? He couldn't trust his father. The thought left a cold knot in his stomach.

Ahvren got some warm pastry and a bulb of juice from the kitchen, and was standing in front of 33 Shakka Street before the business day usually began. If he could see the scholar for just an hour . . . half an hour . . . The door was unlocked. The chime clanged—too loud in the empty waiting room. But the computer secretary was turned off. A surge of uneasiness rushed Ahvren down the corridor to the scholar's study.

"Come in, youngling. I heard what happened." The scholar sat behind his desk, antennae cocked forward. The sun threw light squares onto the floor. The incense smelled like burning sugar, sweet and acrid. Ahvren's chair was in front of the desk, waiting. He dropped into it, sudden relief (absurd relief—what had he been imagining?) tightening his throat.

"I want, I *need* to talk to you. How long until your first client comes?"

"I canceled all my morning appointments."

Ahvren's jaw dropped; his scent must have reflected his astonishment, for one antennae spiraled softly. "When I said I heard what happened, I was overstating the case . . . or perhaps understating it! I've heard eleven versions of what happened, each one wilder than the last, and half of them contradictory. I also read the official statement on the news net, but it's less informative than the rumors. What really happened?"

Ahvren told him, trying to keep it organized and accurate, even when his voice began to shake. "So you see," he finished quietly, "even after all your help, I was still asking the wrong question. I was looking for the men who might want to assassinate Dravik; I never even thought that it might be a conspiracy of women until it was too late." His voice quivered on the final word. The antennae twitched.

"You intend to help her escape. Why 'too late'?"

"I was thinking about her hand," Ahvren admitted. "I know it's not as important as dying, but Sabri . . ."

The Nisol sword shone in his memory and he couldn't finish.

The antennae arced quizzically. "I know it's harder with you softlings, but can't she get a prosthesis to replace it?"

"Oh yes. It will look like a hand and grasp like a hand. But it won't be quick or strong enough to wield a sword."

All the scholar's elbows rose together—what in the world did that mean? "It sounds to me, youngling, as if . . . No, never mind. A flechett scolds the sata who stalks it, and the being who feeds it, with equal vigor. What are you going to do?"

"I'm not sure." Ahvren rose and began pacing the familiar track before the desk. "I've

283

been in battles, but I've never planned or commanded one—much less a prison break. I was just a secondary. I know I'll need men, a strike force, to overpower the guards, but if Grem won't help me, I don't even know . . ."

"What?"

"I do know a fighter. He's a Grishik, Wurrul. A Mirall. He's T'Chin, so I should be able to hire him, right? And he might know more men I could hire."

"Possibly. But for this type of enterprise to end profitably, it's essential that you be able to trust your trading partner. How well do you know this Wurrul?"

"Not very." The memory of springy footsteps running down a dark street, the gentle touch of rubber-tipped claws . . . the soft voice telling lies. Skillful, loyal lies to protect his employer's interest. So employ him. The Vivitare way had failed him, as it had failed Sabri and Roi. Give the T'Chin way a try. "I think I can trust him. Besides, I don't see any other choice."

The scholar stalked with slow dignity down the path to Wurrul's modest home. The address, which the scholar had found in a commercial data bank, was far out in the suburbs. When the T'chin had offered to take Ahvren in his own flitter—"which will be much faster"—it had proved impossible to leave him behind.

"You could wait in the flitter," Ahvren suggested now. "It's not too late, as long as no one's seen you with me. There's no reason you should risk—"

"Nonsense." The scholar pressed the comm-button. "Only a peepoe fish refuses to see for itself. *Grrat mrm rasm Wurrul?*"

"May we speak to Wurrul please?" Ahvren's bracelet translated.

"You speak Grishik? Wait a minute. How can you speak Grishik when the clip in your synthavode is for Vivitare?"

"By 'saying' the words as a Vivitare would say them. It's just a knack, though it takes a few centuries to devel—"

The door swished open. Wurrul was wearing the multi-pouched belt all Grishik used to carry things as they walked. They had thought they might find the night watchman home during the day—Ahvren was glad they hadn't dragged him out of bed to ask their favor.

"Viv Ahvren! What are you . . . Ah, please come in, and accept my sorrow for your foster sister."

A long antennae arched. "How did you know it was the girl," the scholar asked, "amid all the other rumors?"

"I *listen* to rumors," said Wurrul, gesturing for the pair to come in. "I get my information from Odan Mo, who has better information sources than anyone else in the city."

The scholar had to duck though the door, but the ceiling was high enough. The furniture consisted of cushioned half-spheres that looked uncomfortable. No one sat down. Ahvren gazed at Wurrul's soft-furred face. Did the slitted eyes really hold that gentle sympathy, or was he imagining it? No way to know. And no reason to dance around the subject; sooner or later he'd have to say it, entrusting his life and the scholar's (he should have *refused* to bring him!) to this stranger's furry hands.

"I need your help . . ."

Wurrul heard him out, the astonishment on his face rapidly giving way to careful control. Only the flicking tip of his tail revealed tension.

". . . so you see, I need to hire a strike force. Fighters, good enough to fight Vivitars. Weapons, help in planning and—"

"Forgive me, Viv Ahvren, but if you intend to make a frontal assault on a guarded facility, you need someone to rethink your planning more than anything else. I'm not a soldier, but even I can see that would be suicide. And even if it weren't, as soon as they realized we had a chance, what's to stop them from killing your sister? They would, before they'd let us take her."

"I was only a secondary—I've never planned an attack." Despair clutched Ahvren's heart, but hadn't Wurrul said . . .

"Us"?

Wurrul turned and paced to the window. "It sounds like a worthwhile project. Dravik was . . . I had a friend who encountered him shortly after your people came here. She's still recovering. I'd like to help the woman who killed him. But if you're going to do this, you need someone who can come up with a sensible plan of attack. Something devious. And don't look at me, I'm a Mirall, not a tactician."

"I don't know any tacticians!" Ahvren barely kept the words from emerging as a wail.

"Yes, you do." Wurrul's whiskers twitched. "A fine, underhanded, devious one. And he owes you a favor, too."

Odan Mo was not at home, and the tight-lipped Zo woman who opened the door refused to say where he was. Wurrul had declined to go with them, saying that Odan knew him well enough to include his abilities in any plan they formed. Then he went to bed, leaving Ahvren and the scholar to track Odan Mo on their own.

"Leave that to me," the scholar told him now. "If you'll fly us back to the city, I'll make a few calls." He made more than a dozen calls on the flitter's comm-system, changing clips in his synthavode almost every time, so their flight was accompanied by a wild assortment of twitters, growls, and some language that rumbled like a distant volcano. By the time they reached the city, the scholar had the addresses of Odan Mo's offices, both listed and not.

Odan was at the unlisted address and showed no surprise at seeing Ahvren, though his mobile brows lifted at the sight of the tall T'chin.

"You said you owed me a favor," said Ahvren. "I've come to claim it." He was prepared to use blackmail if he had to, but he hoped he wouldn't—he needed to be able to trust this man. If he had to force him . . .

"Come in, both of you."

The office was small and very modern, and it looked cheap until you realized how much the communication and data system built into the battered desk must have cost. Odan Mo's sleeves were mid-length today, and for some reason Ahvren found the small, implicit lie reassuring. A schemer was what he needed.

The scholar introduced himself and made the formal talons-together-rotating-up gesture, which Odan absently repeated.

Then the merchant turned to Ahvren. "I didn't think I'd see you again, at least not so soon. I'm glad of it, though I'm sorry about the circumstances. You want me to arrange a rescue for your sister, don't you?"

"Yes." Ahvren's throat was dry. "It's a lot to ask, but—"

"Child, I'm a merchant, not a miracle worker! And what you're asking—"

"Wurrul said you could do it."

"Oh he did, did he? And did he say how I was supposed to accomplish it? And keep us all from getting caught and executed, if not in the act, then afterward? Do you have any idea how dangerous this would be—for all of us?"

He sounded perfectly sincere, but he didn't meet Ahvren's eyes. Ahvren gazed at him, suspicion giving way to amazed certainty. "You know how to do it."

Odan Mo sighed. "I don't *know*. I have a few ideas, but that's all. My particular curse is to be able to weave together ways and means, and when I heard about your sister . . . Up till now I regarded that trait as an advantage." The corners of his mouth twitched up. "After all the effort I've expended to keep my dealings inside the law, I suppose it's fitting that when I give in and break the law, I should do so in a big way. If you hadn't held your hand over my affairs, I'd be in a cell beside your sister's right now. But before I agree to help you . . ." Ahvren's heart leaped. ". . . Were you followed here?"

"I don't know—"

"No," said the scholar placidly. He had been quiet so long that Ahvren jumped when he spoke. "My flitter has a good scan-system, and I kept careful watch. No one was following him, and no one was tracking us electronically. So far."

"Why would anyone . . ." Ahvren thought of Redahd's suspicions and his voice died.

"Perhaps no one will," said Odan Mo. "If I held your sister I'd keep an eye on all her family, just in case. But then, I'm a notoriously careful man."

The scholar said nothing. His body was still, unreadable, except for his antennae, which flicked from speaker to speaker.

Ahvren thought. "It's not a very . . . Vivitare thing to do, but Redahd is different. I'll be careful about that."

"Good," said the merchant, with no trace of his usual smile. "Because *you* are the greatest danger to all who help you. You're the only link between us and your sister's disappearance; if they find us, it will be through you."

"Then you can get Sabri out?"

"It might be possible. I'll need more information. Fortunately, I know someone who can get it for me. But getting her out of prison is only the first part. Once she's free, we have to get her out of the city—or better yet, off planet. Preferably before they even realize she's missing, so we'll need a ship."

"I thought . . . Don't you have ships?"

"I have twenty-seven ships scattered all over the Confederation. The nearest could get here in nine days, which is five days too late. Most of my shipping rivals are decent men, but to go to one of them for an illegal favor . . . Even discounting the risk, I'd rather not open myself to a lifetime of blackmail."

"I think . . . I think I could find a ship," said Ahvren. "I know someone who—"

"Excellent. Don't tell me who and don't tell them about me—we'll all be safer. And money's no object. I can pay whatever they ask."

"I have enough—"

"Perhaps, but when they're trying to find out who helped your sister escape, one of the first things they'll do is check your credit accounts. *You* are the danger, remember?"

"Yes," said Ahvren slowly. "I'm beginning to see that."

He sent the scholar home. The T'chin went willingly—he had not canceled his afternoon appointments. If he hadn't gone freely,

Ahvren would have insisted—he wasn't about to drag the scholar in deeper. It was bad enough that he was going to join them when Ahvren met with Odan Mo tomorrow, by which time Odan would have his information and Ahvren hoped to have found a ship.

He regretted having to involve Reecheep as well, but it was him or Maffatti, and of the two of them . . .

It was just the right time for midmeal at the share market. Crossing the gracious, light-filled room, the traders' tension no longer seemed strange, perhaps because Ahvren's own nerves were so taut. He found the area Reecheep was serving, and the little Brill appeared as soon as he took a table.

"From the look of you, it was your sister. I'm sorry, Viv. I was hoping it was the duel with the three brothers." Grave sympathy looked strange on the bright-striped face, and something hard in Ahvren's belly began to soften, painfully, dangerously. He couldn't afford to soften now, so he smiled and said, "Don't be sorry just yet, my friend. How would you like to earn some money . . . and have a Vivitar owe you a really big favor?"

# Chapter 18

**A**HVREN SPENT THE REST of the afternoon wandering aimlessly around the city, for he dared not go home. Tense as he was, his father would have to realize something was up—and since he left Mirmanidan, Ahvren had not once succeeded in lying in answer to a direct question. He had no idea what they'd think of his absence; they'd probably assume he was sulking . . . or grieving. Fine. He didn't care, as long as they didn't suspect the truth.

By the end of the day he was tired, and dirty enough that the Bredayma baths were a natural place to go. Lying in the shimmering water, listening to the echoes of conversation around him, Ahvren heard several different versions of Dravik's death, in which Sabri was transformed into an outraged husband, a woman Dravik had abused, a woman who was jealous over Dravik's marriage, and a whole band of political assassins. If anyone ever guessed the truth, it would be lost in the flood of rumor.

When Ahvren finally went home, very late, light still glowed in his father's office window. Ahvren stared at it for a long time before he slipped through a side door and sneaked to his bed. Concealing something this important from his father felt even more strange than plotting against the emperor. Though he wasn't plotting against the emperor, Ahvren told himself fiercely. Not really. Freeing Sabri would harm no one. And Dara was right—it was time to change the system that had driven his sister to kill. Still, it was a long time before he slept.

Next morning Ahvren darted in and out of the twisting streets long enough to be sure no one was following him; then he took the underground. No scanner was sensitive enough to track one being through the seething crowd of morning commuters.

This time Odan Mo's door was opened by a giggling Zo girl, whose age Ahvren guessed at about seven, though her head almost reached his shoulder. Odan Mo and the scholar were sitting in the kitchen, at a table covered with notes and printout. The scholar was the first to notice Ahvren; the long antennae swayed toward him, held lower than usual by the ceiling.

"Youngling! We were about to start without you."

Odan smiled his greeting and gestured for the girl to leave. His sleeves were long, in the privacy of his own home. "Come in, Ahvren. There's tea on the warmer and pastries beside it. Help yourself." The door closed behind the girl, and the merchant switched conversational tracks without pause. "Did you find a ship? It's beginning to look like this might work."

"Re— My friend thinks he can." Ahvren poured himself a cup of tea and, remembering he'd had no breakfast, took several pastries. The smudges under the merchant's eyes spoke of a sleepless night. A surge of gratitude tightened Ahvren's throat. But there would be time for gratitude later. "What have you got?"

"The details of a very tight security system." A smile eased Odan's weary face. "Your father is good at this."

"But they don't . . . they haven't put him in charge of holding Sabri!"

"No, but they're taking the same precautions with her that he designed to protect your emperor. Here, let me show you." Odan Mo shuffled the papers on the table and came up with a plan of the house—all five stories. "Prisoners are held in the cellars—thick stone walls and strong wooden doors. There are two guards, one at each end of the corridor, so you can't take out one without the other seeing it. They carry laser rifles."

"Hm. Could we flood the place with gas or something?"

"Gas wouldn't work fast enough, because now we come to one of your father's better ideas: Both guards have panic buttons on their belts. If anything happens they press the button and an alarm goes off, not only in the guard room but also in the vid-monitoring center."

Ahvren wondered how Odan had come by all this information, but he knew better than to ask. The scholar nibbled delicately at a sweet pastry, his antennae swaying softly.

"The corridor is monitored by two vid-screens and there's one in each cell, so we have to take out three guards—two in the corridor, and one in the monitoring center.

And the guard in the monitoring center has to be first. The center is here"—he pointed—"on the fourth floor."

Ahvren's hand clenched around a pastry, crushing it. "We'll never get a strike force up there, and back down, without raising an alarm."

"If they look and act like a strike force, no. But if they look like the cleaning crew . . . There's a firm that cleans the house every night—just the heavy work, floors, windows, so on. The regular crew is five beings, assorted species, which is our first stroke of luck; they're all species that look pretty much alike to us humanoids." The merchant's eyes crinkled, and Ahvren smiled back as the scholar's antennae twitched irritably.

"Wurrul is going to secure the real cleaning crew when their hover-van picks them up. Someday I'll compensate them for their trouble. For now it will be safer for everyone if they're simply found, bound and gagged, after this is over, and our people will take their places. Our team will go to the house and clean as usual; we want to leave at the regular time. They'll take out the guard in the monitoring room, then go down to the corridor where the cells are."

"Take out the guard how? There has to be an alarm button in the monitoring room."

"Yes, and that brings us to the other intelligent precaution your father implemented." He dredged another set of papers out of the pile. "The cleaning crew is scanned for weapons before they go into the building, but I have the scanners' specs here." They were written in Zo. "And I'm pretty sure a medical stunner could get past them. Those stunners have almost no metal in them, and very small power packs."

"Pretty sure? How sure is . . . Wait a minute. A medical stunner has to be in contact with the person's body—and close to the head or spine to knock him out."

"That brings us to the delicate part of the problem. They'll have to use a ruse to get close enough to touch the guards without making them suspicious. In the monitoring center that shouldn't be too hard—they'll just go in and ask if they should clean there. Downstairs . . . well, there's a chance. One of the other prisoners is a Kelke. They're nocturnal, so he's fed at night. We'll substitute one of our people for the servant who brings his meals. The real servant will appear to have been taken out by force, but she's actually in our pay."

"It sounds . . ." *Insane, impossible, unspeakably dangerous.* ". . . complicated."

Odan Mo laughed, and the scholar's antennae spiraled.

"No worse than taking over a company without letting its owners learn you're doing it. Though there's one more thing."

"Another complication?"

"Most of the cells are unlocked by an electro-key in a guard's comm-bracelet—just one key per door. Your sister's cell needs both the guards' keys to open it *and* a key that's worn by the guard captain your father appointed. My informant says he doesn't take it with him when he leaves the palace, but she doesn't know where he stores it . . . and getting hold of that key is the third thing the cleaning crew will have to do. I was hoping your father's files would tell us where it's kept."

"My father's files are all encoded," said Ahvren thoughtfully. "I'm not much of a data-breaker."

"Don't worry about that. I know several excellent data-breakers. All you'd have to do is get them physical access to your father's computer. He had the good sense to store his security files in a noncommunicating system, or we'd have the information now. Could you smuggle someone in?"

"Probably," said Ahvren. "But there may be a better way. It's even the right time of day to call on a lady. When do you need this information?"

The merchant's eyes dropped to the papers and the scholar's antennae twitched. "It will be difficult to assemble everyone in time, but we were thinking we'd do it tomorrow night, if you can get the ship by then. The night after that is the night before the execution, and they'll probably be more alert."

"You're right." His tea was cold; Ahvren set the cup down. "I'll get a ship. And I'll be ready."

Odan Mo and the scholar glanced at each other.

"I told you so," the scholar said. "Youngling, you're going to spend tomorrow night with me, and several of my friends, talking about Vivitare history and culture and establishing a firm alibi. That's *my* contribution to this affair."

"But I can't—"

"Ahvren," said Odan Mo firmly, "you are the danger, remember?"

"But you can't—"

"Yes we can, and we'll be safer without you."

The scholar said nothing but it lifted one small talon. Ahvren bit his lip. They were right and he knew it, but to send others into danger, fighting his battles while he stayed safe . . . His safety would increase theirs.

"All right," said Ahvren. "I'll find out about the key and come back as soon as I can."

"A cracked bissa egg can produce sweeter meat than a whole one," said the scholar approvingly.

"What?" said Odan Mo.

Ahvren was grinning when he left them.

He had no trouble getting in to see Dara this time. She was in the garden, alone, thank the old gods, weaving lace by hand—something ladies did only as a hobby since the Karg had given them manufacturing technology. She presented a charmingly old-fashioned picture, sitting gracefully among the flowers . . . until you noticed the strain that thinned her mouth and shadowed her eyes. Then she looked like someone who was waiting for her best friend's execution, but Ahvren had no pity for her. He wondered, for a moment, how he looked.

"Dara, if you could help me help Sabri, without endangering your conspiracy, would you do it?"

"If I *was* the leader of such a conspiracy, which I'm not, of course I would."

"Oh for— All right." Ahvren took a deep breath. "*If* you were a conspirator, you might have security information from the servant you bribed, and if you did, would you give it to me?"

Her face was politely blank, but thoughts raced behind her eyes. "Ahvren, you're not serious. If I had such information, giving it to you would *prove* my involvement. If I was this hypothetical leader, I couldn't risk that."

"What do you think I'm going to do with it? Give it to Redahd? You're Sabri's friend— help her!"

"No." She sounded almost abstracted, though she gazed at him intently. "I can't do that." Her voice held a note of utter finality.

"You bitch." Ahvren turned to leave.

"Wait!"

He turned back.

"You're really planning something, aren't you? You're going to try to save her?"

"Why should I tell you anything?"

Dara bit her lip; her hands clenched in the lace, destroying the delicate pattern. If it mattered enough to destroy *her* composure . . .

"What is it?"

"Ahvren, if I were the leader of a conspiracy, which I'm not, I'd have been very concerned about what a member of my organization might reveal under torture."

"So?" Something in her eyes made the back of his neck creep.

"So before she went in, I'd have had her take poison. Something with a timed release, that would grant her a painless death before the five days were up. If she'd escaped, we'd have given her the antidote. If I had planned such a thing, that's how I'd have done it."

Blood drained from Ahvren's face to aid his pounding heart. His fingers were numb. His voice sounded distant in his own ears. "What's the antidote?"

She bit her lip and said nothing. His hands clamped on her shoulders, bruising hard, but he didn't care. He shook her. "What poison and *what* is the antidote?"

She wasn't intimidated by his strength or his anger. Her voice was calm, diminished only by a hint of . . . shame? "If I had done such a thing, I'd have used fellanic. It's easy to bind in a timed-release formula, it's painless, and rejolac will counteract it instantly."

"Timed to release itself when?" His hands tightened until she flinched.

"If I had . . . Tomorrow," she whispered. "Sometime tomorrow. I can't give you an exact hour; the formula isn't that precise. Ahvren—"

But he left the garden before she could finish. He had no more interest in anything she had to say.

Ahvren burst into Odan Mo's comfortable, shabby kitchen without warning. Odan Mo jumped. The scholar had gone, but Wurrul was there—the sharp spines buried in his hackles lifted when he saw Ahvren's face, and his tail began to bristle.

Odan Mo rose to his feet. "What's wrong?"

"You know the plan"—*that detailed, complex plan*—"you were going to try to get ready to bring off tomorrow? We have to do it tonight."

# Chapter 19

THE HOVER-VAN MUTTERED demurely through the dark streets toward the palace. Ahvren tried to convince himself that his being with them was an added risk—that he should feel concern, not this odd, exalted terror that made his heart pump faster.

How he came to be aboard the van was a saga in itself. Odan Mo heard him out with the professional calm of a general learning of disaster on the battlefield, and then he issued orders. Ahvren had been sent to pick up an Olopoli data-breaker to find out where the guard captain kept the third key, and Wurrul was set to rounding up the substitute cleaning crew immediately. Ahvren thought that if he hadn't lost his father's wager, he might like to work for Odan Mo. But he had lost—completely failed to find the conspirators with wits or sword. He would have to go to Zodan. *Worry about that when Sabri's safe.*

After giving some thought to smuggling a stranger into his father's office in the middle of the day, Ahvren decided not to try. He told the servant who answered the door that the Olopoli was a potential business partner who needed to see some records. Which was true, after a fashion. Heart pounding in his throat, Ahvren asked if his father was in. The servant said no, his father had gone to plead with the emperor. The peculiar look he gave Ahvren made him realize that three days before his sister's execution was an odd time to be recruiting business partners.

Ahvren led the Olopoli to his father's office and spent the next hour and a half dreading that his father might walk in. He also found something else he wanted and after a moment's hesitation he decided to take it—why not? Sabri deserved a dowry.

Once the files were open, Ahvren copied them onto a clip and took them back to Odan Mo. He found the merchant sitting with his palms pressed together, staring off into space, thinking so hard he didn't even hear Ahvren come in.

"I've got it. The captain leaves his electro-key locked in his lower desk drawer. We can tear it apart if we have to."

"Unfortunately, there's another problem. A big one."

"What?"

"I can't get a replacement for one of the cleaning crew. The Rembroli I thought would do it has refused. Says it's too risky to throw a plan together so fast, and . . . Well, I must admit, he has a point. We could try to run one short, but the contract calls for five people and it might make the guards suspicious."

"What happens if one of the regular crew gets sick?"

"The company sends a substitute."

"So send . . . I'll go!" said Ahvren. "I'll be the substitute."

Odan Mo shook his head. "No one would believe a Vivitare would be working on a cleaning crew. Besides, I've already had to substitute for one of them; two substitutes would probably be as suspicious as coming up short. Not to mention the chance that the guards might know you—at least by sight."

"But the Rembroli wear hooded tunics, don't they? They're about the same height as we are. How tall is the man you're replacing?"

"About your height," Odan Mo admitted.

"But he's also sixty pounds heavier and has scaly green skin. Be reasonable, child."

"I'll wear pillows and paint my face green. It wouldn't pass close examination, but I won't let them examine me closely."

Odan Mo's mouth twitched. "You have the wrong number of fingers for a Rembroli."

"I'll wear their work gloves."

"You're mad. Though it might . . . No, it's too dangerous."

"She's my sister. Do you have a better idea? I'll do it."

Ahvren told the scholar about the change in plan, and went over the same arguments he'd had with Odan Mo. Then he thanked the scholar for offering to provide him with an alibi, even though it wouldn't be necessary.

"Oh, I'll still create an alibi for you. Instead of having friends in to see you, I'll spend the evening convincing my home security system to show your presence. It's not as good as witnesses—machines can always be tampered with—but you'll have spent the evening with me, no matter what you're really doing. Remember, a reflection is you, only left-handed."

"Thank you," said Ahvren. "But I wish you weren't involved. Barring that, I wish I could make it safer for you by really being here . . . No I don't. I want, I *have* to go with them. Even if it wasn't for Sabri. Is that unprofitable thinking?"

"Yes," said the scholar crisply. "Only a udulu dives into the fire because it's pretty."

Ahvren grinned. But there was a note in the T'chin's voice. "Do you want to come?"

"Youngling, even if there was a T'chin on the cleaning crew—and you'll note that I cannot be disguised by a little green paint— I'm a bibliogoth, not a warrior. You can—in fact you'd better!—come tell me what happened as soon as you're finished."

"But do you *want* to come?"

"All right!" The antennae lashed back. "Yes, I'd rather be there to see it through instead of waiting and wor—waiting. But I can't, so there's no use discussing it. You may choose to back an unknown fleeta if the odds are high enough, but only a fool would bet on one with a broken leg."

Any gratitude Ahvren might have felt was lost in the sudden, outrageous, incredible suspicion. "You're making that up! All those sayings . . . you just make them up, don't you?"

"Upon occasion." Its voice was unruffled, but the antennae spiraled, tighter and tighter. "All things are made up by someone, youngling. Why not me?"

Looking back on it now, it was funny. Ahvren laughed softly and Loba Amm grinned at him. As grins went, it was more fierce than friendly, but Ahvren didn't care. He loved the strangers who sat in the van beside him, as Wurrul steered them through the quiet streets, for they shared the bond of common danger that makes people closer than friends, even if they hate one another. As close as brothers, who can hate or love but are always bound. Close as brother and sister, the old ones help them all.

"The old ones help us," he murmured. He thought he'd said it too softly to be overheard, but Loba Amm glanced at him.

"These old ones are your gods?"

"They used to be," Ahvren replied absently. The van walls held no windows—all he could see past Wurrul's shoulders was a small section of the windshield. "How far to the palace?"

"Not far, I think." The Zo's white brows had lifted. "They *used to be* your gods?"

"Yes. On our homeworld there's a mountain so tall it pierces the atmosphere. No one could climb it, so we believed the gods lived there, with the spirits of dead heroes and bards."

The van turned a corner and stopped. Peering through the windshield, Ahvren saw the palace gates and every nerve in his body tightened. A N'Ssser leaned over Wurrul's shoulder and hissed something into the comm-unit. The gates opened.

"So what happened to your gods?" Loba asked, as the van hummed forward. He was trying to sound casual, but Ahvren heard the tension in his voice.

"We were conquered by a race called the Karg. They leveled the mountaintop and built a spaceport. Thousands of Vivitare slaves saw the place. There was nothing there, of course—no gardens, no palaces, no gods, just vacuum and rock."

"I see." Loba sounded thoughtful. "That must have been hard on your ancestors."

"We survived." Ahvren shrugged. "It was a long time ago."

The van rocked to a stop and settled with a sigh of dying fans. Ahvren took a deep breath and pulled his hood over his face. The paint made his skin feel stiff. The Zo woman who had applied it had given it a dappled texture that mimicked Rembroli scales—if no one looked too closely. Odan Mo must have been desperate for manpower to let him come, but Ahvren had realized that when he saw Odan's nephew in the van. The rest of the crew consisted of two N'Ssser, and a small slim G'Cy woman—one of the furred races, but there was something reptilian in the movements of her long spine. Since there were no Grishik on the crew, Wurrul would stay hidden in the van—guarding their escape.

They hauled the industrial-sized cleaning bots, almost four feet tall, out of the van and over to the servants' door. There were two guards, with scanners and nerve disrupters. Ahvren cast them a cautious glance, but they were looking at Loba Amm. Ahvren didn't recognize them, thank the old ones.

"You're new," one of them said.

"Shirob got sick," Loba replied. "So they made me take his shift. I get paid extra for it."

His casual shrug was a masterpiece.

The guards glanced at each other. One of them shrugged, too.

"Is there a problem?" one of the N'Ssser hissed. Translators were wonderful for disguising voices. "Our contract says five and we are five—you do not have approval of whom."

"No, no problem." But the guard scanning Loba and his equipment took a little extra time.

The guard who scanned Ahvren was watching his colleague and barely noticed his own scanner—not that it mattered. The scanners were designed to register metal or power packs, not pillows and paint. Odan had been assured that the guards didn't search the cleaning crew physically, and they didn't.

The crew took the service lift up to the fifth floor and started working. They had to waste two hours here before descending to the fourth floor, where they would clean as usual until Ahvren passed the monitor center. Ahvren had begged to be the one to take out that guard, and because he was the best fighter among them, Odan Mo had agreed.

But first things first. All he had to do now was spend a few hours running a cleaning bot. He must have seen servants do it hundreds of times. How hard could it be? The controls were fairly simple—he could steer it and direct its roving tentacles. But how was he supposed to keep it from sucking up the curtains? Ahvren stopped the machine for the fourth time, to pull fabric out of a hose, carefully not glancing at the vid-screen that overlooked the hall. There was no reason for the guard on duty to be watching him work, but perhaps he'd better keep those omnivorous tentacles away from anything loose—he didn't care if the place stayed dirty! He just hoped the others looked more professional than he did.

At least wrestling with the cleaning bot passed the time. Almost too soon, they left the fifth floor and went down to the fourth where they separated, as the cleaning crew usually did.

Ahvren ran the recalcitrant bot down to the monitor room. Was he going too fast? Too slow? Being too sloppy? Too neat? His heart thumped against his ribs as he opened the door.

The guard sat in a cage of screens, his eyes fixed on the text that scrolled down one of them. He turned in his chair as the door opened, but there was no surprise in his face. No one running a cleaning bot could surprise anyone.

Ahvren went into the room. "Want clean in here?" he mumbled in a guttural voice. He gestured vaguely and took a step toward the guard.

"No," said the guard. "It's fine. You don't have to clean in here." He was already turning back to his book.

"As you say." Ahvren leaped forward and pressed the stunner against the back of the guard's neck. It buzzed softly, and the man jerked and fell slack on his comm-board, out for about three hours. Plenty of time.

Ahvren glanced at the screens, which were focused on the building entrances, and Lessar and Jennah's rooms. They were both asleep. He called up the cellar. Two guards stood watch in the corridor. Sabri lay curled under her blankets like a child.

Only one servant was awake in the kitchen. Odan Mo's informant—at least, she'd better be. To Ahvren's alien eyes she looked exactly like the G'Cy woman who'd come with them.

Ahvren went out and told the others the monitor center was down. The G'Cy and one of the N'Ssser went with Loba Amm to "take out" the servant. The other N'Ssser came with Ahvren, to help find the guard captain's electro-key.

They located his office without difficulty; it had been marked on the house plans. Ahvren hurried around the desk and tugged on the handle of the lower drawer—an automatic gesture; he knew it would be locked.

It slid open; a few files, power packs for a disrupter, a squirt bulb of machine oil, a toolbox in the back—no bracelet. Nothing that could hold an electro-key.

Ahvren looked up and met the N'Ssser's worried eyes. As one they started opening the other drawers. Nothing. They ransacked the office, pulling out files and dumping shelves as fast as they could do it quietly. Nothing. Ahvren stood in the middle of the wreckage and reluctantly acknowledged the truth. The guard captain had taken the key home with him.

"But Odan said it would be here!" Even

through the translator you could hear desperation in the N'Ssser's voice.

"Well, it's not."

"But why—"

"Doesn't matter. We have to think of something else, that's all. Let's get back to the monitor center. I want to see how the others are doing."

They were just in time. Ahvren's hands clenched as he watched the tiny G'Cy woman carry a tray down the stairs to the cellar. She smiled at the guard and Ahvren's stomach knotted—suppose the servant didn't usually smile, suppose . . .

The guard nodded acknowledgment—the bored expression on his face never wavered. He unlocked one of the cells and stood aside, leaning against the wall.

Ahvren started pushing buttons to activate the vid inside the cell, but it happened too fast. The G'Cy darted out, chittering; the Kelke was ill, she couldn't wake him, please come see, she wasn't sure . . .

The guard looked less bored. He waved a casual "it's all right" to the guard at the other end of the corridor and went into the cell. The G'Cy stood aside, letting him enter first. She had a perfect shot at his back. Now came the tricky part.

She ran from the cell and looked around, which was pure artistry, for she knew exactly where the other guard was. Then she rushed toward him, covering the open space faster than Ahvren would have thought possible for such a small creature.

The last guard laid a hand on his disrupter butt and she skidded to a stop, blinking up at him in bemused innocence. "Sir, your friend sent me to fetch you. The prisoner is ill." She eddied forward, graceful as a dancer, harmless as a child. "I'm afraid he's dying, but Kelke physiology is different, and he is a con artist. Your friend wants you to check."

She moved a bit closer, gesturing toward the cell. The guard stepped toward her, then hesitated, gazing at the empty corridor.

"I'd better call it in." He reached for his comm-bracelet, and Ahvren's heart stopped.

Swift as a striking snake she leaped, jamming the med-stunner against his neck. He barely had time to flinch before he fell. She tried to catch him, but he was too large for her and they both crashed to the floor. Swearing softly, she was squirming out from under him when the others reached her.

"We did it!" Loba Amm's whisper came clearly through the pickup. "Where's that arrogant fool of a Viv? They should be here by now!"

"We must go." The N'Ssser's hand fell gently on his shoulder. "Perhaps between us we can think of some way—"

"Wait." Ahvren prodded the controls and the image zoomed in on a cell door. An old-fashioned cellar door, in this old, rich house, made of thick wood, with old-fashioned steel hinges. Not for nothing had Ahvren spent weeks bumping into archaic doors. He knew how those hinges worked . . . and how they came apart. He looked up and met the blaze of understanding in the N'Ssser's eyes. "There's a toolbox in that desk."

Ahvren slid the edge of the chisel under the cap at the top of the hinge pin and began to hammer it up. It was horribly loud in the echoing stone corridor, especially when metal squealed against metal. He set his teeth and went on pounding.

"You're making too much noise!" Loba Amm hissed.

"We're in a cellar. Underground. No one can possibly hear us." He hoped. "At least they didn't put alarms on the doors."

The two N'Ssser, who had locked the startled Kelke back into his cell, rummaged in the tool kit. They came up with a spike and a smaller hammer and started working on another hinge pin. The G'Cy opened a bot's dust drum, dumped a pile of sweepings on the floor, grabbed a cloth off one of the bots and began cleaning the container. Ahvren glanced at her quizzically.

"So she won't start sneezing."

It took only a few minutes to remove the hinge pins, but Ahvren was sweating in his padded tunic when the last one popped out. Loba Amm caught it before it clanged on the floor. The two N'Ssser slid their fingers under the bottom of the door. Ahvren and Loba Amm, jostling for space, got a grip on the freed hinges.

"Ready? Pull!"

The door came loose with an ease that sent all of them staggering and fell on top of them. Ahvren, who'd been standing toward the outside, was the first to struggle out from under the heavy planks. He left his cursing allies without a second thought, scrambled up, and gazed into the cell.

Sabri was on her feet, staring with open-mouthed bemusement at the door, which rocked wildly as the others wiggled out. When she saw Ahvren her eyes lit with . . . fury?

"You idiot!" she hissed. "You slaver-bait! What do you think it's going to do to Mother and Father if you get caught?"

"*I'm* an idiot? I . . . You . . ." Anger and relief clashed, stopping his voice. He grabbed her shoulders and shook her, then hugged her hard.

"There's no time for this nonsense!" Loba snarled, pulling Sabri out of Ahvren's grasp. He hustled her out of the cell and helped her into the empty dust drum, sealing the lid with long blue fingers that shook slightly.

"Wait! Isn't that airtight?" Ahvren protested.

"She won't be in there long enough for it to matter if you get going," Loba snapped, running the bot down the corridor as fast as it would travel.

The others grabbed their equipment and followed, leaving the door, tools, and guards where they'd fallen. Ahvren scrambled for his bot and caught up with the others as they reached the lift. The tiny G'Cy reached up and tugged Ahvren's hood over his face. Ahvren wished he knew her name so he could thank her properly, but ignorance was safer for all of them.

The guards passed them out without even a scan, though Ahvren's heart leaped into his throat when one of them commented that they'd finished early tonight.

Loba rolled the bot that held Sabri over to the back of the van and the two N'Ssser tried to lift it in. They failed. The bots were heavy— with Sabri's weight added to the load . . .

Trying to look unconcerned, despite his pounding heart, Ahvren went to help them. Between the three of them they got the bot off the ground, but then Sabri's weight shifted and one of the N'Ssser lost his grip. The bot crashed down and would have fallen over if Ahvren hadn't grabbed it.

One of the guards snickered, and the two N'Ssser, rubbing their stinging fingers, glared at him. It was a very natural response, Ahvren thought desperately. It was also a mistake.

"Here, I'll give you a hand," said the guard who hadn't laughed. Ahvren felt the blood drain from his face as the man approached. Sabri's weight unbalanced the drum badly. There was no way the man could lift it and not guess . . .

"No need, good sir." Loba Amm stepped between the guard and the drum. "We'll manage." Tension edged his voice, and the guard who'd come to help them stopped, brows drawing together. The other guard was watching them.

Even as he shifted his balance to spring, despair coursed through Ahvren—they could take the close one, but the other guard was too far away. He'd hit his belt alarm the second they attacked his partner, and then . . .

If Ahvren hadn't been watching the second guard, he'd never have seen it. Wurrul descended in a flying leap, flattening the far guard before he even knew the Grishik was there.

The other guard turned—it only seemed as if he moved in slow motion because Wurrul was so fast. Part cat, part martial art, part dance, the pivoting leap that covered twenty feet and smashed Wurrul's heels into the second guard's jaw was something Ahvren had never seen before, and wouldn't have thought possible if he hadn't seen it then. Frozen, openmouthed, he watched the Grishik bend over his victim's fallen body.

"In the name of the Furred Fathers, get that thing loaded!" Wurrul snapped. "I'll prop them up and tie them so they'll stay where they're put, but the sooner we're out of here the better."

Ahvren stirred. The whole thing had taken only a few seconds. "They're not dead?"

"Of course not. I kill only when I mean to."

Ahvren believed it. Helping the others hoist Sabri's bot into the van, he swore that if by some miracle they got out of this, he was going to introduce Wurrul to Grem.

Wurrul scrambled into the driver's seat, and they lifted off as soon as the doors closed behind them. As they slipped slowly away from the mansion—Ahvren clenched his teeth and managed not to ask Wurrul to speed—he opened the drum and helped Sabri out.

Her face was smudged in spite of the G'Cy's cleaning; under the smudges it was ghostly white. "You cursed fool," she went on, as if she'd never been interrupted. "How do you expect to get away with this? You're the *first* one they'll suspect!"

Ahvren discovered that his voice was back. "*I'm* a fool? None of this would have been necessary if . . ." They argued their way through the grounds and into the city, as Ahvren pulled off his padding. The others were grinning, but it didn't matter. Nothing mattered but Sabri, alive and angry beside him, as the streetlights rippled past. They were still squabbling when the van stopped in a deserted alley. The others hurried off without a word, though Ahvren grabbed the G'Cy woman before she could disappear and hugged her. Her fur felt warm and strange against his bare arms. Loba Amm grinned at him, a little less fierce than before? He was gone before Ahvren could be sure.

Wurrul helped Sabri into his flitter. She moved as if she were old, or ill, and fear touched Ahvren's heart. "The drug?" he murmured as Wurrul went around to the driver's door.

"I know, cub. Next stop is the pharmacigoth."

Wurrul left them in the flitter while he went to buy the antidote. Sabri wasn't arguing anymore. She leaned against Ahvren, her head heavy on his shoulder, though she roused when Wurrul handed her the pills.

"Take one of these every three hours," he told her. "That'll keep enough rejolac in your system to counteract anything. There are enough pills to last four days."

"Thank you." Sabri's voice shook. She fumbled, trying to open the bottle with just one hand. Ahvren reached to do it for her, but she stopped him with a glare and managed it herself. He sank back in his seat, reassured, as she popped a pill into her mouth and swallowed it.

"It looks like you've saved me after all, heart-sib. I have to admit, I didn't expect it at this point."

"If you had any sense, it wouldn't have been necessary. You could have . . . have . . ."

Sabri's exhausted smile was rich with irony.

"Well, you could have *told* me."

"You would have tried to stop me. And you couldn't have concealed something like this—could you?"

"No," Ahvren admitted. "But I might have found some other way to stop it."

"How? You were already trying as hard as you could. You scared me to death when you started tracking that rumor."

"So you set Viv Redahd on me—thanks a lot." But he pulled her against him again as he spoke, and she leaned into the warmth of his body.

"Dara didn't think you could find us, but I knew better. You're only a fair fighter, but you put things together better than anyone I know. Setting Viv Redahd to stop you was the only thing I could think of that wouldn't make you suspicious."

"Not that it mattered," Ahvren muttered. "I went right on looking for the wrong thing, just like Om Loppo."

"Who?"

"An Olopoli fable," Wurrul interrupted. "Which you'll have the rest of your life to hear. Now I want you to change into these." He handed a bundle of clothing back to Sabri. "And this," he offered Ahvren a small jar, "is for you."

"What is it?"

"Cleaning pads. They'll take that paint off your face, and improve your complexion, too. The clerk gave me a very odd look when I purchased it." His whiskers twitched in a smile.

Ahvren was free of paint when they reached the spaceport, and Sabri was dressed in rough crewman's overalls, a grubby cap covering her bright hair. It would do, Wurrul assured her, to get to the ship, and after that it wouldn't matter; they'd lift off as soon as she was aboard. Officially, they'd left five hours ago—through some strange clerical error, the mechanical failure that had forced their return hadn't been noted on the log. Even if the port was closed down, they should still be able to get off under cover of the shield fleet's ongoing traffic. Odan Mo, Wurrul added, had deep fingers.

Ahvren pulled on his sand cloak to conceal his face, though he saw no one in this remote part of the field. When Sabri got out, he retrieved the long slim box he'd asked Wurrul to bring, and followed her.

"What's that?" She didn't sound as if she cared. Her eyes were on the ship; her voice was distant, as if her mind had already traveled on.

"It's something I thought you should have. You . . . Well, it belongs with you. That ship is a freighter. It will stop at a dozen planets, and there's no reason for anyone to suspect you're on it. The captain has money for you. There are forty worlds in the T'Chin Confederation. You should be able to vanish completely."

"But then what?" Her eyes glistened in the stark industrial lights that bordered the spacefield.

"I don't know. What did you plan to do if you escaped?"

"Frankly, I didn't have a plan for that. I didn't expect to escape, so I didn't bother."

"Of all the stupid, idiotic, *unprofitable*—"

She laughed. "Take care, heart-sib." Her arms went around him, and her hand stroking his back made Ahvren very aware of the absence of the other one.

"Take care, heart-sib. And someday, when it's safer, get word to us. I'd hate to have you vanish too completely."

She let him go, and he thrust the Nisol sword into her arms. The luminous tears spilled when she smiled, but her head lifted as she approached the waiting ship. Ahvren thought he heard her murmur, *"Forty* planets . . ." But he couldn't be sure.

● ● ●

Wurrul dropped him off a few blocks from 33 Shakka Street. It was just a few hours before dawn, and Ahvren longed for his bed, but he knew the scholar would still be awake, establishing his alibi. Waiting and worrying.

The question he'd asked Sabri lingered in his mind, for in truth, he had no more plan for his future than she did for hers.

He'd lost the wager. If Viv Saiden demanded that he go to Zodan, he'd have to keep his word—but Ahvren suspected his father might have lost his taste for forcing his children into things. On the other hand, if he asked again what Ahvren wanted to do, Ahvren still didn't have an answer. Or did he?

The last few days had been difficult, often uncomfortable, sometimes downright terrifying, but he'd enjoyed the challenge. Even if he hadn't exactly won in this war of wits.

With practice, with teaching, he might get better at it.

If he agreed to become an intelligencer, Redahd would be his teacher. Ahvren shuddered.

The one he'd really like to have as a teacher—even more than Odan Mo—was the bibliogoth. Who would only consider taking him as an apprentice if Ahvren could figure out why the Vivitare conquest didn't matter. And Ahvren was further from understanding that than he'd ever been.

The more he thought about it, as he strolled sleepily toward the scholar's house, the stranger it seemed. The T'Chin weren't cowards. Tonight had proved that. They were capable of military planning, military action. They had better technology than the Vivitare, more manpower, and they were fighting on their homeworld. They could throw the Vivitare off this planet in a week if they wanted to. Why didn't they do it? Aliens conquered their planet, imposed laws and taxes, stole their homes and goods . . . and it didn't *matter*? Ahvren shook his head. He was too sleepy to make sense of it tonight.

Yawning, he opened the door and heard the familiar clang of the chime. There was a scent in the air—strange, even for the scholar's incense. It smelled like scorched plastic and burning electronics . . . and it was coming from the terminal on the desk. A wisp of smoke drifted from the shattered screen, even as he watched.

Ahvren ran for the scholar's office, his

pulse pounding out the only thought in his mind: *No, no, no*.

The old clay barter bowl lay in fragments on the floor. Ahvren bent to gather them, foolishly, uselessly. The desk had skidded across the room, the cup-chair was overturned, a few papers had flown about . . . slight signs of struggle, but somehow obscene in this civilized room.

At least there was no body.

Ahvren searched for some indication of who the intruder had been for almost five minutes before he thought to try the terminal. The message activated as soon as he turned it on, but he didn't need to hear it. One look at Redahd's triumphant face was enough to tell him that the bibliogoth of 33 Shakka Street had been taken for questioning.

Taken . . . in Ahvren's place.

# Chapter 20

**A**HVREN RAN THROUGH the dark streets; the only sound was the rhythmic slap of his shoes on stone. The scholar's house was less than a mile from the emperor's mansion. He prayed Redahd had taken the scholar there—if he hadn't, Ahvren would demand to see Lessar, wake him up, tell him . . . what? If he told the truth (not a single successful lie in all the months since Mirmanidan), he would implicate not only himself but the scholar, Odan Mo, Reecheep, and all his other accomplices. *He* was the danger. Odan was right.

Ahvren tried to slow down. He had to think about this. He could almost see the scholar lifting one small talon in the gesture he had come to read as *Think it through, block-head, you're missing something.* But what?

Why had Redahd taken the scholar? Why not seize Ahvren? Or, if he couldn't find Ahvren, then Odan Mo, who was far more deeply involved? If Redahd knew anything—and how *did* he find out?—surely that was what he'd have done.

Ahvren realized he was running again, which made it harder to think. *You don't know what's going on. Be careful! Only a fool would bet on a fleeta with a broken leg, no matter how high the odds.* He was breathing too hard to laugh or cry. The entrance to the palace grounds loomed before him. Since most visitors arrived by flitter, and a fit child could climb the estate wall, there was no guard. If Ahvren raced up to the mansion all but hysterical, would the guards even admit him?

Yes, if Redahd had brought the scholar here. They'd be expecting him. That message had been left for him. Bait. And he'd take it—but not blindly, like a stupid peepoe fish.

Ahvren slowed to a walk and kept that pace all the way up the long road to the house. The scarlet-sashed guard at the front door looked interested to see him but not surprised. The skin on the back of Ahvren's neck crawled; he'd been right, he was expected. Did that mean the scholar was here? *Don't assume—you might end up asking the wrong questions again.*

"Is Viv Redahd here?"

"Yes. Are you Viv . . . ah, your name?"

A cold smile crept over Ahvren's face. If he was going to control this situation he might as well start now. "Yes, I'm Viv Ahvren. You may take me to Viv Redahd. Now, if you please."

The guard closed his dangling jaw and led Ahvren into the house and down—to the cellars, of course. But a different area from the one where Sabri had been held. Ahvren struggled to remember the plans Odan Mo had spread in front of him . . . only this morning? Surely this vaulted corridor led to the storage rooms? Why—

They turned a corner; Redahd and half a dozen guards stood by a lighted window set into one wall. One of the guards was his father's friend Wythan—his expression as he gazed through the glass sent a shiver down Ahvren's spine. Deciding he didn't want to know what Wythan was looking at, Ahvren looked around.

The corridor opened into a room that had been fitted as an office of some sort. Desks, comm-equipment, and cabinets full of . . . medical supplies? Straps were attached to

336

some of the chairs, and Ahvren felt the blood drain from his face.

Redahd turned toward him, smiling.

*Let him talk. Don't give anything away until you find out what's going on. And* don't *let your stupid compulsion get the better of you!*

But for all that, words of anger and condemnation rose in his throat at the sight of this sick place. If worst came to worst, he could let those words flood out—challenge Redahd to a duel and slaughter the slaving bastard, law or no law.

*You think he isn't prepared for that?*

Redahd's smile was slipping. He probably expected Ahvren to burst out with demands and then confess.

*Disappoint him. Don't ask. Don't let him see you care.*

"I see you got my message, Viv Ahvren." Redahd summoned the smile back. "I'm glad you could make it."

"Given the context of your message, I could scarcely ignore it. May I ask why you're harassing my business partner instead of talking to me?"

"Ah, but you've been hard to find, these last few days. Your father is worried about

337

you. You were especially hard to find tonight."

They must have picked up the scholar as soon as they discovered Sabri was gone; they *didn't* have any connection between the scholar and the breakout. They'd just seized him because of his connection to Ahvren. But now he had no alibi. Shackles, let them prove it! If it would save his friends, they could have him—but it wouldn't. Under truth drugs, if not under torture, Ahvren would betray them all. His palms were wet, and he fought the impulse to wipe them on his breeches. Redahd was watching his every move, but the smile was slipping again. Whatever he expected from Ahvren, silence wasn't it.

"Where were you tonight, Viv Ahvren?"

Direct question. Words, true words, rose in Ahvren's throat. Quick, something else.

"Where is the bibliogoth? Whatever you want with me has nothing to do with it."

"But I can't know that, can I, unless I question . . . it?" Redahd's smile widened. Evidently that line was in the script. He gestured to the lighted glass square.

Ahvren's stomach knotted. He didn't want to look, shouldn't look, must not look, but his feet took him to the window of their own volition.

The scholar crouched against the wall, down on all of its legs. Its whole body shook, and its quivering antennae rubbed against each other, frantically, ceaselessly. Its big eyes were fixed, sightless.

But Ahvren saw no wounds, no cracks in the chitin, no burns. The room held nothing, no sinister equipment . . . nothing but a puddle of glistening scum that spread over most of the floor. Looking closer, Ahvren could see it on the scholar's talons, and on its side where it must have fallen.

"What is that stuff?" He didn't realize his voice would shake so badly until he heard it. So much for the pretense of not caring.

"Nothing much. Just concentrated ammonia, in a gel that keeps it from evaporating too quickly. It seems T'chin are sensitive to odor. Only fair that an exoskeletal creature should have some vulnerability."

Redahd went on talking, but his voice was overwhelmed by the blood pounding in Ahvren's ears. Ammonia would sear those long, sensitive antennae like acid. Ahvren watched the scholar rubbing them, and something rose within him, hard, cold, and in control.

This was the work of the empire he served. This was what his people would do on Zodan. *Some things were more important than truth.*

He turned to Redahd. "What is the charge, that you think you can do this?"

"I suspect the creature of being involved with the rebels who broke your foster sister out of her cell earlier tonight," Redahd answered smoothly.

"But Sabri didn't . . ." *Act surprised, stupid!* "Are you telling me Sabri escaped?"

Redahd smiled. "Yes. Though I doubt I'm telling you anything you didn't know."

"But if the schol—the bibliogoth was home tonight, why do you think *it* had anything to do with it?"

"Oh, I can think of ways it might be involved but still at home. For instance, it might be the base coordinator for several groups pursuing different tasks."

Redahd thought they were that organized? Ahvren drew in a shaking breath. Forget that. The next question was the one that mattered. "What did the bibliogoth tell you?"

"Very little . . . so far. That you had a standing option to join it in the evening, but you hadn't come tonight. It hasn't said anything since we put it in there, somewhat to my surprise."

It took Ahvren several seconds to master his voice. "It probably can't. T'chin synthavodes work on scent—all that ammonia must be overloading it."

Redahd recoiled from the rage in Ahvren's face.

Wythan stirred, and spoke for the first time. "If that's true, then this is useless. We can let the creature go."

"No," said Redahd. "It serves a purpose. I can't believe that someone Viv Ahvren has seen so often over the past few weeks is wholly unaware of his plans."

"I've seen you more often than I wanted to in the last few weeks," said Ahvren. "That doesn't make you guilty. And I notice you're just assuming my guilt. If I'm not guilty, then the bibliogoth isn't either, right? Or any of my other friends?"

"I suppose that follows," Redahd admitted. "But I doubt it matters. You weren't at home tonight, Viv Ahvren. At three in the morning, your bed was undisturbed. So if you're going to claim you weren't freeing your murdering sister from our justice, you'd better have proof of where you were. And you don't, so—"

"Don't assume, Redahd. It's . . . unprofitable. I was with a lady tonight. Ordinarily I wouldn't name her, but under the circumstances . . ." He glanced at the scholar and wished he hadn't. "I was with Lady Dara, Bard Bredan's daughter."

Redahd's smile vanished. He hadn't expected a name. "Will she confirm this?"

"She will," said Ahvren, hoping he sounded more confident than he felt. She'd better. It was good to have control of his tongue back, to be able to say the lying words with certainty.

"Then you won't mind if I call her right now and ask, will you?"

"Not at all, though you'll probably get her out of bed." Wythan slipped out of the room as Redahd operated the comm-equipment. Ahvren was sorry to see him go; he needed all the support he could get. He turned his back on the window, not wanting to see any more, grudging every second's delay as a servant answered the comm-unit, was convinced to wake Dara's parents . . . Finally her face appeared, tousled and lovely.

"Yes?"

"Lady Dara, I'm sorry to—"

"I had to tell him, Dara," Ahvren interrupted. "I'm sorry. But someone broke Sabri out of her cell tonight, and they need to know where I was."

"Sabri's free?" She clapped her hands. "Oh, I'm glad, I'm glad!" She sounded a perfect idiot—at his best, Ahvren would never be the liar Dara was. For an instant, he almost loved her.

"I know she was your friend." Something rasped in Redahd's voice. "But Viv Ahvren claims to have been with you tonight . . . late tonight . . . all night. Lady Dara, is that true?"

Ahvren heard Bard Bredan's gasp; Dara's mother's face appeared on the screen. "That's absurd! My daughter is a maiden! What you're implying is an outrage, sir."

Ahvren stared at Dara, trying to convey with his eyes what he couldn't say: *Back me up, bitch, or I'll take your whole conspiracy down with me.*

Did she read his eyes, or just reach the logical conclusion?

Dara's gaze dropped. A blush the color of wild roses stained her cheeks. "I'm sorry, Mama, it is true. He came to talk with me about Sabri, to comfort me, and . . . well . . ." She blushed harder, but she met Redahd's eyes as she said, "My maid can confirm it. I'm—"

"Foolish girl, what have you done? No Vivitar will marry a wanton—no fit man would have you! What—"

Dara's image vanished as the connection was cut. Bard Bredan, no doubt. No *fit* man would have her. Was that in Dara's mind when she backed him? Probably. Too smart by half. Bard Bredan would be out for Ahvren's blood when he refused to marry her, but that was tomorrow's problem.

Ahvren turned back to Redahd, trying not to let the triumph show on his face. "You see, I have an alibi. And if I'm innocent, then my friends are too. Release the bibliogoth. Now."

"I don't believe it! She lied and you're lying, and I'll have the truth if I have to break each and every one of—"

"On whose authority do you propose to

do that?" said a cool, female voice behind them.

They all spun. Jennah stepped out of the shadows; Wythan stood behind her. Ahvren wondered how much she'd overheard. He didn't have to wonder long.

"Viv Redahd, you seem to think Lady Dara is lying. A lie that will destroy her reputation. Why would she do such a thing?"

Redahd had recovered his temper. "There are many reasons, Lady, why a person lies. To protect someone they care for, for instance. If she loves this man—"

"If she loves Ahvren, it's news to me, and I'm one of her best friends," said Jennah bluntly. Her eyes swept the room, taking in what Ahvren had seen, and her anger became more dispassionate . . . and more powerful. She looked through the window and her mouth twisted. "Tell me, Viv Redahd, on what evidence do you accuse Viv Ahvren and Dara, and torment that creature?"

"He has motive, Lady; the assassin is his foster sister. Lady Dara was her friend, and the creature is his. I believe he—"

"So your only basis for this is motive? Sabri had lots of friends, Viv Redahd." Her lips

tightened ironically— "Are you going to interrogate all of us?"

"Of course not, Lady, but you don't
understand—"

"On the contrary, I understand all too
well. Viv Redahd, this disgraces my house,
and our people's honor." Her face was grave
as always, but the imperious—imperial?—
note in her voice was new. "I find your justi-
fication for this . . . proceeding inadequate. In
the future you will get my father's or my permission before you *interrogate* anyone."

"Lady Jennah, you don't have enough
experience to—"

"Perhaps not. But as my father's heir"—
she took a deep breath—"I certainly have the
authority. You may raise the question with
my father if you wish, but I believe he will
support my judgment—*he* is a man of honor.
Release the T'chin. Viv Ahvren, you may go."

Another woman, another man, might
have left then. Jennah, the conscientious one,
stayed to be sure her orders were carried out.
She would make a fine emperor. Ahvren no
longer cared.

The guards led him around the scholar's
cell. When they opened the doors, the acrid

stench choked him, burning his eyes. Ahvren hurried to the scholar and dropped to his knees. The synthavode was emitting a discordant buzz. How could they communicate?

Ahvren grasped one of the scholar's trembling shoulders and tugged. The chitin felt like varnished paper. Could the scholar even feel his grip?

Something roused it. The draft of fresher air perhaps. It crawled haltingly toward the door, like an animal, like an insect. It made Ahvren sick to see the scholar so reduced; the tears coursing down his face were not all due to the stinging ammonia.

It took an eternity to guide the scholar through the twisting corridors. Anguish was tying knots in Ahvren's stomach when they finally reached the cellar door. The fresh night air seemed to help, but the synthavode still buzzed softly. The scholar was covered with the stinking stuff, and so were Ahvren's shoes.

Pulling out his sand cape, he tried to wipe it away, but it only smeared—he couldn't get enough of it. There was a small lake not far from the house; Ahvren had seen it when his father flew in. T'chin might not habitually submerge themselves in water, but it was the fastest way to get rid of the gel. He tried to tug the scholar toward the lake, but it resisted.

"Please, you have to . . ." What was the use? It couldn't hear him.

The scholar reared up, trying to stand. Ahvren caught the chitinous arms and heaved, and the scholar rocked upright, wavering unsteadily. Its talons descended on Ahvren's shoulders, piercing his tunic, scratching his skin, though he knew the scholar was trying to be gentle. Ammonia burned in the scratches.

They walked slowly to the lake. At the shore the scholar released Ahvren and stalked awkwardly into the water. Ahvren barely had time to press the buckles on the synthavode straps and snatch it off before it was submerged.

The scholar waded in until only its head was visible above the rippling surface; water splashed as it washed itself. Ahvren stared numbly for several minutes before he remembered the synthavode, still buzzing in his hand. He cleaned it with scraps torn from his sand cloak, careful not to let water seep into the electronics—cleaned it till the metal squeaked under his damp fingers. His shoes were a lost cause; he'd go home barefoot. He threw them as far as he could, into the shrubs around the lake.

It seemed a long time before the leggy figure emerged, dripping, from the dark water. It checked the synthavode carefully with its antennae before strapping it on. Ahvren had to help with the buckles, for its talons shook.

"So, youngling." Was it mechanical stress that made the voice sound so rough? "I thought they had us, but now it looks like they don't. Are we as free as we seem? I want very much to go home."

Ahvren explained as they walked. He'd offered to get a flitter, but the scholar refused. It moved slowly, but aside from that it seemed to be all right, as far as Ahvren could judge. How could you tell, with a creature so different? They reached the scholar's front door and it turned to go in.

"Are you all right? You seem to be, but I can't tell and . . . Please, are you all right?" Tears stung Ahvren's eyes. He hoped the scholar couldn't scent them.

"I will be. Don't worry so. I was young

when your great-great-grandfather was young, and I will probably outlive you, though not by much. This"—all its talons turned outward—"is just one unpleasant incident. It really doesn't matter."

"Yes, it does. Curse you, it does! You're builders, and all we do is conquer and destroy. We have no right to be here, robbing you, taxing you, hurting you . . ." The tears were falling. "How can it not matter?"

"Youngling, if you continue to take this emotional approach, you'll never figure it out. It's the facts that are important, not how you feel about them. Only a subucu thinks it can conceal itself by hiding its own head."

Ahvren smiled in spite of himself. "Then I may never understand it—it matters very much to me."

"It won't, once you understand it. But I thank you anyway. You'll come tomorrow night, as usual?"

"Yes. You should get some rest."

The scholar hesitated. Then one antennae descended, slowly, giving Ahvren time to flinch away, and stroked his cheek. It felt like a stag's horn, bone covered in velvet, utterly alien, utterly warming. Ahvren reached up and brushed it with his fingers, returning the embrace as best he could.

The chime clanged. The door closed. Ahvren stood, fighting rage that his people had done this—that in their fear and arrogance they had come to this place and . . . had come . . . had come to . . .

The realization began slowly, fact adding itself to fact until the whole swept over him in a crashing wave of comprehension. And in the shimmering peace of its withdrawal, Ahvren understood that the scholar, all of them, had been right; it really didn't matter at all.

# Chapter 21

THE INCENSE TONIGHT smelled of fresh bread, with a hint of something green underlying it. The scholar sat behind the desk as usual—a slight stiffness in its movements was the only sign that anything had happened. Everything had been picked up and put back, even . . . Ahvren stepped forward and touched the old barter bowl. Only by looking very closely could he see the cracks where it had been mended. "I'm glad," he said softly.

"Indeed?" The scholar paused in the midst of its greeting gesture. "Last night you would have been sorry."

"Things have changed since then," said Ahvren, dropping thankfully into his chair.

"Really?" The antennae swept out to hover above him. "Yet you seem a bit stressed."

"I am! I spent the whole shackling day refusing to marry Dara. Her father—both her parents—want to kill me. But after she backed me up so splendidly, refusing is the least I can do for her. For Roi, too, though I don't think this was what he had in mind when he asked me to help."

One antennae spiraled softly. "If I understand your culture correctly, I'd tend to agree with you. What of your own parents? Are they angry with you?"

"Not exactly. They know they should be, but they're so relieved about Sabri, they can't quite manage it." A tremor shook the core of peace that had carried Ahvren through the trials of the day. "I wonder what she'll do now." He rose and paced to the window, looking out into the starry desert night. "No family, no friends . . . nothing, really. What can she do?"

"What she has always done," said the scholar gently. "Make her own life through her own choices. Everyone invests their lives differently, youngling, because everyone's ideal profit is a different thing. At least she's alive and free to choose."

It sounded a chord in Ahvren's memory. "Freedom. That was what she wanted. The only thing she wanted. I hope she wants it now that she's got it."

"That too is her choice. Speaking of choices, the problem you originally brought me has been solved—after a fashion. What do you want to do about our arrangement?"

"I won't be able to do anything for a while." Ahvren returned to his chair. "Father is sending me off with the shield fleet, to conquer Zodan. He may not be angry with me, but he does think I should get off the planet for a few months while Redahd's still sniffing around. Though I heard a rumor today that Redahd has lost the emperor's favor. I doubt he'll get it back. But I'll be on Zodan for at least eight months. I'll miss this." He gestured at the warm, book-filled room. "But as my father pointed out, I did lose our wager."

"Did you tell him about last night?"

"He asked me." Ahvren savored the memory. "I looked him straight in the eyes and lied. It was wonderful."

One antennae arced. "Most beings wouldn't boast about that. Is lying of value in your culture?"

Ahvren smiled. "Only if you haven't been able to do it. Only to me." He told the scholar about the bizarre compulsion that had finally released him. "I still don't understand why it happened—now I probably never will." A chill dimmed his satisfaction. If he never learned what caused it, it might return.

"Not necessarily," said the scholar. "If nothing else, the T'Chin do have healers of the mind. You may wish to speak with one. But I could hazard a guess myself. Would this compulsion have prevented you from going to Zodan?"

"Yes," said Ahvren. "When they asked me to take the service oath, if not before."

"And when your compulsion left you, had your feelings about going to Zodan changed?"

"It wasn't my feelings about it that had changed," said Ahvren slowly. "I had realized that I would refuse to go to Zodan. Even if my father disowned me."

The antennae hovered over him again. "Yet you say you're going now, and it doesn't seem to distress you."

"It doesn't matter now. You see, I've figured it out."

Both antennae arced. "Have you? Yes, I believe you have. I'm impressed."

"Didn't you think I could?"

"On the evidence available to you . . .

frankly, no. I was about to start giving you hints," the scholar admitted.

"You gave me several hints. Remember when you told me that the Zo were the second-most-recent species to come to T'Chin? It never occurred to me to ask who the most recent species was. It's us, isn't it?"

Both antennae curled into spirals. "It is, youngling. Welcome."

Ahvren snorted. But . . . "Please, explain this. It seems so outlandish."

"You're the one who's passing a test. You explain it to me. Why doesn't it matter to the T'Chin that you have conquered us?"

Ahvren smiled. "Because we haven't. Not in any way that counts. How many of the species now part of T'Chin came as conquerors? All of them?"

"Oh, no. Only a little more than two-thirds."

"But they don't stay conquerors." He rose to pace. It was such a strange concept, he found it hard to put it into words. "They come, and you let them conquer you. You don't resist, so your cities, your culture, most of your wealth remains intact. You let them impose their rule, customs, whatever they want, and then you just . . . absorb them. Economically. Culturally. You make them rich!" It sounded, absurdly, like an accusation. The antennae spiraled tighter. Ahvren grinned and continued. "You make them rich, and your society is so free and so . . . happy, that they choose to become part of you."

"The fact that there are hundreds of T'Chin for every one invader helps, too," the scholar informed him. "It's hard for anyone to make much impression on a culture that vastly outnumbers them."

"So you let them in, and wait till they change. That's why nothing we do matters to you. Because in ten years, or twenty, or fifty, we'll be just another part of T'Chin."

"You have it, youngling. Though you may have trouble explaining it to others."

Ahvren smiled. "I'm not going to explain it to anyone. Ever. Though I could, you know. I could go to Lessar and explain the whole thing, but even if I could get him to believe me, which I probably couldn't, it still wouldn't matter. Because even if everyone believed it, they wouldn't stop it from happening. In the long run they'd still choose wealth over poverty and reach for personal freedom and happiness. It might take a little longer, but in twenty years, or fifty, or two hundred, we'd still be a part of T'Chin. Though there are some things that matter. It would have been terrible if Redahd had won."

"For you, perhaps," said the scholar calmly. "For me, certainly. But in the end, he and his kind can't win. We find them in all cultures, the sadists, the destroyers. Even, alas, in mine. But for every Redahd there are dozens of Jennahs, Sabris, and Ahvrens who rise up against them. As long as that's true, they can never win. Not in the long run."

Silence fell and Ahvren felt no need to break it. Finally, the scholar stirred.

"You may be only a fair swordsman, but as a bibliogoth you show great promise. It's been almost a century since I last took an apprentice, but I believe the time has come. If you wish it, of course."

"I do," said Ahvren. "That's exactly what I want. Even if my father does think I'm crazy."

"Then come back from Zodan soon—I find I'm impatient to begin working with you."

"Me too. It shouldn't take long, if the Zo don't resist. They won't, will they?"

"Of course not. The Zo may not have been part of T'Chin long enough to like surrendering, but they still remember what happened when *they* conquered us. No, you needn't fear that they'll resist."

"Is that why the Zo have their own neighborhoods? Because they haven't fully assimilated into your culture?"

"That's right. But every year more of the young ones move out into the mainstream. In a few more generations there will be no Zo ghettos. Vivitare ones, perhaps. It's a stage most cultures pass through."

Ahvren shook his head, still astonished. "And I once wondered why you didn't mind using our money. You change monetary systems with each conqueror, don't you?"

"Yes. As I told you, in T'Chin it's the transaction that matters, not the medium of exchange. At least you *have* money. The Fetorg's only medium of exchange was to share 'good stink,' which was rubbed onto them by their queen. Bottle makers became very rich, I understand. Fortunately for us they learned quickly. And in the end, we were all richer for it. That's part of it you may not have grasped yet. Every culture that comes to

T'Chin brings us things of beauty and value. From bathhouses to electronic banking. From pottery to poetry. Always, we are enriched by those we absorb. That's why your people truly are welcome. Because we know you'll enrich us in ways far outlasting any temporary inconvenience you may cause."

"What do *we* have to offer *you*?"

"Probably many things," said the scholar imperturbably. "I hesitate to say this, knowing how you feel about bards, but Vivitare drama is already much admired. Some of my literary friends tell me your best works show a mastery of pace and dramatic structure surpassing anything we've produced. And that's only the first thing of value we've discovered in your people. We'll find much more as time passes. Just as you and I will work to discover each other's value."

"That sounds like a challenge—the best kind of challenge. A clean fight."

"Then return to me when you come back from Zodan, and we'll begin a different business relationship." The scholar's talons came together and rotated down.

"I'll come back as soon as I can," Ahvren promised, and rose to go.

"Youngling?"

He turned. The scholar was holding up one small talon in the all-too-familiar gesture. What . . . of course! Color flooded Ahvren's cheeks and he plunged his hand into his pouch. Had he come out without money again? He sighed with relief as his fingers closed around the hard squares.

"This is the last time you'll need to remember it," the scholar told him. One antennae curved softly. "Apprentices pay in other ways."

Ahvren smiled. "I'm sure we'll both profit by it." And he stacked the silver squares, with careful reverence, in the old clay bowl.